M000105020

IN THE
EYES OF THE
MOOSE

DAVID RANKIN JOHNSON

Copyright © 2019 by David Rankin Johnson

All rights reserved. No part of this publication may be reproduced, distributed or transmitted in any form or by any means, including photocopying, recording, or other electronic or mechanical methods, without the prior written permission of the publisher, except in the case of brief quotations embodied in critical reviews and certain other noncommercial uses permitted by copyright law.

David Rankin Johnson/In The Eyes of The Moose
Printed in the United States of America

Publisher's Note: This is a work of fiction. Names, characters, places, and incidents are a product of the author's imagination. Locales and public names are sometimes used for atmospheric purposes. Any resemblance to actual people, living or dead, or to businesses, companies, events, institutions, or locales is completely coincidental.

In The Eyes of The Moose/ David Rankin Johnson -- 1st ed.

ISBN 978-1-7339410-0-6 Print Edition

ISBN 978-1-7339410-1-3 Ebook Edition

This book is dedicated to My Mother Joan VanAsltyne Johnson, my Father Edward Fuller Johnson and my Niece Alden Landis. Just before my mothers passing I read part of this book to her in the emergency room, I will always remember her smile when hearing the plot unfold, At times while writing this book I could see the rolling of my father's shoulders in laughter and hear Alden`s voice imitating the English and French accents, they are not forgotten.

- CHAPTER 1 -

The sound of a child crying carried across a meadow, past an old barn, through a wooded marsh and on into the deep woods. On a still day you can hear the crashing of the surf. Not on this day. Sky was walking that funny walk of a three-year-old bawling her eyes out for her Mama heading for the old barn. The moose was standing in high wet grass in the wooded marsh, chewing on the sweetness of the earth and listening to that troubled sound. It disturbed the female moose, taking away the peace that was in the woods. With curious concern she went to see what that crying was all about.

She stood for a moment at the edge of the field watching the girl. She had seen the child many times, playing with her mother right there in the field. But she had always made the sound of laughter, never this screaming with despair, never alone. Something was wrong.

Sky fell to her knees wailing at a shrill. Pushed by maternal concern the moose approached slowly, her eyes on the child, her nose smelling human baby, surprisingly comforting. The child felt movement through the earth. With the hope of it being her mother she stopped wailing and looked up to see the moose approaching. Sky had seen the big animal before when she and her mother would spy on her grazing in the woods. Never this close. In her fertile mind they were already good friends for they had watched her a lot. She felt no fear, trusting this animal. The moose and Sky stayed still, only feet apart, just feeling the energy. The child made the first move. She crawled up to those long legs and pulled herself awkwardly to her feet, wrapping her small arms around bony wet fur, hugging and holding strong for the love of life. The moose felt the warm chubby hands then stuck her nose into the child's soft ticklish hair, smelled her baby smell and was moved to protect her. It would be dark soon, and the coyotes would be out picking up the strong scent of the child. She could think of one safe place close by. A place she knew from her past.

On the east side of the barn was a depression in the banking, a safe place in the moose's memory. When she was a young calf she'd lost her mother to a truck accident. Vulnerable in the woods, she was attacked by coyotes, but an old farmer heard the noise thinking they had one of his cows and rescued her. He scared them off with a poor shot of his gun that also took off a piece of the young moose's ear. The coyotes had torn part of her right hind leg with their sharp teeth. The old farmer, with the help of his three young sons, carried her back to the farm. They put her in a pen that was in a depression in the banking on the east side of the barn. The farmer, who was called Moxie, named the moose Tilly, nurtured her back to health and set her free. Free or not the bond was established between Tilly and Moxie. She never wandered far from the old farm for too long, even though Moxie had passed one year ago.

Tilly and the child made their awkward way to that safe place, Sky holding strong to that one bony long leg. Tilly sometimes gave an extra shove with her nose and head. Dusk was taking hold as they made it to the depression. Sky felt the security of this place nestled snug to the old barn. She let go of her strong hold on Tilly and fell into the soft high grass. Tilly swung her long lean head, grabbing bunches of grass in her teeth and tossing it down for bedding. The child rolled in the soft security of earth feeling like she was in her mother's arms and smelling the strong scent of the moose as its breath tickled her. Tilly worked the grass around the child with front hoof and nose, tucking her in for a long night ahead. Sky had eyes only for the moose and she played for more attention, more direct contact. The moose was ever aware of how vulnerable this child was outside in the darkness.

Tilly learned a thing or two during her time on the farm. She could use all four legs in self-defense against all sizes of critters, fighting off everything from nasty roosters, feisty pigs, jacked up dogs and three farm boys looking for a bull fight. She had a mean right front leg move that always caught the offenders off guard in a frontal attack. Then of course her specialty the dual rear piston kick that sent them into the neighbor`s pasture. So to state the obvious, Tilly was a true veteran of self-defense on the day she took a child into her care.

The east side of the barn faced a small open field of high grass, which gave way to deep woods. The coyotes would come from that direction through the high grass that gave way to deep woods. There was a three-quarter harvest moon, but that would not come up till later. Tilly would have to get by listening and smelling for them for the first part of the night. She faced the child keeping her head low to comfort her, listening to the soft breathing that was close to her big ears and keeping alert to the far off movement of danger. The sound of frogs and owls took over the night. The exhausted child fell into a deep sleep.

Being back at this place of old comfort brought Tilly back to images of Moxie and the sound of his voice. He would always approach Tilly with a song and food at hand. His approach first meant food, then relief from the pain of her torn leg. Later friendship. They communicated through different tones in their grunts and voices. Body language, touch and expression of emotion shown in the eyes. Tilly was young and vulnerable without her mother, and Moxie filled some of that void. The memory was held strong in her mind. Small in size big in voice, Tilly felt only compassion from this man, a trust built over time and healing.

The healing of the flesh wounds from the coyote's teeth was quick but that of the muscles and tendons was much slower. Moxie knew that her leg needed to move and get exercised or Tilly would not regain full use. With his wide hands and powerful arms from a lifetime of farm work and raising three boys he rotated her leg daily. Tilly knew the smell of him and of the farm which came in with him. She could tell his moods by the levels of tension radiating from his strong touch. Periods of happiness, a touch without stress for days on end, a grand smile, shiny eyes, then stressful times and clumsy hands and dull inattentive eyes. The young moose learned how much more the emotions of men swung compared to those of the more stable moose. Tilly did have her moods but not with the same level of drama as she witnessed from Moxie and, later, much of the town.

The town spread its lazy self along a sweet spot on the shores of the Maine coast. Tilly could access most of Scottstown from the woods and marshes that surrounded it. The shoreline swung and dipped into a big tributary. An inland lake that moved fresh water and silt into the salt creating beds of mud and eel grass that are a wonderful nursery for the sea. She loved to swim, leap frogging her way along the shore, and she accessed town from many advantages.

Tilly was a common thief. She feasted in gardens, selective trash bins and the rare birthday cake that was left out on that open picnic table. Her favorite meal was pumpkin, which she stole right off of porches in the fall. She also loved to listen to music, Moxie's fault. On top of his singing he had an old turn table on which he would spin his beloved Scottish music and the odd tango. There were others of his ilk in town who played similar music. Tilly would seek them out, lying low in the nearby woods, listening and thinking of Moxie.

One such place was the Dragger Inn. It had a wraparound porch that went completely around the old Victorian mansion, its grandiose days behind it. She was now a bit droopy in the drawers but dripping with character. The front porch faced the sea and the sides gave way to the abrupt woods and steep inclines of rugged shoreline. Tilly heard and saw plenty in those woods.

The Dragger Inn was a place of great democracy on this earth, for it was visited by locals and folks from away who openly mixed. The salt air and crashing surf eased the social barriers between the classes. This resulted in open conversations in which their differences were laid bare and played with in dialogue ending in roaring laughter into the wee hours of the night.

A full, right varnished, mahogany bar, its precious wood stolen from the fore deck of a foregone schooner, gave a deep warmth to the pub that spilled its tables out to the front porch. A wonderful old sound system cranked out Scottish swings and waltzes and a full kitchen provided all the fixings. The staff were family and generational locals, and the continuity of their connection to place gave them a great warmth of character, very much unvarnished and honest. Those lucky enough to stay and play at the Inn would always find their way back.

Moxie was a regular. He liked to sit out on that porch sipping his whiskey and playing backgammon with the boys, a local cast of characters, fishermen, tradesmen and the odd banker. Others would come to sit and watch but they mostly wanted advice from Moxie. He was a jack-of-all-trades and took them all to perfection. He knew all there was to know about a trade from doing, to watching, to talking and reading. Plumbing, carpentry, motors of all kinds. He knew his stuff and he loved to share his knowledge. The go-to man in town. When a guy was in over his head on a project and needed sound advising he found Moxie. Then of course there was the discussing of local politics. Things were voted on at town meeting, but issues were resolved at The Dragger Inn. Moxie had a strong and respected voice in those discussions.

Tilly loved to be out there in the woods listening to the cadence of voices. In the past she could easily pick out his voice, so distinct in its rhythm and strong Maine accent. Always more laughter later after the watering. Plenty for Tilly to hear and see. Even with Moxie gone Tilly would still visit those woods, recognizing all the voices that used to surround his. It gave her some comfort. She had been thinking of going over that night but now she had this problem of a young child on her hands.

The night settled in. Tilly listened for predators. Now she faced out, her eyes taking in the shapes in the field, smelling that mixture of grass, pine and fir so familiar and grounding to her past.

- CHAPTER 2 -

Where is the mother? To understand the answer you have to first hear this story. In 1726 a ship from Scotland landed on shores of Maine there in now Scottstown. Moxie's fifth Great Grandparents were a young couple on that ship, running from the island of their births, not from famine or English landlords, but toward love. Effie Wallace was a Protestant and Boyd McCormack a Catholic. That kind of mixing was forbidden and the whole community was against it. They left all they knew, their families and ties to place to be free of parochial religious boundaries and share their love. Effie and Boyd walked ashore and kept walking inland as others hugged closer to the sea. They walked until they felt under their feet a place of good earth to grow food. Their feet served them right, for the MacCormacks found a rare thing on the coast of Maine, good and deep soil. A spit of sand tossed in amongst those glaciers of ice way way back when. Ages of rotting trees decayed over time finer than wine left the MacCormack family with a wonderful piece to farm.

First they built a storm bunker, then the barn and the farmhouse last. Right next to the bunker, he dug a well. A deep one. They kept it open through the years using it to water their cows.

It stayed that way generation after generation until it dried up and was covered over with six-by-sixes and a low-pitched roof. Through the years it got overlaid with earth, and eventually a rhododendron bush grew there. It was forgotten. Until Jake, Moxie's middle son, found it.

After his initial discovery of the wood planking Jake went back to the house for tools, and when his dad was out in the barn he hacked a hole through it. The black hole gave him no return echo when he dropped a stone. The well was still dry and very deep. He then went back to the house to get his head lamp and long rope. It took him many attempts to find bottom.

He loved all the different rocks, their colors illuminated by his lamp held time. They gave him foot holds for his descent, he also had one foot sections of cut re-bar he would occasionally hammer into tight cracks between the rocks. He soon had to share his discovery with his brothers. It was a great secret keeping it from Moxie for so many years. Always recovering the hole after each exploration with new planking they had taken from the barn and then dirt on top of that.

Marcy had just fed Sky and put her down for some quiet time when she looked out the window and watched a cat limp its way under the big rhododendron bush out front. She had seen it off and on for the last two weeks and was moved to help this cat. She went outside and ran under the bush to catch it. The earth gave way and she fell through rotten planking and down into that well.

Her brain went into instant flight. Away from the anticipated pain and possible death at the bottom. Very clear scenes from her past came to her mind, starting with her and Sky coming to the farm then moving backwards from there. Amazing how much can be relayed in mere seconds before she lost consciousness.

Marcy and Sky came to the farm looking for Moxie. Marcy knew him through letters he wrote to her mother while she was growing up. Mary, Marcy's mom, read them to her daughter often. Moxie was a wonderful writer who described his life in great detail. Marcy felt like she was right there experiencing farm life for herself. She felt like she was growing up with brothers hearing the stories of his boys and all their mischief.

The story of her mother's friendship with Moxie was somewhat of a mystery. She claimed to have met him as a young woman at summer camp in Maine. They lost touch for many years but got reacquainted after Mary searched him out and sent a him letter. That started a correspondence of long letters but they never saw one another again. Marcy felt there must have been some romance from the way her Ma would blush at times in her reading. She never pressed the question.

Growing up on Long Island as an only child, Marcy was in a house with her mother and Father but raised by her mother. Her father Darren was an introverted man who seemed to love his work more than his family. Mary made up for it in spades, spending quality time with her child and exposing her to as much life as possible. She read books that illustrated the world to her growing daughter and went to all the museums in New York City. Mary had had a sheltered childhood and did not want the same for her child. She was open with discussion and explored the diversity of life with Marcy. As a result her daughter was a special person, smart and always curious and never afraid to ask questions.

Her father died of a heart attack. Two years later her mother was diagnosed with a rare liver cancer. Marcy moved back in to be with her. At least she went fast. Mary was such a vibrant woman, and living a compromised life would have been too hard to take. On the last days her mother seemed overwrought with something she needed to tell her. It started out with her mother telling her she must go see Moxie. Made her promise. She was going to say more when pain overtook her. Mary died that night, and Marcy's last words to her mother were her promise to visit Moxie.

The first scene that played in her mind on her flight down to uncertainty was of coming upon the boarded up farmhouse and finding Moxie's gravestone in the back field. He had died one year before her arrival. The date of death on his stone was one week after her mom died. Marcy fell to her knees and cried for this man whom she felt she knew so well but would never meet.

Why had she waited so long to come?

Sky was held tight while her mother cried for a very long time.

Marcy and Sky broke into the farm house under the pretense of staying one night. When they walked into Moxie's living room Marcy felt like she was falling into his arms. His presence was strong. He was there in all his things that he had described so well. This place was in her. For it was true to the words described in his letters she had heard through much of her youth. Marcy felt such a deep connection to this place she could not leave.

She took black plastic that she found in the shed and covered up the windows from the inside so no one could see the light from the lanterns she lit at night. The house was buttoned and boarded up tight. Beyond just gone for the season. Not like anyone came up there anymore anyways since the boys moved away after their dad's death. During the days Marcy opened a back shutter and window to let in air and some light in the living room. Marcy was an artist in her blood. Sky loved art as well. They painted on rainy days and played in the back field and explored the woods on good ones. It was on one of these explorations that they first spotted Tilly. They loved to paint her after that.

- CHAPTER 3 -

She lied there in that soft grass with a moose standing over her dreaming of her mama. She could see her face, her full lips with her loving smile. She had blue eyes and reddish auburn hair so unique in color. It was good for Sky to see her mama smiling and laughing again. Before coming to the farmhouse her mother did not have many smiles.

A sharp high shrill, a kill cry from a coyote close by in the woods, tore Sky from her dream. She felt the earth move as Tilly jumped in response to that howling screech. With her eyes open and looking at Tilly she heard the return howl from the den farther off acknowledging that dinner was on. She knew the songs of the coyotes. Her Ma told her they were really smart and clever.

Tilly was all perked up. Hair standing on end, head moving, eyes bulging. She sniffed the scent right out of the air. Ears alert with that one ear missing its tip. That's how Sky knew it was Tilly. Moxie described her in his letters and her mom painted her that way. There was lots of movement in the woods as the coyotes ate their kill. Nostrils flaring, Tilly stood close guard.

Tilly was showing signs of anxiety. When the air is charged like that all the critters buy into the anxiety and fear of the kill. It becomes a collective of negative energy that gives in. Sky did not give in, and Tilly felt that resonance of peace and strength. She turned and looked at the child's blue eyes and felt calmed.

Sky, with all the compassion that only a child can show, started to hum.

- CHAPTER 4 -

The sound of the coyotes always disturbed Tilly. You can't blame her. After a certain species tries to eat you for dinner it's hard to be trusting. She was trying to stay focused on what was going on in the woods but her mind kept replaying scenes of the past. The sound of feet moving fast close by on the forest floor. Then pain in her behind and hind leg as three coyotes brought her down to the ground, teeth ripping her flesh, deep growling of the coyotes and her own cry of pain. Then a gun shot very close and piercing pain at the tip of her right ear. She went into shock after that coming in and out of consciousness.

She remembered the sound of Moxie's voice. The first time she had heard it, she and her mother had been eating the high grass in the wooded wetland close to the big barn. He talked the way he would to his cows when he brought them in for milking. Soft and strong.

They put her in a pen snug in the side of the barn and fed her milk from a bottle spiced hard with Scottish Whiskey to dull her pain. Moxie spent time with her talking soft and gentle to calm and soothe the wounded calf. In time she fell into the fold of the farm.

There were two dogs on the farm called Rex and Sally. Moxie made them sleep out with Tilly to protect her at night. At first the dogs resented their new assignment, but that young female moose calf won them over. A great and very playful friendship developed. On cold nights lying next to Tilly was like a furnace. It was quite a sight, two dogs and a moose all woven in, sleeping hard like sheep.

Once Tilly could walk the dogs started to chase and play with her. At first it was the head fakes and jumping to a crocked run. Then it got rough. The dogs started it by taking Tilly down one fine day. They both grabbed her right front leg and pulled across and back from under her belly. Down she went hard. Tilly learned then to be proactive and keep them out from under foot by giving them some hoof. She got good and dangerous from any leg in many positions. There were bumps and bruises, mostly the dogs, but they got smarter and in time their play became a great sight to witness.

When the child stopped humming she patted the ground next to her

"Lie down" Tilly knew those words. Drawn in by those blue eyes, Tilly went and laid down next to Sky and cuddled like she had with the dogs.

- CHAPTER 5 -

The next scene that played in Marcy's mind on her fall down was her mom dying. As much as she tried to prepare for it in the last six months, it devastated her. Her mom had always been there for her. That loss left a hole in Marcy's life. For days she was numb, unable to get out of bed. A neighbor watched out for Sky and tried to feed Marcy to no avail. She willed herself out of bed after three days. She had to look after her daughter and organize her mother's funeral. At the time she was a functioning zombie but looking back she saw all the people that were at the funeral. Her mom had so many different friends. She now saw each of their faces and their characters strong in her mind's eye. They reflected much of who her mom was, a woman open to the world. A curious soul always marveling at the wonders of life, her friends so diverse. It was a strong feeling of comfort to see her in this new light through her friends as she descended down.

Then there was the selling of her mother's possessions. Marcy only wanted a few things, a rocking chair, an oil painting and the family photos. She sold the rest to auction. Gave away her mom's clothes to Salvation Army keeping one of her mom's silly hats. The estate was complicated to settle and would take years to free up money for Marcy and Sky to use. She needed to work. They fled to the west in a Subaru wagon doing what Marcy knew. Paint.

Marcy convinced the owner of a commercial building in downtown Boulder, Colorado to do a mural of a wildlife scene on the facade, at cost. It was a big success and several newspapers printed articles on her mural. She got the word out and work took her to different towns all over the west.

They made some friends but mostly stayed to themselves. Men would try to approach her when she was working in public places. She was quite a sight to see from the street up there on the staging with her long auburn hair blowing in the wind. Men pretended to show interest in her work but always ended the conversation with an invite to dinner. She always declined. She used to have a good libido but it was just not there. No interest. With her desire to flirt gone she saw men as very singular in focus. They bored her. Looking back she understood that she had closed herself off to any connection that could end in more loss. All those towns flashed in her mind. She could not see past the pain. She was also weighted down with an old sorrow beyond just that of her mother's death that she noticing for the first time. A chain of suffering in her family she could not place. Stories never told but strong feelings felt. Like it was in her genes. A family that has suffered for causes. How to be true to herself with such a genetic hangover? What is the purpose? Who were these ancestors that died for causes? The legacy of her mother. Would she carry it on, or not? These questions were brought to the surface from deep in her sub consciences. Falling down a well.

- CHAPTER 6 -

Moxie's death brought on great change for his three sons. They were all in their twenties. The oldest, Shawn, wanted to travel, get away from the daily grind. The youngest, Brian, was all about fishing and the sea. But the middle son, Jake, loved the farm and took the death the hardest. For six months after their father's death they all tried running the farm. It was really hard without Moxie. They were reminded of his absence constantly. His presence was everywhere.

What really kept the farm financially afloat was the mechanic shop. Moxie fixed motors and pumps when he wasn't tending to the farm. Brian was the one who had Moxie's touch with machines but he used it on motors in boats not on land. He just wanted to be fishing. To the shock of Moxie's life long customers, they shut down the shop.

Jake and Shawn made up for the loss of income by working carpentry jobs. All three boys worked the farm early mornings and evenings. Those were some long days. The change came when Brian got a job offer fishing in Alaska. That ignited Shawn's dream to travel to Mexico. Jake tried talking his brothers into staying and working through their hard tide. His brothers felt it was time to let go.

"There is the life you are born with then the one you make for yourself as you move on in life. Time to move on" said Shawn.

For the most part the boys had always gotten along. As boys and teenagers they fought but it was what boys did. When it came time to make decisions in running the farm without Moxie, they quarreled. It got in the way of getting things done and was wearing on them and carried over to the home. Not the best of times. But once Shawn and Brian were gone it was lonely.

Jake worked all the time. He ate very little doing carpentry jobs and tending to the farm. He was depressed and lonely. As angry as he was with his brothers he really missed them. There was a huge hole at the farm and it was eating Jake up. His friends were worried about him. He was losing a lot of weight.

Six months after his brothers left, a tragedy happened at the farm. Jake came home and found two cows lying dead in the field. When he walked into the pasture he noticed a lot of very wet cow dung that were not solid at all. The rest of the herd looked feeble and listless. The cows were all very sick. The cows' drinking water, something was wrong with the water. He checked on the small ponds where the cows drank and found E-coli in the water from the farm's leaking septic system. Jake felt a sickening wave come over him. He was devastated. He loved those cows. Knew their mothers and fathers. Had helped some be birthed into life. Next to Moxie they were the farm.

It was like losing his father all over again. By overlooking the failing septic, he had killed the cows. A deep darkness overcame his being and he took to bed. He was in bad shape. Very dehydrated. They moved him to the hospital.

After months of mostly drinking coffee and very little food, Jake`s organs were stressed. As he was trying to give the cows as much fluids as he could, he neglected putting any into himself. His kidneys were barely functioning and his liver was overloaded. Stressed out body and soul, he was treading with just his nostrils above water.

His stay was long at the hospital. The neighbors took in the chickens and the dogs, and the cats were left to fend for themselves in the barn. When Jake was clear headed and coming out of it he asked Moxie's best friend Bert to board up the farmhouse. He could not stand the thought of going back there. His guilt was too strong to face it right then.

After coming out of the hospital he rented a garage apartment behind his good friend Jimmy's house. It was good. It meant Jake would not be alone. He could not even drive out to the farm. He tried to not think about it and made a new life. Making a new life for himself in town building and fixing, relaxing in the evenings instead of working. Johnny sometimes went out and checked on the old place but that got to be too much for him as well. The whole town for that matter stayed away. A place that was so full of life and laughter to now be boarded and listless was too much for any of `em to take.

On the east ridge there was an old fire tower. It was hard to see when looking at the wooded ridge line but she was there. Built after the big fire in sixty-five it had not been manned in years. Jake told himself he was going to look over at the sea but his other self knew better. With binoculars he would be able to see the farm house from the tower. Jake focused in on the old place. He could see the back porch and the boarded up windows around it. He had never seen that scene before. It stung his heart and hollowed his stomach.

"Well at least she is still standing," he sounded off to himself.

It was two weeks later he spotted them. He had not been back since, but one day had an inkling to go back for another peek. What he first noticed was the one window next to the back door open to the air. Then when searching the back field, he saw Marcy and Sky kicking a ball around. He looked with his mouth fully ajar. He felt no territorial impulses to go marching out to the farm and demand to know just what they were doing. He watched in wonder as the mother went about washing clothes in a bucket on the back porch while the girl continued on with the ball. Women living at the farm. He never recalled ever seeing a woman doing chores at the farm. He loved it. Part of him missed not having a mother around or any sisters when growing up, felt cheated out of life by the imbalance in his family. Lost in his emotions he packed it up.

He laid awake that night thinking it over. Squatters at the farm.

And women at that.

"The old man would have a laugh on that one," he told the ceiling and smiled big. Something he had not done in a long time. He would not do anything to interrupt their stay at the moment. He would just keep an eye on 'em.

It eased some of the pain for Jake to watch mother and daughter at work and play around the farm. It was like a different story was being written and he could look at it through that new perspective and breathe. He also loved to watch Marcy's movements. She was beautiful, but that was not what caught Jake's attention. Her body movements seemed so familiar. He felt calmed by watching her work. Life at the farm, new life.

- CHAPTER 7 -

The Henney Family owned and ran The Dragger Inn. It'd been in the family generations, built by Great Grandpa Henney as a seaside retreat for his big family and friends back when the family used to have oodles of money. His son lost it all on the market and booze. After big stock losses he made a big gamble on a bootleg run during prohibition. It went bust and into the papers. Henney Jr. went down with a show. The mansion by the sea somehow stayed in the family but sat empty for some years until one of the sons of Junior and his wife wandered to Maine. They put some life back into the old place and turned it into an inn. It started out with a few beds and a fine pub and grill. The locals were the first customers. They set the tone for the place and kept the bills paid.

After a bit they were dying to know who would be the first highlander customers. Then the newlyweds from Chicago showed up. Some the locals were so wound up from all their projected stories they did not let them sleep. They had found out about the inn in an ad in some obscure travel magazine.

It started out as a joke. One night after a few, Johnny Magee brought in this magazine with a free coupon to write up your own ad. Well they took it upon themselves to help the Henney family out by writing the ad themselves and submitting it. They took many liberties with the truth. Boat rides, scenic tours, bikes for rent. All lies.

In time they forgot about it until the first official out of town-er customers finally showed up.

John and Peggy did not have a chance when they stepped out of the taxi. The happy hour boys were out on the porch with some of the waitresses having some lazy laughs. When they first stepped out of that cab the locals started hollering all kinds of nonsense.

"Bout time!"

"Can't believe it!"

They all ran out to greet them. Before they could even check in the crowd ushered them out to the porch. The view from that porch of the sea was a stunner.

"Oh my God John will you look at that," said Peggy with her mouth ajar.

"What ain't you seen the sea before?" Arthur Wallace kidded.

"No we haven't." It was the locals' turn to hang their jaws.

"I can't imagine that. You are grown people. Have not seen the sea. Nope can't imagine it," Kenny went on.

When the Henneys got done introducing and welcoming they asked how their guests from Chicago found out about The Inn.

"From the ad."

"What ad?" Lucy Henney asked.

The boys got real sheepish as Peggy pulled out of her purse that very ad of bullshit the pranksters had put together. Lucy could not believe what she was hearing when Peggy went on about how they couldn't wait to take one of those boat rides and get out on the sea for their very first time. Lucy caught the look on the guilty faces and lit into them with her eyes.

"I will be talking with you boys later."

She cornered them in the parking lot trying to make a retreat. Lucy Henney could make a pirate blush with her sharp tongue. When she got done ripping them up and back down. They claimed they would make it right by taking the folks from away out on Magee's lobster boat.

"And the singing minstrels? Who will do that?" Lucy taunted them, then broke down laughing and yelled out, "You Bastards!"

The boys did all they could to make up for it. They really spoiled that newlywed couple from Chicago. The whole town did for that matter. Never let them rest. They took them out on boat rides and found bicycles for them to use. The women came over and counseled Peggy on married life. The church choir got out on the porch and sang matrimonial songs. So because of a prank, a tradition was started. One of an informal economy of boat tours and bike rentals and the locals making sure that those from away had a good time and left with a good understanding of local perspective.

Tilly could smell the salt on Sky's sweaty skin. She used to lick the salt off of Moxie and his boys` skin. She did it right then. Sky giggled. It tasted different from the males. The only other girl Tilly had licked was Sally Sweeny. It was over at the Inn. Back in the heyday of the mansion they had a small pen and lawn for a milk cow. Trees had since taken over the lawn and a stone retainer wall backed up to those trees. It was a spot where smokers and lovers sat and looked at the sea. Moxie's son Jake was sitting on that wall with Sally thinking real hard on how to get that first kiss. Sally was waiting real hard. What they did not know was that they had a witness very close by. Tilly was in the trees right behind them keeping an eye on Jake. It was a hot summer night. That beautiful neck of Miss Sweeny's was wet with perspiration. When Jake pointed out the lights of the ferry she looked away to the sea. Tilly saw that open shiny neck and went in for a quick lick. It was not the kiss Sally had anticipated. Instead it was rough as sanded paper and slimy wet. She ran screaming. Wondering how a boy with such a nice face could have such a nasty tongue.

Jake was devastated and went home to complain to Moxie. His dad laughed so hard and long that Jake finally saw the humor in it. He never did get to kiss Sally Sweeny. When she went on to marry and divorce one of his buddies he finally felt thankful to Tilly.

Moxie's wife died shortly after the birth of her third son. It devastated Moxie changing all of their lives. To hold himself together he set a course of action on how he would raise his boys. One of the things he wanted to honor and support was their diversity from one another. He knew each of his sons was different in mood and what they wanted to do with their time. Support their interests is what he did.

Jake had an interest in carpentry, far too restless for the mechanic shop. So Moxie took him along when doing his carpentry jobs. To keep things going financially he was a caretaker for two houses "up on the shore" as the locals would say. There were always things that needed doing on those places. Besides all the maintenance, every so many years there was a new dormer or kitchen he would build. From the time Jake was able to walk with a steady foot he had helped his dad on those projects. Because of his small size Moxie had him climbing and crawling into all kinds of troubled situations.

When Jake was twelve there was a leak in the roof at the Ellsworth place. The very high roof peered down cliffs to the sea below. His dad did not have a ladder long enough to reach the leak. In his great ability to come up with solutions he signed Jake up to take the risk. He tied a rope around his son and walked him out the upstairs bedroom window onto the porch roof. On the roof was a ladder going up to the edge of the big roof. He then threw that big honking hemp rope over the peak. Jake could hear the other end hitting ground on the small lawn.

Moxie handed his son a shingle thief and hammer and said "Jakie boy I am going to the other side. When yah feel two tugs start climbing until you come to where those missing shingles are."

Jake knew to trust the rope and lean away from the incline of the roof. He could walk right up that way. He hollered over to his dad and went to work pulling out shingles around the wounded area so he could slide new ones in.

The view was killer. Jake loved being up high like that and when the wind lifted his hair he felt close to flying.

He was working away, fully supported by that rope when his dad hollered up on Jake's side, "How they coming up?"

"Hey Dad! If you are over here who is over there holding the rope?"

"Ah don't you worry son I got' er tied off. Have faith. She's a good knot."

Jake went back to work wondering on the trust thing with the rope. His dad came out on the porch roof, hand lined some shingles up to Jake and went back in through the bedroom window. With the nails he had in his apron he wove and tacked those shingles in just as slick as you please. It took some time.

When he finished, he hollered for his dad to lower him down. After no response Jake untied himself and used the extra rope to lower himself down to the ladder on the porch roof. When he stuck his head in the window he was greeted to quite a sight. The other end of the rope was coming in the other window and tied right off onto the cast iron bed that Moxie was lying flat on. Snoring away with a Louis L'Amour novel lying on his chest. The bed had wheels and in front of the them were wash clothes to stop the bed from sliding across the room into the window.

Jake woke up his Dad and questioned his choice of an anchor, "Don't worry Jakie boy you only would have fallen a few feet until the window stopped the bed. Ah boy! You got to have faith in the rope." When Jake was sixteen Moxie sent him to the Ellsworth place to fix some board walks. It was Monday, Memorial Day. His dad said there would be some kids staying there and not to worry about them. "Go in, get 'er done."

Well when Jake pulled up to the Ellsworth place late morning he got an education badly needed. The first words to himself where "They sure ain't kids."

The places up on the shore all had outdoor showers. No one lived close enough to see, so why not feel the wonders of being outside when showering. Sitting on towels in the sand were five naked women waiting to use the outdoor shower. Other than Playboy, he had never seen a real live naked woman, let alone five. He froze and turned bright red in his truck.

Kirsten Ellsworth, a stunner at twenty-one years, stood and wrapped herself in a towel and walked over to Jake. She remembered him from some years in the past. Always so shy. Those green eyes and dark hair looked good on him now that he had grown to almost six feet. She laughed at him blushing.

"My Dad said it was O.K. to fix those boardwalks by the shower, but I think I will go," Jake said while just glimpsing at her naughty shiny brown eyes.

"Oh no, we can just go inside and shower," she replied and rested her hand on Jake's for a moment before walking away. He sat and swelled.

Jake was using the sawzall to cut away rotten pieces of old boardwalk when out came Kristen still wrapped in a towel.

"I don't want to wait. I'll just use this shower real quick," and dropped the towel with her back to Jake, wearing nothing but a thong. Her bottom was a work of nature's wonders. He stared with his mouth wide open. She stepped into the spray of warm water and cupped her breasts in the crook of her arm and gave Jake a side glimpse of a breast and pink nipple. Delivered with a coy grin. He spun away going in circles with that sawzall just a`humming away. The other girls looked out the window laughing.

Lying next to Sky and tasting the salt got Tilly thinking past Sally Sweeny to the boys. When she was an injured young calf just getting up and running around, they came looking for her. They were age six on up with a year between `em, dressed with pillow cases hanging off their shoulders and armed with a red shower curtain, rod and all, to wave before Tilly the bull. She was excited for the company and went running at the boys. Shawn waved that red curtain in front of Tilly and she stopped dead in front of it. Well they could have none of that so Shawn hollered at Brian to get a stick and whack her in the ass.

"That will get 'er jumping."

The youngest of the boys found a stick and whacked poor Tilly`s behind. In the act of true instinctual self-defense, her right hind hoof came out quick as lightning and sent Brian flying against the barn. When he come to his brothers were hauling him back to the house in a wagon with that red shower curtain dragging behind.

That bullfighting experience earned Tilly some respect with the boys. They decided to promote her to horse status, "running with mankind". Soon after Bryan's ribs healed they took after Tilly with their trusty cowboy boots on snug. They knew she would be skittish from the last time the three of them appeared, so they had a trusty lasso. Tilly had free run of the farm during the day. They found her up by the chicken coop sniffing up cultch. Shawn just plain missed on the first attempt. On the second when she was on a run Shawn got her clean. Once that lasso took hold he got the ride of his young life. Tilly took off for the barn and Shawn held on. He could not hold out long on a dead run. He fell head first and was dragged the rest of the way to the barn on his stomach. They were both huffing and puffing not moving when Jake and Bryan caught up with them.

"Nice going Shawn."

"Good work bro," as they grabbed the rope.

They led a tired Tilly up close to the wooden fence, where Shawn was upright on the top waiting to jump on Tilly.

"Throw me the rope once I jump on!" He jumped fast and so did Tilly.

The boys argued for years about what exactly happened. Shawn claims he rode Tilly and was thrown off. His brothers claim he never made it that far, that she moved out so fast his leg caught, then he was hung up in the rope and fell wrong. The end result was irrefutable: Shawn broke his arm. It was a long summer for that boy with a plaster cast and no swimming allowed.

- CHAPTER 8 -

Still falling, Marcy could see Sky's face when she was first born-clear as day, nothing else. How glad she felt for that birth. Then came visions of what was before the birth of her daughter. How for the first month of being pregnant she did not know if she was going to keep the baby. So much uncertainty, or so it seemed back then. She met Paul at an outdoor concert. A guitar player passing through with the band. Marcy fell in love with his charisma not finding out who he was until it was too late. She left college to travel with him and the band. When she became pregnant and told him he freaked out. A baby was not in his plans. End of discussion on his part. He turned cold and broke her heart. She stepped off the road and let Paul roll on.

The news did not surprise Marcy's mother. It was almost like she expected it. She was very supportive for Marcy having the child though it still did not feel all right.

Marcy went back and forth.

After a month of very little sleep and lots of confusion she made the decision. One day at a bus stop, there was a young woman with a baby sitting on the bench. The mother had eyes only for that baby. She had that maternal glow and looked so happy. Marcy wanted that glow of love.

She moved to a small town in West Virginia where as a child she went with her parents on summer vacations. Sky was born there.

Falling and looking back Marcy could not imagine life without Sky.

A sound like a young girl screeching brought Tilly to her feet and Sky to tears. Tilly was not afraid of the fisher cat, but Sky had never heard that noise before. It sounded human and horrible. She covered her ears with her hands and wailed back. It was out there hunting with its mate, scaring the prey out of hiding. Now with the child crying every predator in the woods would be aware of them. Tilly was back on full alert scanning the woods for movement. Sky would not stop crying.

Sometimes with the dogs, Tilly would nibble them with her fronts lips all perked out. The dogs loved that. She did it to Sky to calm her. It worked. At first she laughed through tears the way all kids do, then she just giggled. It was a site - a moose nibbling a child with those bulky lips.

More noise in the woods. Both child and moose looked out into the night. That screech had gotten critters scared and moving. Two of the barn cats came and sat surprisingly close to Sky. A wild screeching, then yelping of pain announced a nasty brawl with the fishers and some local raccoons. It was really more drama than action from outside the woods, but it sounded ugly. Sky was in awe, beyond tears. Tilly knew the sounds of a skirmish.

The yelping stopped, then three raccoons ran out of the woods right at them. They were just running for cover, but Tilly took no chances. When the first one tried to run by she got him with a rear left hoof that sent that him flying. The other two got out of there.

The next thing Marcy relived was her childhood love, Keith. Click back to a specific day of teenage-hood. A classic. They were both sixteen and hanging out in Keith's room. They had been neighbors all their lives. She was lying on the floor studying and rolled over towards the bed. Something caught her eye. Marcy reached under the bed and pulled out three playboy magazines, "Ahhhh you naughty boy. What do you have here?"

"Hey put those back!" Keith turned very red.

"What do you do when you look at these women?" She was flipping through the pages humiliating Keith. "Do you wank?" She looked at Keith for the truth.

"Come on Marcy it`s personal"

"Hey we all do it. No need to get so red in the face"

"Really, you do it?"

"Of course, silly. Girls do it to. Let's do it together right now."

"Jeez Marcy what are you crazy?"

"Come on do you remember when we were six and played doctor?"

"Oh god I try to forget that stuff."

"Well I don't. Let me see it now?"

"You are a pervert."

"Hey I am not the one with the girly magazines stashed under my bed. Don't you wonder how I look naked now?"

"Well kind of..."

"Come on Keith let's play doctor again..."

"We`re not kids any more, Marcy."

"Oh! You are such a chicken shit."

"Ok, ok. Who goes first?" growing excitement in his face.

"Let's flip to see."

Keith lost and had to strip first. He had developed nicely since he was six and she liked what she saw. He was so shy and awkward standing naked before Marcy. She smiled and stripped looking at Keith the whole time and watching his reaction. When she was naked he got hard fast.

"I guess you like my body."

He blushed again and asked, "Ok now what?"

"Show me how you do it. I want to see."

"You have to, too."

"Ok, let's sit opposite each other on the bed."

Keith's mother came home early, and hearing strange noises from her son`s room, she walked in. Marcy could not see Keith for a long time after that. Their parents made such a big deal out of nothing. Marcy thought they were just being honest about what everybody does. After that she saw adults as hypocrites.

They did eventually lose their virginity to each other. Their parents could not keep them apart forever. After high school he went out West and she to NYC. Looking back Marcy felt the personal act in which they were caught was much more memorable than the loss of her virginity. It was more open and honest. She wondered what happened to the brazen girl she once was, the one who could talk the pants off of a boy.

Jake was lonely. Beyond the loss of his father and missing his brothers, he needed female companionship. Three months before his Dad died he had broken up with a woman he had been dating for three years, June. She had gone off with one of his friends. That stuff happens, but it was the way Jake found out that destroyed him. He showed up at her house one early afternoon- something he did not normally do, but they had finished up a job and called it a day. He was thinking how pleased she would be to see him. She had been complaining for a long time about not seeing enough of him.

He went waltzing in like he owned the place. The first thing he saw were the crazy rainbow-striped socks he had gotten June that Christmas. They were on her feet and her feet were sticking straight up in the air above the couch. Between her spread legs was his buddy Neil. What really hurt and what stuck with him for years after was the sounds of her moaning. He had never heard her like that before. It really stung hard.

June and Neil heard the door slam and got up to see Jake jumping in his truck and driving off.

"You said he never shows up during the day."

"He never did until now."

Once Jake got over the initial shock, his anger was the most dominant emotion for the first twenty-four hours. He raced down Route One out of town and drove for several hours, his mind racing with the images of what he saw. Then he put the pieces of their relationship together, looking for signs.

He turned around and drove back, Neil`s betrayal stoking his anger. He ran up the steps to Neil's house and kicked in the door. His roommates were playing cards. They looked up in surprise at the door flying open and a very angry Jake standing with his fists tight at his sides.

"Where is Neil?!"

"Took some stuff and left, man! Hey what the fuck is with kicking in our door?"

"Fuck off" was all Jake said as he turned and ran down the stairs. He went back to June's house to confront her. The place was pitch black.

June and Neil took off to Canada for a very long weekend then decided to move to California together. Jake did not see either one when they came back and moved out. One month later he got a letter from June with a San Diego postmark.

I know you hate me right now. It just happened, Jake. You were not around when I needed you and Neil was. It surprised the both us when it first happened. Now it feels right. I am sorry Jake, June.

Short and bitter.

The anger was replaced with a hollow ache. Jake lived in its shadow for a long time, just barely going through the motions and torturing himself with the image of those rainbow socks and the sound of her moaning. Over and over.

After Moxie died he would often sit in the woods and wait for Tilly. She had long since left the farm and been back out in the wild. She would come in the late afternoons and feed in the wooded marsh behind the barn. Jake wanted company but no conversation. Tilly was the perfect friend for that. She chewed on grass and looked at Jake with those dark eyes.

When the first chilly fall winds came she charged at Jake for old time's sake. That funny moose was a part of Jake's life. A constant, consistent, loyal friend. He needed her presence. The peace. It helped in the slow climb back, finding center for himself, rebuilding.

"I wish you had licked June and sent her running before our first kiss, Tilly," he laughed long and hard.

After the break-up, Jake's brothers were quite cavalier about it. Shawn slapping him on the back, "Tough one Jakie boy. But hey, you been going together a long time. You are too young to get hitched. She did you a favor really." Brian was even worse. "No shit, I did not think the old girl had it in her." Moxie surprisingly had the most compassion for his pain.

Jake had taken over Moxie's caretaking jobs and expanded a carpentry business from there. With all three boys bringing income to the farm, Moxie could focus on the shop and farm. Two months before he dropped from a heart attack he came along on a carpentry job with Jake. "Jeez boy, starting to lose my touch with the old hammer. Time for a little practice," he chatted away while climbing in the truck with Jake.

They set up on one of those big porches up on the shore. Building screens to enclose the porch for July. It was off season for the big porch people. Moxie was doing all the talking.

"You got some pain going son, that is plain as day. Just hang on best ya can." Moxie held Jake's eye.

"Before you were born I went with a girl named Mary. She'd been coming up for summers working as a counselor over at the camp. I worked on keeping all those outbuildings standing. You know all that. But not about her." Moxie walked away from his tools and placed both hands on the hand rails looking out at the sea and drifting back in time with his story.

"That first summer we got to know each other. When she came back for the second it got hot from the get go. But she broke my heart when she went back to college in the fall and got back with her old boyfriend. She went on about how sorry she was but she did not like being alone and he was right close by and all such rot. Then I found out she got married that very month."

"That fast?"

"She was pregnant."

"Wow that must have really hurt."

"Well I survived. Come out of it a better man."

"How so Dad?"

"The pain. Forced me to find strengths I had in myself that I did not know were there."

"But what I got to tell you is this. All those letters I been getting from my so-called pen pal over the years were from her."

"You got to be kidding me?"

"Nope, right after your mom died she sent me a sympathy card. Softened me up on that one. We been writing ever since. She has a girl just older than Shawn. She gave me some great advice through the years on raising you boys. Aye! all that anger and bitterness. Had it in me for years. It weakened me. I finally forgave her. By doing that, I was free from all that nasty negativity and could thrive. The sooner you can forgive June the better."

"No way, have you forgot what she did to me?"

"No Jake, but she did it for herself. Exploring her passion through someone other than you. Hard to take I know. You loved her. You feel betrayed by love, but love is pure Jake. People

44

will let you down in life. We are all just trying to struggle along. Don't be so hard on `em. Don't stop believing in love son."

Two years later Jake was lying down in his garage apartment. He had taken a nap after work and in that spot between wakefulness and sleep, June's face was vivid as day before him. When he came all the way to wakefulness he was reaching out into thin air trying to hug that image.

"Shit! I still love that women," he ranted to the rafters. He got to thinking back on that conversation with Moxie on the porch. "Dad is right I need to forgive her. Time to move on. Time to love again."

He had a thoughtful dinner alone, sitting in his chair with a standing lamp next to it, reading and thinking until 1 A.M. The hole in his heart was keeping him from the farm.

"Time to face all this sadness, Jake. Get her back up and running," he told that open book. He had to make more money to pay the property taxes and start a new herd of cows. Needed to find a good woman.

"Woman! Shit, I got to deal with the one squatting at the farm." Yes, time to go back.

When Marcy was eight she named her dog Rex after Moxie's dog. All the stories of the two dogs and Tilly in his letters had influence. Rex was her favorite. They spent a lot of time together. That silly Shephard always followed Marcy around. She never wanted to tie Rex up and was always getting into trouble with animal control. For the most part he kept all the action in the neighborhood, but there were times when he would roam. Rex was a people person and needed to expand his social horizons beyond what the neighborhood had to offer. He would wander far.

One time they got a collect call from Rex. A couple from Connecticut found him sleeping in the back of their car when they returned from visiting Long Island. Apparently he crawled in the open hatch back when they were packing and got under a Hudson Bay blanket they had over their luggage. The couple were quite surprised to find Rex there in the back when they were unloading. They called the number collect on his tags. He spent the night there, and Marcy and her Mom drove to Connecticut the next morning to get him. It was a really big and fancy house.

"My, my and they called collect," Ma said as they walked up to the front door. When they walked in Rex was lying in the middle of a shag carpet looking like the King of Sheeba. Ginny Wentworth said they had no dog food so she had fried him up a steak for breakfast, "What a Dog!"

Rex had this antisocial habit of sticking his nose up women's dresses and taking a big whiff and a lick. He surprised and shocked quite a few women with this habit of his and there are some great stories. The most memorable was the day Rex went downtown and visited The Law Office of Shaw Whipple and Earnstein. The office was on the fourth floor. Rex had walked right into the open elevator on the ground floor. When someone on the fourth floor pushed the button, up went Rex.

The partners and associates were out in the hall mingling while having a coffee break. Beth Barnard, an associate being reviewed for partner, was bending over getting coffee when those elevator doors opened. The first thing that Rex saw when the doors opened was the bent over form of Beth and the opening at the hem of her dress. Rex wanted to reward his lonely ride up in the elevator with a friendly sniff and lick. He bolted for the opening and went right up her dress. Now, the offices of Shaw, Whipple and Earnstein are very conservative. All employees dressed accordingly. The women wore business suits that went from the shoulders straight down without showing any knee

Her scream echoed off walls lined with expensive oil paintings as Rex made contact. Because of the long length of her dress Rex got stuck underneath.

Finally Beth had to lift her dress up to let the dog out. Creating a great deal of embarrassment for Beth Barnard. She pushed the law to the max on that one, making it very expensive to get Rex out of the pound.

Pinch Face Parker was one of Marcy's neighbors. Her real name is Florence Parker but the kids for years had called her Pinch Face because she was always scowling and yelling at them. Well, Old Pinch Face Parker was always after Marcy about her not tying up Rex.

"We have leash laws in this neighborhood, young lady," or "Marcy that wretched scoundrel dog of yours has been digging my rose beds again. I will call animal control if you don't tie that dog up!"

"Oh Sorry Mrs. Parker he just loves to dig in the dirt. He don't know no better."

"Yes, well you do, so tie him!"

Then came that fine summer day when Pinch Face was having a Garden Club luncheon on her front porch. She was really trying to put on a show for that bunch of battle-axes. In front of her porch she had a big lawn. She had the sprinkler adjusted to just the right section. It was a nice one, could really put out some water.

Rex loved to lie in the cool dirt under the rose bushes along that porch. The hose to the sprinkler was coming from a spicket close to Rex's hiding spot. The hose was in competition with his comfort level so he took care of the problem by taking the hose between his teeth and yanking the hose out of the way. That changed the direction of all the water coming out of the sprinkler, aiming it right at the gathering Garden Clubbers. There was not a dry face left on that porch. The mascara ran, making it look more like a Halloween party than a Garden Club Luncheon. Through blurred vision, Pinch Face saw Rex running away from the noise of all the screaming and knew who the culprit was. She called animal control and Marcy's dad had to fork over more money to bust Rex out of the pound again.

When Marcy was fourteen she was walking home from school and spotted a crowd of neighbors out in the street near her home. When they turned and saw her coming the expression in their faces alerted Marcy to the tragedy. She went running through the crowd and saw Rex lying in the road.

It was a hit and run. Killed him right away. It devastated Marcy. What really destroyed her was how her parents just expected life to go on as normal. She felt betrayed by their lack of compassion for her pain.

One of the visions during her fall was of the day Rex died. Of herself holding his lifeless body in the street and crying like she had never cried before. All the individual faces of her neighbors, watching with those expressions of pity and collective embarrassment That day marked the end of her innocence.

Sky had wonderful red curly hair. Just amazing to look at. Perfect little curls. Tilly had never seen anything like it. Moxie and the boys were all short-hairs, just like most critters. But this one was long and shiny red. The child stood next to Tilly, her hair right there just below Tilly`s long head. While the child was standing close, she put her nose into Sky's hair and snorted it in. This created quite a tickling sensation in Tilly`s big nostrils. She sneezed. It was a funny sound to Sky. While Tilly`s head was down Sky reached out and touched the ear with no tip. "Boo-boo." She looked into Tillys eyes and craned her head to the side with a look of true compassion. Those expressions of this child, so tender!

Sky was having the adventure of her life that night. At times it was scary but being with Tilly was very nice. She had camped all her life with her mom. When they were drifting amongst towns out west they camped a lot, all that public land provided lots of free places to camp. Marcy had a tent, but when the skies were clear and bright with stars they would sleep out, looking up at the galaxy above and dreaming of other worlds.

Sky wondered where Mama was. She held tight to Tilly`s big head and looked into the open field hopeful for the sight of her mother approaching. Instead a flock of turkeys with a large Tom leading the hens towards the barn came into sight. The hens looked funny to Sky, the way they walked thrusting their long necks and heads forward in rapid sequence. They were gobbling away to each other, getting louder as the flock approached. The Tom got a sight of the moose and child and felt they were a threat to his domain. Thrusting out his chest and wings, squawking at attack speed, the big Tom took on Tilly. It was a sight to behold, turkey and moose butting heads. Tilly's nose hit the chest, lifting the Tom up and over. The Tom a bit dazed and confused from the rugged landing, picked himself up and strutted on as if in victory towards his beloved hens. Sky giggled.

- CHAPTER 9 -

The images from her life were moving faster. She was coming to the end of her reel. A quick shot of herself in that big elm tree in her childhood. She spent a lot of her youth in the limbs of that old elm. Marcy loved that tree. It always made her feel a part of something bigger than herself.

Then she watched herself learn to ride a two-wheeler the day her father took off the training wheels. She had a clear image in her mind of him running behind her on the bike. His hands letting go of the seat. Being set free to find her balance. She felt like she was flying, took off on a wobbly run down the driveway and made the turn onto the sidewalk. She kept going and going, laughing with the joy of her first flight. The ability to be mobile with wheels marked the beginning of independence from her parents. It was also the last thing she and her father did together. Other than those stressful drives to bust Rex out of the pound, they were rarely alone together.

Her father, her father was echoing in her head.

When Marcy was three she spent a couple of nights in the hospital. She had fallen from her first journey up the big elm and broken her collar bone and wrist badly. They kept her in the hospital to control the pain through an I.V.

She had a mental picture of the tray of food in front of her. They kept the food covered on the ride up from the kitchen with a stainless cover. It had a hole in the middle so she could stick her finger in to lift it away. She loved that cover, the mystery that lay underneath. You did not know what was for supper until you lifted the lid.

A clear image of her mother's face glowing with maternal love as she is held Marcy as a baby. She felt complete trust and security she felt in her mother arms.

When Jake and his brothers were exploring the well, they hammered pieces of rebar into the earth for footholds. Just below Marcy on her fall down the well was a trap door she'd fallen through. It had fetched up on one of those pieces of re-bar and laid across the well creating a platform. Marcy's fall came to a sudden stop when she landed feet first on that platform. The impact collapsed her legs underneath her and brought her head hard against the earth. She was knocked out cold.

Jake was dreaming of his dad. That last week before his death he was acting out of character. He had gotten a letter from his so-called pen pal Mary and seemed deeply disturbed. He wanted to get all his boys together, said there was something very important that he needed to tell them. Brian was out at sea fishing. When he came back they would have their talk. They never got that chance. Jake found his dad lying on the floor next to the phone, which was off the hook. There was no pulse. Jake called 911 and started CPR. They continued trying to revive him in the ambulance with the defibrillator. The doctor in the emergency room declared him dead and stopped the CPR. Jake could not accept it. He kept hollering at the nurses to keep trying to revive his Dad. Two orderlies had to subdue him while the doctor gave a fast acting sedative with a very big needle. When Shawn arrived at the hospital, he was greeted with the sight of his father dead on one bed and Jake out cold in the one next to him.

Moxie's sudden death was a great shock to his three sons and the whole town. Those days after, much of the town came out to the farm to pay respects and share in the boys' suffering. The women brought casseroles and the men helped with the cows. Some just wandered about in a state of shock, standing in Moxie's shop trying to absorb some of his presence that was still lingering. For so many years he had been a constant, helping with their mechanical problems and having some good laughs in the process. Losing him would leave a deep hole in the town for time to come.

The boys hand dug his grave on the farm, taking turns with the picks and shovels, working in silent grief. Many gathered around his grave for hours, each talking in turn about Moxie. Stories of affection and much needed humor. The strength and significance of his soul being reflected back to Jake as he relived that period of his life.

His dream shifted to the present. He went out to sit on the rock wall by The Inn and his dad was there, sitting like he had all the time in the world and grinning up a storm.

"Dad what are you doing here? You're dead."

"I know son, but we can do this from time to time."

They talked about various things, mostly about the farm. Moxie pushed Jake to get it back up and running.

The last thing he said to him was, "Jake you got to replace that trap door over the old well."

"How did you know about that?"

"Yah, I always knew what you boys where up to."

"How come you never said anything?"

"Figured you all needed some adventuring."

Jake's dream moved onto that well he had explored as a boy. What an adventure that gave him, seeing time in the layers exposed by the hole. All the work to get to that hole. The layers of roofing and planking and six by sixes he had cut through with the hand saw. The make shift trap door he had made. How he hid that door with dirt and grass. The door was made rugged, even put shingles on it. He was seeing that door, the seams without flashing, water coming down through the grass and dirt down the seam to that vulnerable wood. If he had built it now he would have flashed that seam. How unstable it must be now. The roots from that rugged rhododendron must be the only thing holding it up. What a booby trap!

Jake awoke sitting bolt upright. The little girl out at the farm played under that rhododendron bush like he had as a kid. She could easily fall through that trap door. The image of it struck Jake with terror. Something was wrong. He could feel it in his bones. It was just after four in the morning. He grabbed his big flashlight and for the first time in over a year went out to the farm driving very fast.

Flying down Farm Road Jake visualized what he would find. How he would get her out from the bottom of the well?

"Be alive. Please be alive."

The ladder in the barn would not go near far enough. He turned on the C.B. radio that was still in his truck from the days when he was a volunteer on the Fire Department. He was surprised it worked after being turned off for so long. The head lights illuminated the boarded up farm house. Jake observed them but stayed focused on getting to the well. He drove across the front field to the rhododendron bush. Jake jumped out of the truck with the flash light and got down on his hands and knees to crawl under the bush.

As the light shone on the sides of the natural tunnel of the bush, Jake had a flash back to his childhood when he and his brothers would play flash light tag, remembering how he was exposed by his brother's light hiding in the bush. Now his light revealed what he feared. He could see one of the exposed six-by-sixes. He swallowed his heart as he crawled up to the open hole and peered down with his light.

"Holy shit it's the mother!" She was propped up on what was left of the door. One of her legs was at a bad angle to the side. It was obviously badly broken. She was bleeding from her head and unconscious.

"Hey! Wake up! Hey!" Jake hollered down that well so loud you would have thought he was trying to will her up and out of there.

He got on the radio and yelled.

"Chief get up!"

The fire chief was an old friend of his dad's and Jake had known him all his life. He knew he would have that radio on that was right next to his bed.

"Yah I'm up, who is this?"

"Chief, its Jake."

"Jake! Christ boy, good to hear your voice. How are yah?"

"Chief this ain't a social call. I am out at the farm and there is a woman unconscious in the well."

"Jake, you been drinking? There is only a drilled well at the farm."

"No sober as a sailor. Listen it's an old abandoned well from the 1700s. She is down in that."

"Abandoned well from the 1700s? What is ailing you, Jake?"

"Trust me on this one chief. I need the ambulance and the wrecker to haul her up with the cable winch. Oh and some chain saws."

It was Jake's tone of voice that finally convinced the chief to act on his commands. It sounded like the old Jake before he went into his dark funk.

After the chief set off the emergency tone and gave the details of the call. He headed out the door telling the dog, "This is going to be interesting."

Tilly heard the truck barreling down the road. Sky was under her feet curled up in a ball, covered in grass, sleeping. Tilly was listening hard into the night when she recognized Jake's voice yelling down that well. Help had arrived but Tilly knew she had to move Sky to get it. She first tried nudging the child with her nose to wake her. Not a chance. Tilly ended up picking Sky up by the back of her jumpsuit that was complete with attached bootees. What a shock to poor Sky to wake up from her sweet dreams dangling from the teeth of a moose. She squirmed and squealed until Tilly finally put her down. She let her sit there and cry herself out, then got her up and walking. The two of them made their way to the farm house with Tilly pushing most of the way.

It felt like forever before the crew showed up, but the boys made good time getting out to the farm. Jake was already going at the bush with an ax from his truck when they pulled in. The boys looked with sadness at the illuminated boards over the windows.

"What you whacking on the bush for Jake?" The chief hollering while stepping out of the ambulance.

"The well is under this bush. Hey Tug Boat and Clipper get those chain saws and get this bush out of here." Jake hollered to his childhood friends who had just stepped out of the wrecker.

They looked at the chief then back to Jake, then shrugged their shoulders and took down that icon of a bush that had always sat stoically before the farmhouse. It hurt to do it and took some time. She was a fighter.

The chief was the first to look down.

"I'll be, there is a woman down this well that I never knew about."

"Now ya believe me?" Jake saying while looking down with Chief.

"Who is she and how did she get down there?"

"She's been squatting here and obviously fell."

"How did you know she was squatting? You never come out here."

"Saw her with binoculars from the fire tower."

"Saw her squatting here and you did nothing?"

"Figured it was good someone was living here."

"Holy shit boy! How did you know she fell down this mystery well?"

"Had a premonition."

"A premonition?" the chief asked with raised eyebrows.

"Look, forget it. Let's get focused on getting her out of there" Jake yelled while going over to back the wrecker up to the hole.

They took the tri-pod for lifting motors from Moxie's shop, placed it over the hole and ran the cable winch wire over and down that. They lowered Jake down in a boatswains chair with an emergency kit to stabilize Marcy. He was very relieved to feel a steady pulse. He put a collar on her neck and tended to her bleeding head. They had to send a second cable down with a long board. It took some careful work to get her up in a position to long board her. She had to be vertical. Using safety harnesses, placed around her inner thighs and using the other cable they were able to get her vertical. Jake then had to tend to that broken leg. She had a pedal pulse so he was able to move the leg into a straight position for the splint. With Marcy hanging vertically he slipped the long board behind her and very carefully strapped her down. They were brought up one at a time, Marcy going first while Jake stood on a piece of re-bar, just as he had as a kid.

It was just coming into the light of day. They were putting the mystery woman onto the gurney of the ambulance when Tilly and Sky appeared from around the corner of the farm house. Time froze right at that moment when they all saw each other. All those grown men with their mouths hanging open looking at a moose with half of one ear. With a child that had a halo of red hair filled with grass hanging onto its leg.

"I'll be a monkey's uncle," the chief loudly whispered.

"Tilly, what have you done now?" from Clipper.

"Holy shit! That's her daughter," yelled Jake as he ran to gather the poor child in his arms.

"Where's mama?" cried Sky into Jake's neck.

"Your mother is over here on this bed resting."

"I want Mama!"

"OK Darling. What is your name?"

"Sky."

"That is a nice name. Your Mom has fallen down, Sky."

"Why?"

"It was an accident. She has a boo-boo on her head. That's why she has that bandage."

Jake took Sky over to see her mother. He put two of her tiny fingers over her mother's wrist to feel the pulse.

"Feel that. Your mom is doing good. She is sleeping real deep right now."

"Kiss Mama."

He held her at her mother's side. It touched Jake's heart to see such a precious act.

Clipper was in the back of the ambulance giving Marcy oxygen and an I.V. Jake was sitting in the passenger seat with Sky hanging tight in his lap. Chief was driving looking over at Jake from time to time giving him the old "You got some explaining to do" look. Jake ignored the chief. Holding that child was catharsis; she was melting into him with no resistance, just total trust. It caught Jake by surprise and disarmed him, thawing some of the ice around his heart. After a bit Sky softly pushed herself away from Jake's chest and looked up into his face. She tipped her head to the side and whispered into his open face.

"Jake."

"How did you know my name?"

"Pictures."

"From the family album in the farm house?"

"Uhhhhh."

"Sky, where did you sleep last night?"

"With Tilly."

"Ahhh, how did you know we call that moose Tilly?"

"Mama said."

"How did she know?"

"Tilly," Sky saying with affection.

Jake was trying to put it all together. When they went to the shop they discovered Marcy's Subaru in hiding. The name on the registration in the glove box was Marcy Crawford. Crawford, Crawford... Jake kept running through his mind fishing for that name. Then it hit him. The name on the return address on all those envelopes to his dad for all those years, Mary Crawford.

"Holy shit, Chief!"

"Out with it Boy!"

"You know Mary Crawford, that woman Dad's been writing all these years?"

"Imagine."

"That woman in the back must be her daughter."

"I'll be," the chief groaned out while looking over at Jake.

"They must have come looking for my Dad. Is that why you came here Sky, to see Moxie?"

"Uhuh, but he is dead."

"Yes Moxie is dead."

"Just me and Mama."

"Yes," Jake whispered into that pile of red hair and held Sky tighter.

They rode in silence, each lost in their own thoughts.

Once at the hospital, Jake, with Sky asleep on his shoulder, went to the front desk. Linda Magee, a friend of Moxie's since grammar school, was working there. Jake asked her to hunt down a phone number for Mary Crawford in Long Island. He needed to let her know what happened to her daughter. Linda's first search through information had no listing. She went to the computer and used a search engine for finding missing persons. From that she learned that Mary had died of liver cancer two years prior. Linda wrote the date of the death on a piece of paper in front of Jake.

"My God that was a week before my Dad died, Linda."

"I know" Linda breathed out. "Mary Crawford, how could I forget her. Your Dad was some smitten. A summer looker, knocked him clean for a loop. Oh how we all tried to tell him he was just a passing fancy to a city girl. He would have none of our talk. Well, we were right. It`s a good thing your mom come along when she did. She had the persistence of patient love. Helping him to pick up the pieces and set him right. What a pathetic mess he was," Linda shaking her head.

'He still wrote to her," Jake declared while thinking back.

"He got a letter from her a week before he died. He was some strange after he read that letter."

"How do you mean?" Linda looked concerned.

"He was lost in thought, wandering around kind of looking lost. Said he wanted to get us all together, had something real important to tell us."

"What was it, Jake?"

"He died before he could tell us," Jake choked back the tears. After a long pause he went on. "The phone was lying next to him off the hook when I found him, Linda."

"Good Godfry Jake, do you think it was a call telling him of her death?"

"That's what I am starting to think."

"Oh my, I guess he never stopped loving that woman" Linda looked into the past.

"Now I am wondering what was in that letter that threw him so off course."

"Jake you need to find that letter. It must be somewhere in the farmhouse."

"In the farmhouse?" Jake squeaked out, his face turning to despair.

"Yes Jake. The farmhouse. It is time to face the skeletons in your closet. Go and feel all that sadness then let it go. Jake you can survive the pain," Linda said with strong conviction while putting her warm hand on Jake's.

Marcy was unconscious in the hospital but active in her brain. Her mind took her to the night before her fall. She was at the farmhouse lying on the window seat in the den, looking at Moxie's chair, which was cast in partial light from the moon. That lovely soft glow just touched the arm of the chair next to where Marcy lay. To her it was like he was right there sitting with her, helping with all his wisdom to guide her. She had been crying for hours since reading the letter. At first there was the initial excitement of finding something written in her mother's hand writing then reading into it and discovering the shocking truth. It completely unearthed her. Feeling numb and lost she had been lying there for hours in and out of tears. The moonlight was a much needed comfort. From the photos her and Sky had so often looked at on those rainy fall days, she could see him in her mind's eye, his blue eyes and that smile radiating out with strength and understanding. His presence was so strong coming out of that chair. She hung onto it and floated in her pain.

Jake sat next to the hospital bed looking at Marcy with growing compassion. He had been there for hours with Sky asleep in his lap. Watching her struggling with her deep thoughts. So many expressions of sorrow came to her face. He felt the need to comfort her. A poem his father used to say to them sometimes before bed came into his mind.

Jake said the first line out loud. "Be the grace of twilight here today in our hearts..."

Marcy heard those words. It was like a hand lifting her up and out of her unconscious world. She too knew that poem; her Mother would read it to her often from one of his letters. She formed the words of the next line in her own voice, bringing her to the surface.

"Here by the sea we are set free."

She then opened her blue eyes and looked at Jake.

He was struck hard and deep with the recognition of her soul.

He then asked in a soft amazed whisper, "How do you know that?"

Marcy could only smile, slowly putting his face into memory from looking at his photos on the walls at Moxie's house. But now in the flesh she saw her truth and slipped back into the clouds of her dream world.

Jake left the hospital shortly after Marcy fell back into unconsciousness, while Sky was under the growing affections of the nurses. He could go and face the weight of his past and verify a truth he suspected. He drove into the door yard of the farm house and parked, sitting in the truck for a long time. Looking at the shuttered place of his past. Driven for answers he knew would be in a letter inside, he finally struck out of his fear, got out and walked in. He was blown away by what he saw. There on every wall surface in the kitchen and living room, on art paper, was the fruits of Marcy and Sky's rainy day painting projects. Murals of farm life from his youth--the fulfilling highlights all there in living color. Moxie, his brothers, Tilly, the old barn. There they were as little kids with capes standing in front of Tilly. Even painted a red wagon with Brian in the back. It was scenes of all the good times from his life and none of the bad. It was really amazing what they had done.

"How could they know all this stuff?" he kept asking the walls.

Then after seeing a new scene from his past, "Son of a Gun."

The continuity of his life was laid right in front of him, so powerful. He sat down after looking at it all, buried his face in his hands and cried for the realization of how his pain has taken away his ability to see the good in his life.

Hard to say how much time had gone by, but when Jake came out of it he was in a better place. The letter was open on Moxie's desk filled with Marcy's tear stains. He looked at the familiar hand writing he had glanced at over the years and started to read.

Dear Moxie,

I thought I would never write you this letter but my circumstances have brought on the need to confess a great sin. The cancer in my liver is taking away my life. I am days away, I fear, I see it reflected in the faces around me. Way back when we had that wonderful summer together. I did not plan on getting back with Frank when I went back to my college. I felt so lonely without you. I got drunk at a party and he was there. When I got pregnant I really thought it was his child. But when she was born and opened her eyes I knew you were the father. She has your blue eyes and brow. The truth seemed too unbearable to speak. I told myself I would bring this secret to my grave. She has my face so we joked I had the dominant genes. I think deep down Frank knew but he never let on. He buried himself in his work and provided quite well for us. Moxie your letters were so important. I read them to Marcy over and over so she would know of your life and her brothers. I plan to tell her the truth in the day ahead. I will send her to you. I know you must hate me now at this instant. Please don't hate her. She is an independent wonderful woman but she needs the anchor of family and you will be all she has left. What a fool of me to be more concerned of what others would think, now Marcy has to face the pain of my actions. You know her because of my letters to you. Now, see her as your daughter. There is so much more I wish to say but am too weak to bring it all out on paper. I never stopped loving you Moxie. I am dying having to accept a horrible decision I made years ago. My only consolation is that you will be living and can be with Marcy and Sky, the continuity of our Love.

Jake dropped the letter. Knowing now what he first felt in his gut when he saw Marcy from his field glasses. Those mannerisms so much like Moxie's.

"I have a sister!" he yelled to the world.

To Jake it was a great truth, a spark of life in his withering soul. He gathered up that letter and ran out to his truck.

Marcy was close to the surface, in and out of healing dreams. In her subconscious she was feeling empowered from her journey into her past on that short trip down the well. Since her mother's death she'd felt so rudderless, lost, just going through the motions of life. She kept herself focused on providing for herself and Sky. Stimulated by her fall, the dreams were telling her subconscious that the past was in her but did not define all of who she was. She could just free herself from the dark shadows and move into the light of the present. With that realization, she had more strength to feel the depth of sadness for her mother and fathers, then let it go and embrace having brothers.

"I have a family," her voice brought her back to the surface.

Jake was there holding her hand with a loving smile.

"Howdy Sister," he said with soft clarity into Marcy's awakening face.

"My brother," she whispered back while opening her arms to him.

They held each other on that hospital bed with Jake smiling and Marcy crying for all the emotions spilling over.

- CHAPTER 10 -

Being the oldest, Shawn had no footprints to follow. Only his dreams lay ahead. Shawn had always wanted to explore the world. His dad's bed time stories set a seed in his fertile brain. All the stories came out of Moxie`s head, inspired by all the reading he did. The central character was a Scotsman, Ned McNealy, who traveled the world looking for a particular woman. He never found her but all kinds of things happened to him while looking. Shawn wanted to experience the random events that happen to a traveler and see how people from other cultures lived. He loaded up his old ford sidestep with the necessary equipment to car camp and then go by backpack if he had to. He was confident traveling alone. When a teenager, he would go on his own for weeks, walking with his pack right off the farm into the woods and beyond.

Shawn was not nostalgic like Jake. He loved his upbringing on the farm but saw it as the beginning not his whole life. It was hard to say goodbye to his brothers, especially Jake because he knew how angry he was. But being the oldest he was used to his brothers being mad at him. Time was the great elixir on that one. They all knew the parting would be for a long time. Brian on his way to Alaska and Shawn headed south for the slow road to Mexico.

He visited friends on his way south, spending some nights sailing Casco Bay with an old friend who had moved to Portland. After three weeks of being on the road he started to let go of his worries and live from each random moment to the next. When he could he slept out under the stars on a mat in a cozy sleeping bag. In the big towns and cities he slept in his souped up camper, eating breakfast at diners and cafes. Enjoying the conversations around him indulging in some. The farther south he went the more his accent stood out to the southern drawl. He had not thought of the Civil War since high school days but Southerners brought it front and center. "Yankee huh" some would say after looking down at his plates on the truck and then walking away. But he had a way with people and given the time he would have them laughing.

In South Carolina he got a three-week job on a framing crew building apartments. He had the New England work ethic and knew his stuff so he got reluctant respect on the job site. There was a lot a talk about Gettysburg and Chamberlain and the Maine boys; their Great Grand Daddies had kicked some of them boy's ass, in the big battle.

He made friends with a local boy they all called Cotton because his hair was so white. After working together on a hand rail project Cotton said, "I don't care if my Great Grand Daddy fought yours it got nothing to do with you and me," and shook Shawn's hand securing a friendship that would last well beyond their short working relationship.

Cotton was a talker and Shawn was a willing listener. The south was all new to him and Cotton's stories taught him about the South and some of its culture. He had supper at Cotton's house filled with family. The food was great and the conversations lively. On a couple of Sundays they took an old canoe and paddled into a maze of tidal creeks through marshlands catching catfish and crabs. The landscape was so different from the rocky Maine coast. He drank it all in savoring the taste of exploring new territory. Cotton tried talking Shawn into staying on but he was hell bent on getting to Mexico.

"Only thing going to happen to you down there is you will get the clap and have your precious side step stolen from yah." Cotton would insist, but Shawn would just laugh and move the conversation along.

During his stay in town he slept in many different places, always moving to avoid suspicion of vagrancy. There was a park with public toilets and water. He would pull the old Ford into the parking lot after dark and get water and shave in the sink. One hot night he slept out on the fine cut grass looking up at the southern stars. Other nights he would drive out into the country and pull over on a side road and crawl in back reading with the light of his headlamp. The town of Strose had three cafes and Shawn did his best to support all of them equally. He tipped better than the locals so all the waitresses liked the sight of him coming in. The young ones liked his Maine accent and the older ones jibed him for being a Yankee. Growing up in a small town you get used to major ribbing so he thrived on it all, taking some, dishing some and always ending in a laugh.

Saying goodbye to Cotton has really hard for Shawn. He had never shared so many of his thoughts about life with another person. Their differences in upbringing and culture brought them closer together. After getting a bear hug from his friend he climbed in the side step and headed for the coast of Texas.

While he rolled down that road he moved backwards in his mind, replaying the story he just lived back in Strose. Making it a part of his life. Funny how things become real after we have relived them in our minds.

By nightfall he was back with it, feeling the combustion of his Ford and the hum of the road. The moon lit up the landscape as he moved along looking at the tops of cattails and tall reed grass with the occasional big openings of marsh and tidal creeks. Easing nice and slow over the small bridges with the windows down he took in the sweet rich smell of marsh salt. He made miles along the coast of South Carolina heading down from Georgetown to Charleston.

It was in the wee hours of the morning when Shawn finally pulled the Ford off the road and found a safe place to sleep under the stars. He walked a ways with his bed roll under his arm along a creek until it opened up around a fresh water pond. He found a soft and dry safe place to lay down feeling quite content with his life as he looked up at the night sky and made out the big dipper until he fell into a deep sleep.

Moxie came to him in his dream sitting there in the passenger seat of the side step.

"Holy shit, Dad! Where did you come from?"

"Calm down son I never left just changed form a little."

"You look younger."

"Hey it's the best of me right here for yah."

"Nice seeing yah Dad."

"Not too bad looking at you either. What's this road trip all about?"

"You ought to know you planted the seed. I got to see the world. I don't want to read about it anymore. I need to see, taste and feel it."

"What about your brothers and the farm?"

"Dad we tried to work together it ain't the same without you. You raised us to be different and now we can't agree on nothing."

"All my doing, huh?"

"Well you were a strong influence on us."

"Hey I needed to make up for your mother not being there."

"Pops I ain't complaining just saying how it was."

"What about the farm?"

"Dad that farm was and still is you. It is not me."

"So you going to find you on the road?"

"Maybe, but at least grow some from different experiences. I have to do this Dad."

Moxie paused for a long time with an inward smile and then said, "Huh, you are a piece of work. You got me thinking about something I took to heart one of my Uncles told me years ago. There is the life you are born with and then the one you make for yourself as you move through it. O.K son, be safe," then he was gone.

Shawn woke up at sunrise still feeling the presence of his father.

- CHAPTER 11 -

Jake drove Brian to the airport in Bangor for his flight to Anchorage. He was traveling light with a duffel bag that held his toothbrush and foul weather gear and one change of clothes. He sold his beloved Camaro for cash and figured he could get the proper clothes for the local conditions in second hand stores. He was mostly thinking about being on the sea, fishing for big money and testing himself in one of the most dangerous fishing grounds in the world. Moxie's stories had taken Ned McNealy fishing in the frigid waters off Alaska. He read many books on his own about it after he heard those stories.

Ever since his dad helped him build a small skiff when he was eight, he could not get enough of the sea. He felt at home, totally himself, out on the water. He struggled with life on land, found it hard to navigate the artificial boundaries of society frequently crossing them and causing misunderstandings. With fishing there was a natural order to things and he could rub hard against the boundaries and be respected.

Heading west to the sea he was also running away. Chloe Baxter had been stringing him along for years. He was mad for her. She got just close enough to build intrigue but not enough to consummate the relationship he wanted. Brian was aware that she was doing the same with several other guys, but he figured it was just a ploy to raise her stock with him. Sometime after his dad died she consummated with one of the others and ditched him. After fighting with his brothers all the time about simple decisions on the farm and feeling heavy in the heart, he wanted out.

He landed in Anchorage and bought a Chevy Impala for six hundred bucks and headed for Southeast Alaska. He had never seen such wilderness, such a true expanse of nature. "Holy shit will you look at that," he said again and again to the Chevy during that remarkable drive to the town where he had work. When he drove into the fishing village of Boyd and stepped out onto the dirt parking lot of the wharf, a calm come over him. He had found his place.

It was late afternoon but still quiet. He took in the layout of the wharf and the boats moored around it. All sizes of fishing boats the bigger boats were way bigger than what he grew up with and he was thrilled. With hands on his hips he stood and gawked.

A female voice came from behind him, sure and smooth, "Stand there much longer we might have to charge yah for long term parking."

Brian turned around to see a woman around his age walking towards him with a big full-lipped smile and confident green eyes taking him in.

"I would guess you are Brian," she held a hand out in greeting.

"Do I stick out that much?" he took her warm strong hand.

"Oh yah, this is a small town, you will stick out to everyone. Welcome, I`m Judy," with true feeling in her voice.

"Good to be here. Wow quite the state you got here."

"Enjoyed that drive did you? Well, all the boys are still out fishing till tomorrow. I`ll show you to your digs."

Brian followed Judy down to the wharf and up some stairs to a small rustic apartment looking straight out to sea.

"This is great," he told her.

"I love this little place. I lived here for a year and a half"

"Did I kick you out?"

"No, I moved out to be with my boyfriend."

Of course a boyfriend, Brian thought then asked without thinking "Still living with your boyfriend?"

Judy paused for a moment then looked him straight in the eyes and said, "No, I moved back home when he was killed at sea."

"I am sorry," Brian says with feeling.

"Ya, not as sorry as I am. It happened eight months ago. I am just past the shock of it and really miss him now." It was awkward for a moment, then she walked out saying, "Let's get your stuff."

When they got to the car and he only had the duffle bag, she commented on him traveling light.

"Not even a box of photos with family and old girlfriends?"

"No, kind of want to start over."

"I see, so you burned the photos of the old girlfriends?" Judy said with a wicked smile. "I will let you be, but come over to the house and have supper with me. I could use the company."

Brian went up to his apartment and sat down on the couch and looked out to sea and expunged.

"Holy shit, she is beautiful!"

He went over to the house and Judy greeted him at the kitchen door. Her hair was pulled back in a ponytail giving Brian a full view of her face and green eyes. The kitchen was big and open with a gas and wood fired cook stove holding court. She had settings for two on the cutting table. She was making fish hash and the kitchen was rich in the smells of fried fish, potatoes, and cilantro. Judy told Brian it felt too lonely out at the big table without all her brothers and father around it.

"No sisters?" Brian asked her.

"No, three brothers."

"Did you learn to throw a good punch?"

"Of course," she says with a smile. "And you, Brian, any sisters?"

"No, two brothers and yes I learned to throw a good punch," smiling back. "Your mother?" looking with concern in her eyes.

"Died when I was little."

"Mine too," Judy said and patted Brain on the shoulder as she walked around him fixing supper.

She was used to being around men, and he was not used to being around women. It became very apparent to Judy. It was different for her than being with her brothers. She liked Brian's manners. He was trying to hide his attraction to her but she could tell. She had to scold him with her eyes when he tried to make shine later in the night. She liked feeling she was still attractive to men but she was no way ready for any romance.

"Of course, you dummy she is still grieving." he said to himself after picking up on The Look.

"Two months after Josh died I went down to the lower

forty-eight. Had to get away from these fucking fishing boats. I hated them, hated the sea. I was a wreck with grief. I waited tables in Madison and took some art classes but I missed home, my family, Alaska. Just don't get the strong sense of community and belonging in the lower forty-eight. I have been home for a month now helping with the books and keeping order on the wharf when they are all out."

"Do you still hate the sea?" Brian pushed.

"No, just more afraid. It was a rogue wave that took him. One minute he was there the next gone. So random. The sea, it don't care. It gives and it takes."

"Ya, it is part of the trade. We all accept it as a possible outcome."

"Oh God, you sound like my brothers. It is the ones left on land got to suffer the long haul of that outcome" with that Judy got up and cleared the table looking angry.

Brian sat in the growing tension in that big kitchen knowing he had crossed the line again. He finally pulled some words together. "I am sorry. That was cold."

There was silence as Judy went about the kitchen. Then she said, "No, it is not you it's the truth that is cold. I don't want to lose any more of my loved ones. Sometimes I think you guys are so selfish in accepting it. They don't have to fish outside in the Bering Sea where it is so dangerous, pushing that edge. I want them to get over it and fish inside, protected by the islands so they can come home every night."

"It was like a rogue wave of sorts that took my Dad. He was a healthy vibrant man and just dropped stone dead. He was standing on solid ground when it happened. There ain't no sense to it. Death strikes like lightning, land or sea."

"I am sorry about your Dad, Brian." Judy said, walking over to him and resting a warm hand on his arm and looking in his eyes with compassion.

That touch went through his whole body and rested in his heart, left him awestruck with a new hope.

"I don't think it is all random." Judy said, getting her last word in on risk.

Judy sat back down at the chef's table and looked at Brian, her green eyes smiling. Her peace said she was over the matter. She moved the conversation to lighter things.

"I thought you would be older," she goaded.

"Why is that?"

"Well, we get this big letter of recommendation from Dad's old buddy from Maine on what a hot shot mechanic you are. Figured you might need years of experience to back up that kind of talk. You don't look to have the years on you."

He smiled at her banter and replied.

"When you start playing with motors at four and are around 'em all your life it kinda just comes to yah."

"Oh a boy wonder," she smiled with some laughter in her eyes.

"My dad ran a machine shop on the farm. He pushed me for a bit to learn all I could about motors. He expected I would take over the shop but I really wanted to fish."

"Did he begrudge you that?"

"No, once he saw what it meant to me he was supportive. I think he took some pride in knowing I could get on just about any boat working out of the harbor. Knowing how to fix things raises your stock."

"Bragging now?"

"Well you asked."

They found more to laugh at after that, finding comfort in each other`s company. Brian went to bed that night feeling more content than he had felt in a long while.

- CHAPTER 12 -

It was the way he was standing that caught Shawn's attention. He had his thumb out but you would have thought he was standing in front of a girl asking her to dance. Cowboy hat on his head and a smile on his face. Shawn pulled over.

"Where you going?" he asked when the hiker stuck his head in the window.

"Sassafras Island," the cowboy stated with southern relish

"Where is that?"

"Down the coast a ways across some bridges and onto a ferry," delivered with a big grin.

"OK hop in."

The cowboy had a small bag that he threw into the cab next to Shawn and off they went down that coastal byway. His name was Clint, claimed to be a master of all trades including his abilities as a chef and oohhh by the way a chauffeur, excellent driver. Basically a survivor who had done all kinds of work while kicking around the south. From a small town in Alabama running from a woman in Georgetown and heading for the peace and quiet of the island.

He never stopped talking from the moment he got in.

"If you ain't never been to Sassafras Island you got to go. This place is far out dude. It`s got these crazy oak trees with wild branches covered in Spanish moss. Still got ruins about the place from mansions and forts from the Civil War. The place is a time warp dude."

"Sounds too good to be true," Shawn played it back.

"O.K. man I`ll prove it to ya. I`ll show you."

"Nice trick to get me to drive you to where you want to go."

"Dude, if I am wrong I pay for all the gas."

"O.K., you got yourself a deal, Sassafras Island it is."

"You won't regret it, man, not even for a second."

With that taken care of the boys moved on to other things.

The small ferry took only twelve cars. A big truck bringing supplies out to the island residents took several spots. All of the passengers got out of their vehicles and stood close to the side rails looking out at the blue green sea. Clint struck up a conversation with the trucker while Shawn stood and took in the beauty of it all. The smell of southern salt, marshes and raw fish. He looked out at a maze of islands rich in life with estuaries, fresh water ponds and loggerhead turtles. It was a wonderful hour-long ride. At one point twelve dolphins came along and played in the wake off the bow.

"Dude listen I am an ace mechanic, you got any problems, I am your man." Clint worked his angle, trying to stir up some work.

"Fix my own truck. Don't trust anyone else touching my girl."

"Oh one of those guys."

Shawn could only smile listening to his new friend in action. It looked to be an adventure ahead staying on this island with this character.

Part of the island had homes, the rest was left to the wilds. The boys drove the wild side step along the beach until they found a nice camp spot between some dunes. Clint walked along the beach gathering the right drift wood and built himself a small shelter. He used a tarp from the truck for the roof, and he was home. Shawn walked a ways down the beach collecting driftwood for a fire. He dug a hole for a fire pit and set up camp. They had stopped at a store before boarding the ferry so they had some vegetables and meat to fry up for dinner. Clint insisted on cooking but he kept getting distracted by playing with the fire so Shawn took over. It was a great meal sitting by an open fire on the beach on an island with a night sky all around them overflowing with stars.

"Well, in the beginning she was as cool as could be. Not possessive, free and easy. Then after eight months of bliss she lays the bomb on me, asking to get hitched. Shit Dude! I tell her darling I loves ya but I ain't the marrying kind. She goes to tears for a bit and I thought all was said and done. Then she gets to hollering, calling me all kinds of names. I thought some of the names was funny and I get to laughing. Big mistake, that just turned up her steam. The next thing I know that frying pan is coming right for my head. Good thing for my athletic abilities, I ducked in time. Whoooomp, in the wall goes the frying pan. Can still hear that noise, yes siree mister, man I am telling you. Well she ain't done, she goes for the carton of eggs that was out on the counter. So there I am gathering what I could of my things dodging eggs from my girl gone psycho."

"How many of them eggs hit you?" Shawn asking with a big grin.

"Now I was good at ducking, but there was one in particular got me clean in the back of the head when I was going out the back."

With that the boys broke into laughter.

"What about you. Got any women back in Maine pining for your sorry Yankee ass?"

"Ohhh not really, I was dating a girl but nothing serious. My brothers had enough drama going with the women. That seemed enough for one household. There were no eggs when I left town." That ended the talk on women so the boys moved on to other things.

The next morning they got up to a soft spring day and the sound of crashing surf. Clint made a small cooking fire and fried up bacon and eggs.

"The party line around here is that the old mansion was built by a cotton baron during the Civil War. They clear cut this whole island to build ships to fight you Yankees then cleared the land for cotton. That old mansion made for a sweet summer pad. There is all this bullshit history about this place but I know the real story. It was built by a French privateer for his mistress who was from a cotton baron family. You can still feel the love vibe about the place. Steamy love affair sidelined with deception and blackmail of the locals." On and on went Clint trying to get Shawn excited about their day's adventure of exploring the old mansion.

They made up some sandwiches and packed a ruck sack and off they went along the deserted beach full of sandpipers and sanderlings. They walked for a couple of miles when Clint decided it was time to head inland. They walked into a maritime forest of scraggly oak covered in Spanish moss and pines.

"Far out," Shawn said.

"Dude, I told you this place is awesome."

The sound of grunting and pounding earth rang out and the boys turned to see four wild pigs bearing right down on them.

"Shit Yankee run for the trees!" Clint yells, moving like a jack rabbit for the grove of oaks.

They both found their own trees to climb as the wild pigs grunted and snarled below them, flipping their heads, flinging snot and showing awful dangerous teeth.

"Holy shit boy what a rush!" the cowboy hollered from his perch with the big hat still on his head.

"That was some close," said Shawn, feeling the real adventure had begun.

They were up there a while when a high-pitched yelp from one of the boars brought on some change. A few more yelps and off the wild things ran.

"You boys going to stay up in them trees all day?" came a young male voice from behind one of the oaks. The tree-bound men looked out on a teenage boy with a sling shot in his hand and a smug grin on his face approaching out of the trees.

"The trick misters is not to go on the run. Got to stand your ground and have a sling shot or a long stick," the boy said with young gusto. The boys climbed down and shook hands with their savior, Clive Adams from right there on Sassafras Island.

"You guys were faster than most. Usually them hogs get to 'em before they reach the tree. Then I got to go get my dad and he brings down the rescue cart and sews 'em back up. Those nasty bastards will go right for a guy's sack from the back. We have to airlift those poor bastards."

"Boy, I think you are talking local nonsense to us folks from away," Shawn not giving to the young buffalo.

"Noooo, now you all saw the teeth on those bad boys. No problemo."

"Damn close to getting a piece of my ass," Clint added with a smile.

"Where you all going?" Clive moved things along.

"The ruins dude," Clint answered with conviction.

"Just where I was headed. Good time to catch the horses grazing about the place."

"What horses?" Shawn asks with joy in his voice.

"Wild horses are all over this island. Surprised you got this far without seeing any. Hey mister, you sound like a Yankee. Where you from?" the kid held his ground.

"Maine. How many wild horses?" Shawn asked, not letting it go.

"A couple hundred at least. I never been north of Washington D.C but I want to. Hey let's get going if we are going to catch the horses," the boy took the lead.

It was a beautiful walk through the maritime forest of oak and pine, walking along tidal creeks and taking in the strong smell of salt and marsh, scaring up the herons that where feeding along the banks. Clive talked away about his life on the island. He had two sisters, lived there all his life. His dad was the go-to guy on the island and kept the small island infrastructure going with all kinds of trucks and equipment. Clive knew how to drive a truck by eight. Could change a transmission in his sleep or so he said.

"But right now I got horses on my mind and this one particular stallion. I aim to ride that one." Clive talked and walked fast, on a mission.

The trees changed to small spindly oaks that gave way to dunes covered in high grass. They walked into a cut in the dunes and Clive stopped and whispered for silence. They stuck their heads around a high bush and saw a wonderful scene. There was a big opening in the land-- a field in the middle of all those dunes. In that field were three high walls of rock and mortar and all around it were beautiful horses, golden blond in color with long sweeping white manes.

"Awesome," Shawn whispered incredulously.

There were about twelve mares and the one stallion who was bigger and darker in color. Clive told them to stay put and walked out in the clearing pulling from his pocket some sugar cubes. He proceeded to make a noise that was like a song. It was the sound of a boy that still had the mother in him. Sounding both male and female in his pubescence. A remarkable sound, and the horses responded by stopping their grazing and looking with wonder.

The stallion was moved back and forth both protective and curious. He must have known from past encounters what was in Clive`s hand. Temptation moved him close but caution kept him away. Clive moved slower and closer. It was remarkable to watch this dance going on between a boy and a wild horse. Caution won out and the stallion made bigger and wider circles.

Clive put the sugar down and walked backwards to Shawn and Clint. When one of the mares tried going for the sugar the stallion moved in like a bolt and gobbled it up with his eyes on Clive. Clive watched with a smile of victory on his face.

"Soon he will eat from my hand, then I will touch him, then the bridle. One step at a time," the boy stated with conviction.

The stallion moved his tribe along and the boys took to the ruins, each wandering and exploring on his own. On the walk back to camp Clint went on about being able to visualize the privateer's mistress.

"Isabelle; eyes of the southern blue skies, auburn hair, bold cleavage with all the fixings."

"Dude, calm down, yah getting all worked up," Clive said with a smile of amusement.

Clive was getting a big kick out of Clint's version on the history of the mansion. He and his sisters had made up all kinds of bullshit stories to tell the snow birds. They loved it when years later they would hear the stories quoted by others. It was easy to see that Clive and Clint were peas of the same pod. Shawn was enjoying the banter brewing up between them. Reflecting in that moment on the joy of making friends on the road.

Those first weeks in Alaska were a time of daily wonders. The sea, the landscape and the people all so different for Brian. He was loving it. The brothers where testing him both as a mechanic and as a man at sea. He thrived in the challenge. They took him through all stages of the operation, teaching him how they fished and what species of fish and why, checking out all the engines on the boats. Then the generators, ice machines, hydraulic winches, he went through them all noting what he knew and what he needed to study up on. His nights were spent going through schematic drawings and visualizing each part so it was in his head.

His enchantment with Judy gave him plenty to dream about in his times of rest at sea. Back at the wharf she was busy during the days. At night her time was taken by her brothers and father who obviously loved her and were really enjoying having her back at home. He was never alone with her like that first night and struggled with his affection for her, trying to hide it and act nonchalant, but inside he was melted when she was near. It was spring, and spring in Alaska is powerful. He was burning with nature's desire, but he knew he had to be patient.

The youngest of the brothers, Kevin, was the most protective of his sister. He was closest in age to her deceased boyfriend, Joel, and did not like the idea of Brian being his replacement. He had no problem voicing this to Brian, who took it quite well knowing he would have been the same way if the roles were reversed. The two other brothers, Cole and Sawyer, were older and looked at things differently, open to what Brian had to offer their family. They also had girlfriends who took much of their attention when back on land. The father, Rich, who they all called Pops, was a happy man who laughed at the circus of his family at home but was a hard and focused man at sea.

Brian's world of desire for Judy took a hard hit one Saturday night when after dinner she announced to her brothers, "Why don't you take Brian to the Dragger Inn so he can meet a girl. I am sure he is interested in more than engines." She gave Brian a look like she was one of the guys.

It was like a slap of rejection. He tried to laugh it off on the outside but inside he was crushed.

The brothers and their girlfriends took him out to the bar and Judy stayed home. Everyone was very friendly, glad to be finally meeting the new greenie in town. There were single women, which was surprising because usually in small towns the young women are all snapped up. Boyd was settled by five families in the turn of the century. Their offspring had a dominance of women despite the desire for more men. Many a daughter grew up fishing but some preferred the finer things of life and either moved or got involved in the local commerce. Most of the few businesses in town were run by women.

The bar tender, Clara, had broken up with her boyfriend and was clearly ready to move on. The brothers' girlfriends made plain to their mission at hand. She responded by openly flirting with Brian. She was a pretty woman, with auburn hair and shiny brown eyes but he was not interested. His heart was set on waiting it out for Judy. He was polite and all, but Clara took as him playing hard to get, which encouraged her all the more. She liked challenges and was ready to try something new and from away. Just before they left for home she offered to show Brian "around town." With the brothers right there egging things along he could not turn her down.

Clara showed up mid-morning the next day driving an open Jeep.

"Better bring an extra layer, she gets cold on the open road," she hollered to Brian when he stepped outside. He went back in and grabbed his hoodie. When he stepped back out Judy was out talking with Clara.

"You two have fun," Judy said with a wink at Clara.

"Oh man this is not the way I want things to go," thought Brian. It hurt his pride and wounded his heart. She was obviously not interested in him.

"You don't look so hot. Did I over serve you last night? Clara called him on his mood.

"No, just the wrong side of the bed this morning. I`ll snap out of it," he stalled for time to pull himself together. He shook off his mood as best he could and tried to show a happy face as he listened to her telling him about the town of Boyd.

They drove a ways out of town then down a two track road by the sea. The beauty that surrounded them lifted him and he started to actually enjoy himself. Clara was twenty-seven, confident and funny. Her perspective on life behind a bar in a small town was enlightening and at times hilarious. In no way ready to settle down, she was a wild cat.

"What about you Brian? Tell me about home," she said, reaching over to touch his arm.

"Well, I grew up on a small farm on the coast of Maine. My two brothers and I were raised by our dad. We ran kind of wild as kids. I loved life on the farm but once I got on boats I was all about fishing. The coast of Maine is raw and rocky, nothing like the expanses you got here," Brian gestured to the view in front of them of snow capped mountains going straight to the sea.

"Nice huh, I love it here. What is going on now with the farm?" Clara picking up on a tender issue.

"Ohhhhhh, my dad died just over six months ago. We tried working it together but it was just breaking us apart. Fighting all the time over stupid stuff. I had always wanted to fish Alaska so I took the job offer when it came. My other brother Shawn took that as his cue to head out for Mexico. Jake is there alone keeping her running."

"I am sorry about your Dad," she reached over and held his hand.

"Yah me too, still hard to believe he's gone."

Clara pulled off the track road into an open meadow by a tidal stream. Then took his hand in both of hers and smiled at him with affection. He liked having his hand held. Hers were warm and soft, his hard and calloused. They said nothing for a long time just taking in the beauty of what was before them.

"Hungry?" Clara asked, breaking the silence.

"Come to think of it yes."

"I made us a picnic lunch complete with cold beers."

She reached into the back and pulled up a small cooler. She handed Brian a honking roast beef sandwich and snapped open a beer for him.

"Always the bar tender," he took the beer with a smile.

They ate, making yummy noises over the delight of them wicked good sandwiches. Clara worked the eye shine while seductively biting into hers.

Her noises sounded more sexual than just dietary delight. While drinking the six pack between them she told stories about some of the fishermen in her bar. She was a good story teller. He laughed at her imitations of the different male voices. She touched him more and more, and he started to really like it. The beers were kicking in, surrounded by wild nature on the coast of Alaska, on a hot spring day.

Laughing at the end of one of her stories she rolled her head onto Brian's shoulder, her hair falling across his chest the smell of it taking over his senses. Her hand on his thigh was hot through his jeans. He was a goner, Judy was in his heart but Clara had his moment of desire. He kissed her. She gave him her hot tongue. Hands explored. His on her face and neck, hers on his inner thigh and lower back. When they came up for air Clara swung her leg across his lap and flung her self up on his saddle looking right into his blue green eyes with her naughty brown ones.

"Wow, you Alaska girls are something," Brian squeaked out.

"What those Maine girls don't take control?" a wicked grin.

He could feel her heat through their pants. He swelled, she smiled in victory.

While looking deep into his eyes she outlined the contours of his penis, her pupils dilating with her passion. She slowly unzipped him and took out his hardness.

"HhHmmmmm, such a nice cock you have Brian" her tone soft and hot.

"You are something." in a voice of awe. He reached up and feeling her breasts through her sweater, smiling when he did not encounter a bra.

She took one of her hands, put some fingers to her mouth and got them wet. With her moist hot fingers she slowly stroked just the head moaning slow and soft like. He moaned back leaning forward for a long kiss then left her lips to go lower biting her hard nipples through her sweater. She yelped in joy.

He guided his hands under her sweater and onto the naked flesh of her ample breasts. He took them in his skilled fingers and softly played with them until she was moaning loudly while stroking hard on his prick.

Mad for each other they tumbled out of the Jeep. Brain bent her over the hood of the Jeep and pulled up her sweater, licking her back while reaching around and undoing her pants. He slowly pulled them down over her beautiful behind trailing his tongue down her cheeks going deep and tasting her wet desire. She yelled into the wilds.

They were reclined in their seats relishing in the after glow when a big smile swept across Brian's face.

"What you smiling about?" Clara wanting in on his joy.

"I was just remembering this dream I had last night about Tilly."

"Who is Tilly?" in laughter.

"A moose" he replied nonchalantly.

"A moose? Is there something I should know about you Maine boys?" she raised an eyebrow.

Brian laughed on that one.

"My Dad saved her from coyotes when she was a young calf. She stayed at the farm for a bit until she was fit to be on her own. We thought she was our pet but Tilly kept reminding us that was not the case."

He told her the story of him getting sent into the side of the barn via her hind legs. Then he went on and told the one of his brother Shawn trying to ride her. Clara thought it all very funny.

"What was the dream about?" she asked.

"It is kind of hard to explain but I saw her dark eyes and she was looking at the farm from the edge of the woods. My brother Jake was far off in the field and he looked very alone. It was like Tilly was worried about him."

"Why did that make you smile?"

"Well it's kind of funny that a moose has to come to me in my dreams to remind me to call my brother," the smile came back.

On the drive back to the wharf Brian fell silent and Clara, knowing men, said, "Feeling trapped, like because I had sex with you, I now have some ownership in yah?"

There was silence for a bit as the truth of her words sunk in. He replied with weighted breath, "Something like that, I just met you, seems things are happening real fast all of a sudden," with weighted breath.

"Brian, I just got out of a relationship that ended badly. The last thing I want now is a BOYFRIEND. Hey, we are two horny people coming together on the wild shores of Alaska in spring time. Relax enjoy sex for sex and thank you. I really needed that. You are a good lover for such a youngster," she reached over and pinched his cheek.

"Youngster?" in hurt reply.

"Yes, how old are you twenty-two?"

"No, twenty-four," in defense.

"Oh such a baby face," she taunted more.

It lifted his weight. He was thinking how all this would affect his relationship with Judy. Her rejection of him by passing him off to Clara only deepened his resolve to win her over. He knew it would be a long-term project.

When they drove into the wharf it seemed everyone from the house had found a reason to be outside. Clara picked right up on it giving Brian a big kiss goodbye and then whispered in his ear, "I guess you get to do the walk of shame," with a wicked giggle.

Brian tried to hurry his way up to his pad with just a wave to the wharf crowd when Judy hollered out knowingly. "Have a good time?"

Oh man!

"Yah, was a nice time," Brian said to the sea, unable to look her way as he slipped into his door.

- CHAPTER 13 -

S cots-Irish is not a mix of blood but refers to the lowland Scott Presbyterians who, in the 1600s were relocated by the English to Ulster in Northern Ireland to replace the Irish that were rebelling. They hated their English landlords who kept them in poverty as tenant farmers and, in turn, the local Irish Catholics hated them. After a succession of crop failures in the 1720s they migrated in masses to the new world up until 1770. During that time one seventh of the immigrants into America were Scots-Irish. Shawn's ancestors came over in the beginning of that wave and settled in Maine in 1727 but many other Scotts migrated to Georgia. A small number of them settled on some of the Barrier Islands.

Clive told the boys around the fire that his father's family is Scott and his mother's a mix of Swiss and Native American, "You all, I am the living example of genetic conflict. The jacked up Scott versus the spiritual Native American and introverted Swiss," he said with a smile.

"Where you get all this genetic talk?" Clint wondered.

"My ma-- ever since I was a little kid she would go on about genetic personalities and all. My ancestors from so many differ-ent cultures making up my general character. Of course when I get into trouble she say oh that's your dad's genes taking over in a weak moment. Then when I do good oh why that is her genes keeping the balance. I pretty much ignored her all through life until I got into these horses. She got me interested in genetics when she told me these horses' ancestors come all the way over from Spain. I got me these books on Spanish horses sent to me from the library in Savannah. Took three weeks to get to me out here on the island. I learned heaps of shit from them books. I can see similarities in certain breeds to the ones here. Yup if you want to see genetics, study horses. All about it now," Clive preached.

"No shit," Clint chimed in, "Well, besides being Ali Bami I am English, Scots-Irish and Native American. I get my powerful thirst from the Scotts, me balance in nature from the Native American and my sense of entitlement from the English."

"Sense of entitlement?" Shawn asked, taking the bait.

"Dude, my English ancestors were fucking royalty. I deserve a higher place in the pecking order," Clint said sticking his nose in the air.

"Ya, like now we should be serving you?"

"Yes of course."

"Hah like that is going to happen," Shawn was not having it.

They were all sitting around the fire talking and playing harmonicas. Both Clint and Shawn had one that they had been learning on. Clive got into it as well taking turns with each of theirs. It was going on two weeks since the boys had come to the island. Just about every evening, after a day of exploring, catching crabs and shrimp, Clive would show up and hang with them.

He was an interesting young lad full of stories of the islands and knowledge of their rich ecosystems and the sea. He told them that the salt marshes were the nurseries for shrimp, crab and fish. The chain of islands and marshes protected the shoreline of the mainland from erosion and also acted as a purifier filtering out pollutants. He was always going on about how delicate the marshes were and how the recent development of seasonal homes was destroying them.

On one of his first nights around the fire he said, "My Dad makes some of his living from the snowbirds but he is always going on about balance, don't want too many of `em. We generally try to discourage them from buying. Most land stays in the local families."

"We got the same thing going on in Maine, used to be nobody looked at land to sell for cash. It was for family. Now some are starting to sell for the big money from away," Shawn weighed in.

"Bloody bastards," Clint kept it simple.

"Damn right, why they got to build so big and dig up the marshes to make room for their fat boats. The locals live in smaller homes on stilts and respect the tenderness of nature on these islands."

Their conversations were often about the ways of life at home. Not just the threats but stuff like what each learned from his family about how to have a proper barbeque or traditions of celebration from thanksgiving to birthdays. They each came from different upbringings and environments, each in turn finding great joy in learning about the details of those differences.

"In the fall on weekends we would pick apples from the trees right on the farm then spend whole afternoons chopping them up. Squeezed some with that old wooden press to make cider. What was left we boiled off in big old pots for apple sauce for the winter."

"Cider huh, you mean Maine moonshine don't ya?" Clint said, being smart.

"Well, some of them jugs did get put down in the basement to go hard. My first drunk was on cider at the ripe age of fourteen. Ended the night worshipping the white porcelain with my dad yelling down the hall, 'That will learn ya.' It did too."

"Shit fourteen-- I was twelve my first time, Glen Levitt, Man oh Man what a wine," Clint had spirit in his voice.

"Oh that shit is nasty," Clive chimed in.

"OK boy wonder, what do you drink here on the island?" Clint got defensive.

"Peach wine, Dude!"

"Oh you little bastard I love that stuff. Can you get your hands on some?"

"Of course. Going to cost you though."

"I'll pay, I'll pay just bring it on."

He did bring it on. Clint got very drunk and ran off into the bush with a big stick to take on the wild pigs. He found them alright and they chased him up a tree taking pieces of his jeans on the way up. They heard him from camp hollering for help.

"Leave 'im up there for a bit to think it over," Shawn told Clive when he picked up his sling shot for the rescue.

After a while they got tired of hearing him howling up in that tree and they both went and chased away the pigs lurking at the bottom. When he got down he said nothing just marched off towards camp with the boys in laughter back at the tree.

Some nights after that Clive's dad, Dale, showed up at camp. First the dog, Sycamore, made its grand appearance, then they heard the four wheeler before the headlights came into view. He wanted to meet the two men that his son was spending so much time with and wanted help on some of his construction projects. They had hinted to Clive that they were open to such a prospect. Dale reminded Shawn a lot of Moxie. Small but strong, confidence delivered with a grand smile.

Clint was tasked with helping him put in a new transmission in his big hauling truck. He wanted Shawn to rebuild some of his docks that had taken on some damage in the last big spring storm. Said his boy was talking up their talents so he thought he would see if there was any truth in all the hot air.

They worked hard for Dale and were rewarded at the end of a long day of work with some island cooking from Clive's mom, Claudia. It was a small but cozy house that looked out past the rickety docks and boats of the salt marsh to the sea and more islands. Such a soft and powerful view. The cats took to the new-comers' laps and made them welcome. Clive's sisters Trudy and Sandra were shy at first but came into themselves in time and started to plague Clint on being chased up a tree twice by the little piggly wigglies. He of course took it with relish and am-bushed them back with some of his Ali Bami nonsense, claim-ing it was a sign of bravery and athletic ability. Young teenage girls, each uniquely beautiful in their own way, they were true to themselves. They came from the island life and knew who their ancestors were. Each was aware of which great aunt she resembled the most from all the old family photos their Mother had around. A sense of place in the family. They knew who they were but who they were to become lay ahead of them. It was a hoot of a night.

So the boys were taken away from their life of leisure to one of working every day as Dale found more for them to do.

When Moxie died Tilly felt the void of his presence gone. No longer could she hear his voice in song coming across the open field into the woods. It was like when her mother was killed, a great sense of loss. She watched the boys from the woods when they dug their father's grave. It was painful to see their bodies move in such sorrow. Then the days and weeks followed with no more music coming from the house, just silence followed by the yelling. The harmony gone. During those hard times she spent more of her time over in the woods by The Inn. Laughter and music over there, familiar voices. A cadence of different tones of voice expressing emotions.

During that time when Jake fell ill and ended up in the hospital, Brian was out at sea and had no idea what was happening back home. He was in a pickle himself. They had been out on the Bering Sea for three days when a big blow came upon them and stayed constant for two days bringing on forty-foot seas too big to fish. They were steaming for home when the distress call came over the radio from Winter Heat, a fellow fishing boat out of the harbor. They were dead in the water with both engines down. The Blue Water was the closest to her so they changed course and headed for their brothers in need. Brian was summoned up to the wheel house to listen over the radio as the captain, Buddy Winters, of Winter Heat described what happened to his motors. Several rogue waves brought sea water into the engine room and and water came in the exhaust valves and flooded the cylinders of both motors. The heads of both would have to be taken off and the valves purged clean of the salt water along with removing all the old oil that was

inseminated with sea water as well. It needed to be done quickly before the cylinders froze up from the salt. Brian had done it once with Moxie but not at sea with forty-foot waves. Buddy was a somewhat of a mechanic but he needed trained hands on this one. Without electrical power generated from the motors they had to save battery life by using the hand bilge pumps, pumping hard to stay afloat.

When they came upon Winter Heat it was a hard sight. They had taken some of the nets and balled them up to make a sea anchor off the bow. That kept them into the wind and waves. Without power to go into those big waves she was getting pounded. It was way too rough for the Blue Water to go alongside to let Brian board so he agreed to go over by breech buoy. Dangerous in these seas. They talked it over on the radio laying out the plan. Brian shot the lead rope over with a potato gun. With the lead they attached a cable, pulled it over and secured that to the bridges of both boats. Brian was harnessed into a seat with metal wheels that could slide along the cable. The lead rope was then attached to his harness so they could pull him over.

"Brian if that cable snaps hang on for your life. They will reel you in and land you like a fish," Captain Bill told him straight.

He then looked at the rest of the crew who were at their stations. The risk he was taking was apparent in their eyes.

Hundreds of miles away Judy sat in the kitchen listening to
what was going on by short wave radio. She heard the first distress call from Winter Heat when she just happened to come
into the kitchen to stoke the wood stove. She'd been sitting and
listening ever since. When she heard they were sending Brian
over by breach buoy she got scared. Josh had always referred to
that as flirting with death. The cable between boats can easily
snap in high seas. Even with a line attached to haul in the un-
lucky soul the cold water of the Bering Sea was deadly. Please,
please keep him safe, she pleaded upward. She could not stand
the thought of losing anyone she knew to that sea, not again. In
the past six months Brian had been working with her family, she
had come to see him as a good friend. His little rendezvous with
Clara made her feel more comfortable being with him. It took
away some of that sexual edge she did not want to deal with. But
she was a little surprised just how worried she was that Brian was
the one in danger. God it's all family out there what a horrible
choice. But Brian was the only one to go. He was the mechanic
on board. She sat and listened to the silence and static. In her
mind she saw the boats and high seas and Brian going across by
cable.

Standing on the hand rail of the bridge of Blue Water, Brian
knew how to adjust his mind for what lay ahead. It was like racing
cars back in Maine on late Friday nights. No room for fear. Just
wanting more speed. All focus, no doubts. He set his mind for
that. The ride of my life, bring it on. He raised his arm to signal

then jumped. He was moving fast, riding down the slack in the cable. The huge waves were just below his feet and he could see the profile of Winter Heat being pounded. When he was heading up towards the bridge he felt a great shift in movement upwards like he was being catapulted. The cable went tight fast as two opposing waves shifted the boats away from each other. Just as fast as he went up he came down into the sea. The cable snapped.

The cold water was a total shock. He felt movement forward from the lead line, but the sea was strong and unwilling to let go of him. He was hanging onto the rope keeping his head above water, focusing on staying conscious. He was losing that battle, going into hypothermia and feeling the sea absorbing him. His thoughts were foggy; he could not move his hands rigid around the line and his legs were completely numb. A wave lurched him upward and flung him from the sea's hold. He skipped forward along the water as the boys on Winter Heat hauled like mad.

Judy heard some of it as her father hollered over the radio that the cable had snapped. Then radio silence as all hands on Blue Water were glued to the handrails looking and willing for Brian to be hauled in alive.

He looked listless as they brought him over the side of Winter Heat. He was rigid but conscious. His eyes were blurry, pulse slow and he kept muttering "what a rush" over and over. They took him down below into the ship's kitchen where the kerosene stove kept it warm. They stripped off his rain gear and layers of wool and were surprised to find he had on a short dry suit. It had kept his core body temperature high enough to keep him alive. Jake had sent it to him a couple of months earlier. It was a token of forgiveness because it was Jake's and he cherished it. He had put it in his sea bag at the last minute before leaving the wharf, running below and putting it on under his clothes before getting tied into the sling. They stripped that off, rubbed him dry, then covered him in wool blankets and put hot water bottles under his armpits. Half an hour later he was lucid enough to take in warm liquids. They gave him bullion laced with brandy. When he smiled after the second sip they knew he would be alright.

"Fuck! What a ride!" Brian delivered with a wicked grin, the boys had a good laugh in relief. Then he said, "Thanks for hauling me in."

"Hey man you are one heavy dude," said a relieved Sherby Bates, second mate.

They left Brian alone in the kitchen as the crew had to go back to man the hand pumps to keep afloat. Buddy went up to the bridge to inform The Blue Water that their boy from Maine was down below sipping brandy. Robert hollered the good news to his sons and they cheered back.

Judy was so relieved to hear the silence broken by the good news. How had he survived that frigid water? She wondered in relief. She went to the liquor cabinet, poured herself a shot of Wild Turkey and swallowed it down. Letting its woody musky scent ease the tension in her body. She had another and then went about the kitchen making something to eat.

Just when she had finished eating the phone rang. It was Walter Wallace, her dad's buddy from Maine, the one responsible for bringing Brian to Alaska. He wanted to speak to Brian. Judy told him he was out at sea not revealing the pickle he had just been in. He sounded upset, said it was urgent, that his brother Jake had gone ill and was in the hospital in bad shape. Was there any way to reach him? Judy told him she would try to relay a message by radio but there was no way of going ship to shore by phone. It would be days before he got back to shore. Walter then confided in her that all the cows on the farm had died of E coli and Jake had taken it hard and fallen ill. Such a tragedy. He sounded frustrated on not being able to reach Shawn as well.

"Who knows where he is," Walter mumbled.

Judy then confided that Brian was trying to help a vessel in distress at the moment and it was not going well.

"Good God. What is going on with this family?" Walter said mostly to himself.

Judy took his number and said she would call when she had more news on his status and to let her know about Jake. She hung up thinking how hard it would be for Brian to hear the news of his brother and the farm after all he was going through out on the Bering Sea.

Brian slowly got up and started pacing the galley of the kitchen. He was getting pitched hard about the place but he knew he needed to get up and moving. He turned his dry suit inside out and hung it to dry on a chair before the fire. Then he ate some beef stew that was in a pot gimbaled over the stove. Halfway through the bowl he poured what was left of his bouillon brandy into it for good measure. His strength was slow to return but he knew they needed him so he pushed himself to keep moving. The vessel would not take much more pounding before she would capsize in the growing seas.

It would be cold and wet down in that engine room so Brian put the dry suit back on and found the clothes the captain had left him along with some rubber boots. He found some cayenne pepper on the spice rack and sprinkled that into his socks. It was something his dad would do before they went out skating into Maine's winter cold. Kept them tootsies good and warm.

He walked into a grim sight. Water surged on the engine room floor. Two men pumped and the captain was starting to take the head off of one of the engines. Buddy was surprised to see him so soon.

"You feeling up to this?" Captain asked with concern.

"Got no choice Captain, we get these motors going or go under."

"This girl ain't going under!" Buddy threw it right back.

Brian looked over what Buddy had done and gave him some pointers before going over to the other motor and turning head bolts. It was slow going and he was exhausted from his little swim. He needed those strong hands that were manning the pumps. He was looking around in frustration when he spotted the gas generator forward on the port side.

"What is the status of that generator?" Brian asked Captain Buddy.

"Been down since before we got flooded"

"What is wrong with it?"

"Carburetor."

"Captain if I can get that going that would get the electric pumps moving and free up the boys to help us."

"OK but don't waste much time on her she could be a lost cause."

Brian went and looked it over. He found the problem after doing some troubleshooting. The gasket between the carburetor and engine was shot and too much air was coming in. He needed to make a new gasket but with what? He saw his solution. Sherby's nice fat leather belt would make a perfect gasket.

"Hey Sherby I am going to need your belt for the cause," Brian said.

"What for, man?"

"To make a gasket."

"Fuck off man! My girlfriend gave this to me."

"Hey if you want to see her again fork it over."

"Sherby, give it to him!" The captain stepped in.

He reluctantly handed it over. Brian was quick to cut out the gasket from the belt using the old one for a template. He then soaked it in oil and put the carburetor back on. It took some tries but he got it going and switched the ship's power over to run on that. The electric pumps kicked in and the crew hollered in joy.

The seas were too big for Blue Water to tow Winter Heat, so they tied onto the sea anchor to keep slow momentum forward so they would not get so pounded by the sea. There was radio silence for a long time as all hands were down below. Captain Richard was watching his fuel gauges and knew he had only so much fuel to get home. Time was running out. When the cabin lights of Winter Heat went on they knew progress was being made and Brian was doing fine.

Even with the boys turning wrenches and Brian supervising things were going slow. The water was gone from the floor but they were getting thrown around quite a bit. Brian had been knocked against the bulkhead several times and was getting beat up. He was going on pure adrenalin at this point. The rest of the crew was tired too from hours of endless pumping.

Once the heads were off they siphoned off the saltwater that was pooling in the valves, then flooded them with motor oil and turned the motors over.

Captain Rich was getting concerned about fuel. His gauges showed they had just enough to make it back home. He was able to reach Buddy by radio in the engine room.

"What's your progress Buddy, we are running out of time on fuel"

"Shit! Rich get on home! We can go back to the sea anchor."

"Yah we were real impressed with how that was working for yah. Hey how about calling the Coast Guard for back-up?"

"Fuck off Rich you know I would not call that bastard if my ass was on fire."

"Come on Buddy that was a long time ago, time to let go."

"Hey there Captain Advice I got my hands too full over here for that kind of fucking talk. Get on home Blue Water, I promise to bring your man from Maine back in one piece."

"Stop wasting your time talking to me and get back on those motors we are staying for the moment OVER."

Buddy cursed at the radio and went back to cranking on the wrench.

Brian tried asking Sherby about the bad blood with the Coast Guard, but he was still sore over watching him cut up his love belt so he returned the question with a glare.

When Brian arrived back at the wharf a very relieved Judy

met him in the door yard. He looked exhausted. She gave him a surprisingly long hug and then told Brian about his brother and led him into the kitchen to call Jake. By that time Jake was in stable condition. He was grieving over the loss of the cows. When Brian said he was coming home Jake was adamant he stay in Alaska.

"You are out there living your dream little brother. Nothing to do here now."

When Brian hung up the phone he was totally spent. Judy hugged him again and said how sorry she was about his brother's health and the cows dying. She told him to go take a hot shower and she would be up with some soup in a bit.

Judy went to Brian's apartment with some hearty chicken soup. After she knocked and had no answer she walked in with justi-fied concern. He was sound asleep, just wearing boxers, curled in a ball. She studied the side profile of his face for some time, seeing a softness he kept hidden. She sat on the edge of the bed and felt the warmth of his sleeping body and looked around his place. Wow, there were hand drawn sketches of boats and men at sea everywhere. He was good. She was surprised by this side of himself that he never talked about. She picked up his sketch book that was lying on the bedside table and flipped through it. Very nice stuff--abstract works of land meeting the sea. Then wham! One of her. It caught her completely off guard. It was a close up of her face straight on. Her hair was partly across her eyes, which showed her pain and sorrows. The truth of it seared through her. She had felt that pain for a long time but never saw it expressed before her, face to face. Crying softly she lied down, wrapped her body around his curled form and took in his warmth and sleeping presence. He knew her pain.

Judy had thought he had a simple crush on her. That sketch showed a man who looked beyond her outward persona and saw something deep inside of her. That perspective does not come from lust but love. He loved her, that was as plain as day to her now. It comforted her and also scared her. She had seen him as a friend. Simple, uncomplicated with no connection to her past. She cared for this man. He came into her life when she needed a male friend. She held him for this love he had for her but most of all because he was alive.

- CHAPTER 14 -

Mexico:

S hawn was starting to feel too settled on the island. The pull of the road, his itchy feet, drew him away. When he told Clive and his family he was leaving, they were sad. It was a really hard goodbye, and Shawn was torn knowing it would be this way for a while. That side of him won out over the stability of familiar people and places. It would be a lifetime dichotomy for him.

He made his way across the border into Mexico after getting all kinds of advice from travelers on the beaches of Texas. Some told him to leave his truck and go by bus since the chances of it getting stolen were high. Others said he could play it safe, not traveling at night or leaving it alone all night in city streets. He took the Ford, no talking him out of it, but he did listen to the warnings of the dangers.

Crossing the border was easy, but life in that border town in Mexico was something Shawn had never witnessed before. The streets were full of vendors selling anything from tacos to fried potatoes, watches, pineapples, and yes further down into the streets, women. He had never been propositioned before. She spoke good English with an accent, approaching him by asking,

"How such a handsome man is walking without a beautiful woman?" She held his arm and walked with him, asking if he would like to have sex. Just like that. She was so confident yet casual about it he could not help but laugh while saying no thanks. She did not take his no.

"Why not? You don't like me?"

"No, you are very pretty but I don't move that fast."

She laughed this time.

"OK I will move very slow, first at your toes and work my way up."

She casually brushed the crotch of his pants with the palm of her open hand. He started to lose his no. She felt the loss of resistance and moved her body closer so the side of her warm and braless breast rubbed against his naked arm. She kept talking, and he kept walking and swelling as she led him down a side street. It was a look of caution from a local man walking by that broke him from the trance of his desire. He looked around and realized she was leading him into a setup as two big men appeared behind them. Shawn reacted fast. He turned and ran right at his supposed attackers and went low. The two men were not expecting that, used to having the element of shock and surprise when they pulled out their weapons and got whatever they wanted. No time to reach for their hidden knives. Just standing with their hands out, their mouths hanging open. Shawn's wide shoulders and hip took their feet from under them, and down they went as he rolled past, got up and ran up the street. It happened so fast his adrenalin was cranking. Some people further up the street asked in Spanish why he was running. He yelled banditos with his Maine accent and kept running until he got back to where his Ford was parked. It looked unharmed, so he went into a crowded bar. He sat by the window and looked out at his new world, laughing at what just happened.

It was early afternoon. He had lots of time before darkness. He felt they would not approach him in a crowded place and so planned to have a few beers and then drive a couple of hours and find a small village to spend the night. Shawn was into his second beer when his lady of the street walked into the bar. She did not see him right away, focusing on her next prey, a young American male. When she did finally look at him there was no look of surprise, she went to him and asked with complete innocence why he ran off and knocked down those men.

"They are not happy with you, Amor," she reprimanded him.

"Come off of it! You know why."

"I think you are a paranoid American and need a woman to give you release," she said in a sexy purring voice while reaching over and rubbing his inner thigh.

"You are something else," Shawn spit out in disbelief.

"Yes, I am very special woman you will be lucky man to have sex with me."

"I am not having sex with you."

"Oh so hurtful to Miss Clara. You have girlfriend?"

"No."

"See you need me. What is your name handsome?"

"Shawn," he said before he could stop himself.

"Oh such a lovely name. You call me Clara," as she reached

over and took his beer and put it too her lips, slowly sipping it in a most seductive way.

He couldn't believe this was going on. She just tried to set him up to be robbed, now she is back trying to seduce him like nothing happened. Shawn had never met a woman like her before. He was intrigued more now by her gall and stellar performance than her hand on his thigh. Well almost, she did have a very warm hand.

"Where are you from?"

He saw no harm in being truthful so he told her Maine. When she heard that she smiled and looked at him with interest, saying she had an uncle who lived in Maine, Snowy Point.

"He works on a big fishing boat. He says he big fisherman now but we know he is the cook, no fisherman. He sends home lots of money so the family forgives him his false talk," Clara delivered without seduction in her voice.

"Snowy Point, my brother fished a boat out of there two years ago. Do you know the name of the boat?"

"Yes of course, Helen B."

"No fucking way, that was the same boat my brother fished on. Man oh man wait till I tell him this one. What is your uncle's name?"

"Manuel Ortega. Is your brother here? I wish to talk with him about my Uncle."

"No he is fishing off Alaska right now."

"Oh that is very far. Life is something that we find this connection."

"Life is a trip," he shook his head and laughed.

Clara changed after that. She asked many questions about Maine. Made him describe the color of the sea. Was there any sand or just all the rocks his uncle wrote about? What kind of man was his brother? Her hand was still on his leg but with less purpose for seduction, more of a hand hold for the conversation.

Laura had been keeping an eye on Shawn. She was attracted to him when she spotted him on the street in front of the bar. Since moving to Mexico months before to teach English in a small village two hours away, she had not had sex. She was looking for the right guy to have a weekend fling with and get some needed release. She was talking with some NGO volunteers she had met six months earlier that worked in another Village. They would all come to Felice for occasional weekend socializing and watching the madness. This particular weekend Laura wanted more than conversation and people watching. She was getting up the nerve to go and talk with Shawn when Clara sat with him.

She had been around long enough to know the score with the working girls. There were the ones who just wanted to turn a trick. Then there were the decoy girls who were very beautiful but teasers not pleasers, leading the men to a side street to be robbed. She had seen it many times. Sometimes the ones who got robbed came back to the bar looking for sympathy and free drinks. They just got laughed at. She felt they deserved it in a way. Come to a bar and in the first minute a beautiful woman hits on them and they leave together. "Come on! They deserve what they get for being that stupid," she thought.

She recognized Clara to be a decoy girl. She wanted to see how her crush would react. They had been sitting together for more than twenty minutes. They never lasted that long before walking out with her. She could tell the change in body language in Clara. They looked to be actually having a conversation. She was impressed with her crush and moved him up a notch, wondering if she should tip him off. Not a wise move. Snitches never walk back in a bar. But if she could do it without anyone knowing…. Her mind went to scheming.

Clara was talking about her family when Shawn happened to look out the window onto the street. A driver's door opened. He could see the reflection of people on the street from the driver's mirror. The new angle gave him a quick view of his tackle buddies lurching to the side of the entrance of the bar. He then looked at Clara. She saw the change in his face, reading that he knew the score outside. She liked Shawn, his brother knowing her uncle made him a person to her. So she took a huge risk by helping him.

"I have no choice in what I am. They will hurt the ones I love if I do otherwise. But I have this moment with you to be honest. You cannot go out the front door. Next to the baño is a door to the back alley. There is a delivery truck for beer there now. I can see the driver at the bar, and he is almost done with his beer. The truck will go soon. Hide in the empty bays. The next stop for their delivery will be safe for you to get out onto the street."

With that said she kissed Shawn on the cheek, looked him in the eyes and whispered in his ear, "Go now mi amor."

Laura had worked out her scheme and was in the middle of executing it when she ran into Shawn as she was coming out of the ladies room after having set the trash can on fire. Her plan was to be out in the bar when some woman yelled "FIRE!" after seeing the flames. She envisioned a panicked bar, and when her crush was rushing out with the crowd she would go to his side and tell him of his danger. She did not expect to be face to face with him so soon. His eyes were green blue and he was looking right into her brown ones. They both froze for a brief but powerful moment.

"You are in danger!" she loudly whispered.

"No shit!" he replied as he brushed past and felt with his chest, through her thin t-shirt as he headed for the back exit.

That brief contact lingered on her wanting breasts, leaving something, as he felt the heat of her on his chest as he slipped out the back door. What was that all about?

Laura knew if she followed him she would blow his cover, so she made a bee line for the front exit. When she first saw him in front of the bar he was checking on an old Ford side step, and when he was sitting by the window he would check on it. He looked to be a Ford man so she planned to hang by that old Ford and hopefully hook up with him when he circled back. She wondered who alerted him to go out the back when she heard "Fuego!!" from a high pitched young Mexican girl. Smoke was coming out of the ladies room by then, so the crowd rushed in mass for the door.

Clara was pushed out of the bar with the flow of the crowd. The criminal boys were fighting to maintain their position by the door. They were big but no match for the collective might of people that was pouring out onto the street. By the time they found Clara, Shawn was hiding in the back of the beer truck as it was flying down the back alley trying to beat the crowd. When they came to Main Street, traffic was at a complete standstill. Shawn knew he was a sitting duck, so he got off the truck and slipped into the crowd staying low and keeping his face down as he worked his way back to the truck.

Laura was leaning against the Ford driver's door acting like it was her truck. When her crush showed up her plan was to offer to drive while he hid on the floor behind the seats and then drive away unobserved. By this point one of the bartenders had put the fire out with two pitchers of Tecate beer. They aired the smoke out of the bar and told the waitresses to go out in the street and tell people it was safe to come back in. A surprising number did just that.

Shawn had made his way to his beloved Ford. He planned to slip in the passenger door and lay low till darkness and drive away then. But first he wanted to look across the street from under the truck hoping to see but not be seen. His view was blocked by the feet and tan, shapely lower calves of a woman leaning against his truck. What were the chances she was a part of the scammers? No, she was a gringa, that is a tan not natural color. She must be a bystander using his side step for a leaning post."

He slid further under the truck and tapped her on the ankle.

That touch surprised Laura. She was waiting for him but was not ready for that. She jumped, dropped her sunglasses and looked under the Ford right into those green blue eyes. Just seeing her upside-down head, he did not recognize her right off.

"Give me the keys to your truck. I will let you in then drive off," Laura stated with purpose,

"Hey aren't you the woman from the hall who warned me of danger?"

"Yes, I am glad you remember me."

"How did you know I was in trouble?"

"The company you keep. Now give me your keys."

"I clearly recall there being a trash can on fire right behind you. The look in your eye told me you set that fire. Why would I give my keys to a pyro?"

"Hey I set that fire for your benefit, Maine boy! I am the only friend you got within hundreds of miles of here, so let me help you get out of here safely," her brown eyes got more beautiful with her conviction.

"You are wrong. I made a friend in that bar and she warned me of the danger."

"Oh man you are a bigger fool than I thought. Do you know how many times I have seen that woman work naive American men like yourself into a setup?"

"Hey I know what she does but she helped me. Now why do you want to help?"

He got her with that question.

"I wanted a victory for the fools for a change," she tried to change the truth.

"How did you know this was my truck?"

"I got you pegged for a Ford boy from the get go. Me and my friends were betting on how long you would last before she got you to leave with her," she said, taking the lie further for the ruse.

"Did you win?"

"No, I lost. You surprised me. It's kind of why I decided to help you."

"You decided to help me. Right now I am not in the frame of mind to trust beautiful women offering to help me."

"So you think I am beautiful?" it came out before she could stop herself. Her desire revealed itself in the tone of her question and the dilating of her pupils.

"Yes and full of trouble. Now, can you see Clara with two big men?"

"Yes, she is talking to them, pointing to a Chevy with Nevada plates across the street," she tried to show him she can help and be trusted.

"See, she is trying to help."

"Don't get your hopes up. I am your only help. Now, fork over the keys and let's get out of here!"

"No, I don't trust you."

"Hey I am an American," she gave him a big wide-eyed look before standing back up to avoid suspicion.

"You got to do better than that. I know a lot of Americans I don't trust."

"Come on, you are from Maine, can't be that many."

"How do you claim to know so much about Maine? You don't strike me as a Maine girl."

"No but I spent some summers there as a camp counselor."

"Oh one of those."

"What the hell is that supposed to mean?" her head went back down and looked at Shawn with burning eyes.

"The type that spends a couple of summers by a lake in fantasy land and think they know Maine," Shawn laid it on her.

"Listen! Those were troubled kids and that camp helped them. So piss off!" and off she went down the street.

With the knowledge that Clara diverted the boys from his truck, he crawled out from under it and slipped his key into the lock, unlocked the door while crouching out of view, and slipped into his Ford to hide under a blanket behind the seat.

After some time he slipped between the seats and put the key into the ignition in preparation for a quick getaway. The passenger door surprisingly opened and Laura slipped in and crawled over and into the driver's seat, turned the key and started up the old Ford.

"Lucky for you I forgive quickly," she said as she put 'er into gear and pulled out into the street.

"For Christ sakes I don't want your help," he yelled while pulling the blanket from his face.

"Well you got it now, you can thank me later," she shifted higher in gear with ease.

Shawn could just see the movement of her thighs and her arm moving the stick. It was poetry, truck and woman coming together. She knew a Ford, and he was seeing her in a new light.

"Where did you learn to drive a truck?"

"On the camp you was making fun of. It was a working farm that took in children from violent homes. I drove all the farm trucks and machinery. My name is Laura by the way."

"Shawn," he said in a warm truce.

"Is it safe for me to sit up?"

"Yes, come up and sit with me. I am taking you to a small coastal town two hours from here. There are lean-tos on the beach for a couple of bucks for the night. How does that sound Shawn?"

"Oh so now I have a say. I was planning on going to the coast. Sounds good," Shawn was warming up to Laura as he crawled up front.

"I have been in this country for six months, teaching English in a small mountain village. I love the sea so I go to this village when I can on weekends. I have been many times. It is safe. But no girls like Clara. Maybe you will get bored," she was still taunting.

"You might be right. I like Clara. She told me how to safely get out of the bar. She has no choice in her own life so she gave me one by helping me. Brave lady, I don't want to think of the consequences for her if they find out."

"What are you trying to tell me?"

"That people are not always what you think they are."

"Did she really help you?" Laura said with a touch of jealousy in her tone.

"Yes and taught me something as well."

They drove in silence after that, aware of each other's presence and the changing countryside of Mexico. Each aware they were sitting next to someone who they felt very comfortable with and very, very attracted to. Shawn thought how up until that moment he had never trusted anyone else driving his truck. Her skirt was hiked up high above the knees so she could lift them to work the long winded pedals of the old Ford. She had nice legs and worked them in time with the changing motor on inclines. From the side he could see the set in her jaw that gave her the grit to be with him now and her lovely eye lashes shadowed by long auburn hair. Her lips, full and eager. He could feel the heat of desire in the space between them. It had been a long time for him as well.

Laura broke the long silence, "I like this countryside. It makes me excited for the coming sea. You can almost smell the salt mixed in with the cactus and junipers."

"You are right, it is intoxicating my first time in a country like this. Why don't you stop? I want to get out and take it all in."

"Probably not the safest thing to do at night on this road but O.K. Quick one," she pulled the old side step off the road.

Shawn got out and on his way got some wonderful eye shine from Laura. He walked off a ways into the night, stood and inhaled the smell of Mexico. Full of life of the land, animal and people. A rich scent of the earth, salt and burning pinion from the hearths of homes far off. The sound of coyotes, prairie owls and dogs barking from a distant village. The wild mixed in with the domestic. Strong and light. He could see the silhouettes of juniper and cactus and the occasional palm tree. He had dreamed of this all his life, and now here he was for real. Laura came and stood close, not saying anything, just feeling his excitement for being someplace new and wonderful. He moaned a few times in awe of it and she smiled and looked at his profile, feeling more attracted and feeding the heat in the short space between them.

After a good bit of time she put her hand on his arm and whispered, "We should go." Shawn broke free of it and turned and walked back to his Ford. They stood before the front bumper just looking and smiling at one another. Laura placed the keys in his hand and held him with the key between their palms. Looking, shining and feeling.

"You drive Laura. You know the way."

She liked that he trusted her driving and even more the way he said her name. The way he pressed the key back into her hand and touched the tips of her fingers with a lingering look in his eyes.

They had fun talking on that road, in the distance left to the coast of Mexico. Laura told of her days as a counselor on the farm in Maine. Shawn relayed stories back from his days as a boy. She had a wonderful laugh. He had great stories but she was a better story teller. They came down around a bend and were greeted by the strong smell of sweet salt, the comfort of the crashing surf of the sea and the village that sat next to it. Laura shifted to a low gear and moved slowly through the main street of the village so Shawn could take it in. She drove around the zocalo and the tiendas and bars and cafes with tables that spilled out into the street. The loud sound of salsa music and the smell of cooking corn and carne filling the cab. Families, lovers, teenagers and dogs milled about. Laura took a lazy sandy road down to the beach toward the lean-tos where they would spend the night.

When Shawn opened up the back of the camper to get his bedroll it dawned on him that she had no belongings.

"Where are your things?"

"I left them with a friend. She will bring my bag back to my village."

"I have an extra blanket in the truck," he offered with a smile.

Laura stood close and held his arm and said, "I was hoping I could share yours" with total confidence.

That being said it took away all that awkwardness on the subject of sleeping arrangements. She led him to a lean-to close to the sea. He made them a nest for the night. She patiently waited and watched. A man came out of the darkness with a lantern and greeted Laura warmly in Spanish. She gave him some small bills and he bid them good night.

They walked out to the edge of the surf in bare feet and felt the warm sea. The sky was all stars, right down to the horizon. The constellations were vivid and strong, timeless. Shawn had never seen anything like it. He was so lost in it and not aware that Laura wanted all his attention. After getting no response from rubbing her breasts against his arm, she reached down and splashed water on him. That did it, full on retaliation with splashes of water until they were both soaked. She completely surprised Shawn and tackled him into the sea. They wrestled in the surf, tossing each other into the crashing waves. She was strong and knew how to use her weight. They ended up laughing and in each other's arms, slowly finding their lips. It was a kiss that started out with such tenderness but moved quickly to match their desire that was fueled by the taste of their chemistry. They explored their bodies with hands, lips and tongues, removing the wet clothing feeling the honesty of their bodies. She held his hardness in one hand and his face in the other, telling him ever so sweetly that she wanted him in the nest he made for them. Her nipples just grazed his muscular chest. He did not want to stop, but she settled it and grabbed her wet discarded clothes and ran away from him, her beautiful bottom swaying in rhythm with her graceful stride. He ran in hot pursuit. She waited for him at the foot of the makeshift bed, naked and full of hunger and need for him. They grabbed each other and kissed without fear. He broke free of her hot lips and slowly kissed her neck and nibbled on her lobes then he moved down to her collar bone and found tender flesh to kiss and lick. He teased her with his tongue, in her cleavage and around her eager nipples, and finally took them each in turn, into his mouth, sucking while she found his hardness with her warm and confident hand. At times he took control, at others she did. When her need was so great and she tried to mount him, he stopped her, his hard, hot head just touching her moist lips. Laura moaned in frustration, Shawn laughed while he threw her below him and rubbed the inside of her thigh with just the head. He kissed her and whispered her name while he slowly entered. The intensity of that act changed random passion to a deep connection. It was like part of their being was being drawn into each other, meeting in the middle and expanding. Never had they felt anything like it before. They cherished the moment and took each other to the edge several times only to hold off and look with wonder in each other eyes. Finally, the passion winning over, they devoured each other, crashing together in a pile, exhausted and totally satisfied. They lay in each other arms completely at home and in peace.

Laura broke the long silence by saying, "It is amazing! what a girl has to do to get laid these days."

They both fell into deep laughter.

They had a wonderful weekend together in that lean-to by the sea, exploring the beach for miles on end, finding tide pools to swim naked in and look below the surface of life in the sea, making love in the crashing surf.

Shawn drove Laura back to her village and stayed. When he saw the condition the school was in he could not leave. He fixed the bathrooms, then the class rooms and got help from the students and even some of the parents. The school ran on a shoe string so he bought supplies with his own money. Shawn loved being needed. The skills he took for granted were so much help to that village school. The kids soaked up all they could of his knowledge and skills.

He was falling in love with Laura and she with him. Shawn took his own apartment, respecting how it would upset the locals if he was living with a woman out of wedlock. They took turns visiting each other's apartments, cooking with their neighbors, eating and laughing, enjoying the compassion of the Mexican people. It was a very joyous four months for Shawn.

Then one night, Tilly came to him in a dream.

In the dream he was at the vista he had stopped at that first night with Laura, but this time he was alone. Tilly came out of the darkness and made a big fuss, ran around him in circles and shook her head up and down, then walked off. He followed her into a small glade of trees. When Shawn went into the glade he found himself in the dooryard of the farm back in Maine. The house looked bad. The front door was off its hinges. No presence of his brother or any of the animals in sight. Tilly stood off at a distance looking at the farm with big, sad, dark eyes.

Shawn woke up with concern for his brother Jake. He went to a calling center and paid cash to call long distance, no phone in his apartment. There was no answer at the farm, so he called a good friend who lived in town. From his friend he learned what happened to Jake. He called the hospital when Jake was past the worst of his illness.

Shawn told him he would come right home, but Jake talked him out of it and said, "We all need a break from the farm."

He talked about losing all the cows, confessing his guilt with the bad septic. Shawn tried to tell him it was not his fault. They talked for a long time. It was good for the both of them to find things to laugh about and heal some of the chasm between them. When Shawn hung up he was left with the edge of old emotions he had tried to run from. The mood carried over and started to disrupt the bubble of his romance with Laura.

- CHAPTER 15 -

Alaska:

Brian woke up late the next morning after sleeping for twelve hours. A strong vision of his night's dream came before his mind with Judy hovered over him, her eyes full of love and fear. The pillow even smelled of her, so unique to her, a mix of spruce, salt and lavender. When Judy had hugged him after he heard the news the night before she craned her head against his, sure yet soft. It must have taken to his hair and then the pillow, he explained to himself. He loved that he could still smell her, having part of her right there with him. After he took a shower he finally snapped out of it and thought of the conversation with his brother Jake. He wondered how Tilly was doing at the farm without other life. He was concerned but relieved in a way. Jake would be free of it for a while. Away from some of the shadows from the past. He felt some guilt. Needed to talk to Shawn but there was just no way to get ahold of him. He'd just have to wait it out for him to call.

When he went over to the house Judy was the only one home, sitting at the kitchen table working on the books for the wharf. She got up and gave him a hug. Brian smelled her hair and held on, and she let him and held right back. When they separated

Judy held his eye for the briefest of moments revealing some compassion. A crack in her wall.

She fed him a fisherman's breakfast of three eggs, pancakes, sausage and hash brown potatoes. They said little while he ate just taking comfort in each other's presence. That peace abruptly ended when Clara came bursting into the kitchen with concern for Brian. When she finished hugging him she kissed him deeply and Judy felt a surprising tinge of jealousy and came up with a quick excuse to leave.

Clara picked up on the change in Brian's energy when Judy left the room and asked, "Is there something going on between you two?"

"What are you talking about?"

"When I walked in here it felt like I was interrupting something. Then you return my hot kiss with a cold one and Judy walks out."

"Christ Clara! There is nothing going on. I just got some bad news about the farm from my brother Jake, so give me a break," Brian snapped back.

After some silence Clara asked him about the farm. After he told her, they cleaned up the kitchen and went out and sat on the wharf.

Shawn did call Brian, and they talked for a long time. Each was concerned for Jake, getting the angle from each other on it. Both feeling it best to let him ride the hard tide out away from the farm. They talked about Tilly. Shawn told Brian about the dream that made him call home. They laughed about it. Then Shawn asked, "Hey, you had a visit from the old man yet?"

"You being foolish?"

"No! He came to me in one of my dreams one night. Clear as day asking why I left the farm."

"No shit! What did you tell him?"

"That the farm was all him and I needed to find me."

"What did he say to that?"

"He said I reminded him of his uncle and laughed."

"No shit, well why the fuck has he not come to me?" Brian sounded hurt.

"Beats me little brother but stay open to it," Shawn said with hopeful laughter in his voice.

In the months that followed Judy seemed to avoid being alone with him. Clara, after declaring she did not want a boyfriend, was acting more like she did. He could not get Judy out of his mind. That look she gave him in the kitchen lingered strong, giving him hope. He avoided Clara and tried to be with Judy and failed at both.

They started fishing inside after Judy gave them all an earful at dinner one night. With the savings in fuel and some favorable currents they did make out a little better. Brian had to admit he did like it. He got a mouthful of the outside to last a bit and there was so much more to see being close to land. That hard contrast from sea to mountains. Beeeeaaaauuuuttiiiiffulll. During the down times when they were just cruising and all the deck jobs were taken care of, he would draw. Porpoise, stark in contrast with their black and white colors. Orca whales, sharks, walrus, sea lions, all mixed in with a deep green of the coastal sea. Since his ride in the breach buoy the brothers had some respect for him. They still loved giving him shit though. They all fell into a groove working on the ship. They knew their roles and each other's moves and achieved less command and more rhythm in getting 'er done.

They all rolled into the bar one night knowing the crew of Winter Heat was in there. Brian presented Sherby a new leather belt, raising the hackles on the girlfriend. That just egged the boys on more. Did they bust some chops. Lots of giving and taking, hard laughter. Judy showed up, which was out of character but a very welcome sight to the brothers and Brian. They were all crowded around the bar stealing the stools from one another. Somehow Judy and Brian ended up sharing a stool together. They folded into one another and found a place to rest between them. Brian fell silent while Judy took up on the jokes. He loved the feel of her body moving against his when they both laughed. He could smell her hair and body, all her. She was leaning with her back partly against his chest feeling the rhythm of his heart and smelling the sea that was with him. That position changed when Judy leaned back to talk with Sherby`s girlfriend, her chest now against his back. He was warm and her breasts were soft. Judy's nipples got very hard and for the first time in over a year she had strong desire for a man. His back got hotter, her hand now on his thigh. Then Clara showed up drunk and dragged Brian off the stool and onto the dance floor, breaking the spell.

After that night Judy started coming up to Brian's room and sketching with him. They would both pick an item then draw their own versions of it. When observing each other's work, their hands and bodies would shyly touch, each knowing what was to come but not quite ready to get there. Savoring that place of mystery and anticipation. Talking of the simple things of life and then not, comfortable in the silence.

- CHAPTER 16 -

Shawn was eight when his mother died just after giving birth to Brian. It shattered his heart, his stable world. When he heard the news, he ran away. They could not find him for twelve hours. Moxie finally found him hidden out in the barn after he had been running in the woods. He was carried back in his father's arms to the house that had always felt warm but now was cold. He felt the emptiness in his heart and his father's as well. The innocence of his boyhood had been taken from him. He became a survivor. Being the eldest, he helped care for his little brothers. He became stoic about it, putting away the pain by focusing on them. He helped feed them at the table, made sure they did not put on their t-shirts as pants and later protected them in the school yards. Even though time moved on the farm held that sadness for him from that great loss. He stopped trusting love. In his few relationships in high school he was more of a friend and protector than a romancer. He never let go. Until he met Laura. For three months he lived with such happiness in that small village, without fear and giving from the heart. He was in the moment in that place in his life without the farm without his past fogging his lens. It awakened places inside of himself, a new found freedom.

The dream of seeing the farm, abandoned, awakened that old wound deep in his heart. That's was how he felt at eight, abandoned. He buried all of that, not having the emotional awareness and support to process that pain and let it go. That time of being shattered was buried in his soul. He found a way to survive, made a safe place for himself by not taking risks of the heart. Being away from the farm, in a new country and surrounded by children that showed him so much compassion and the magic of being with Laura, sent happiness to the core of his being. That bubble was burst by the image of the farm house in his dream and the knowledge that happiness can be taken away by forces you have no control over. Then you are left only with the pain. All of this was deep in his subconscious. He started to resent Laura and showed it by snapping at her over small things. She was confused and hurt by this. She knew how the news of his brother and the farm had made him sad but she did not expect this anger vented at her. They both withdrew from each other, Shawn out of anger caused by a deep fear he could not explain and Laura because she felt rejected by that anger.

The reason why Laura came to Mexico was to get away from a man who could not commit to her. She was a giver of the heart, ready and willing to give and take risks. Bill, the boyfriend, was not. He was fun to be around, but the problem was he was just around for the good times and none of her bad times when she needed support. She called him on it and he talked change but never made any. She got really depressed, finally got tired of it all and found the teaching job and moved to Mexico. That was why she was celibate for so long. When she went after Shawn it was for pleasure; she had not planned on it turning into love. But love it was and she was surprised how willing she was to give it another try. Now this change in Shawn.

When Laura left, Bill finally got it. It caught him by total surprise. Laura had always been there for him. She gave him a hard time for not being around enough, but he saw it as something to put up with, not to deal with by making changes in his behavior. She never returned his pathetic letters asking her to come back.

When Laura started getting depressed by Shawn's behavior, she called her sister back in Virginia. She talked her heart out. Missed home and even missed Bill. Her sister, who still ran with the same crowd as Bill, told him he was missed. Bill saw his window and headed for Mexico.

While all this drama was building, the village where Laura worked was having a celebration for the end of school and the start of summer. Shawn was helping build the float for the school in the parade and she with making costumes for the kids. It kept them busy and gave themselves an excuse to not spend time together. The anticipation and excitement was too much for the kids, and it was next to impossible to hold class time with every kid bouncing off the walls. Finally they just put all the day's energies into the preparation for the celebration.

The thing with the float was that you were an open target for the pedestrians who were well armed with water balloons and foam spray. The trick was to build a theme on the float that could protect you, like a moving castle, and have offensive abilities well under cover. Shawn and the kids designed and built a water cannon that was hidden in the fake mountain they built out of chicken wire, wood and papier mâché. Inside was a massive water tank and cannon that essentially was a water hose, mounted on a pivot block, pilfered from the fire house. They could shoot out water under pressure from the tank provided by a hand pump. Genius really.

Meanwhile Bill is in route to rescue his beloved. He found that the cheapest way to get to Laura's village was to fly to Texas then take a bus to the border, walk across, spend the night in a lively border town and take the local bus the next morning. He walked across the border through customs just as it was getting dark. A street hawker showed him to a cheap hotel close to the action. Checked in, dropped off his bag and took to the streets finding a lively bar to hang in. There was a good mix of people in there. Locals and tourists young and old. Plenty of women, some dressed very well. After his second shot of tequila a stunner walked into the bar. Long dark hair and shiny emerald black eyes dressed sexy but with class. She held herself with such confidence. She scanned the bar and her eyes settled on Bill. He melted when she cocked her head while locking his gaze and walked towards him, her hips swaying with desire, her eyes on fire.

"Hello handsome, why you sit alone?"

"Ahhhhhhh I am traveling alone."

"Oh that is so sad. May I join you?"

"Ahhhh sure."

She sat across from him at the small round table, resting her velvety soft and very warm calf against his. Bill was wearing shorts, it was a hot day.

"Why such handsome man travel alone in Mexico?"

"To visit a friend."

"A Mexican girlfriend?"

"Ahhh no, a buddy of mine from high school," Bill said, not revealing his truth.

"Then this is your lucky day. I am single too and looking for a handsome man like you to bring joy to my day," she reached her hand under the table and rubbed the inside of his naked knee.

"Where you come from?" she asked while holding his eyes and rubbing up his thigh. Five minutes later they were walking out of the bar after the beautiful Mexican woman suggested they go to another bar that was smaller and more intimate. In the street filled with venders, hawkers and tourists Bill asked her name.

"Clara," she told him, rolling that R.

- CHAPTER 17 -

The day of the parade finally came, and the kids showed up dressed as their favorite heroes. The float was looking real good. All that hard work shone with pride in so many faces. They talked a local farmer into towing the float with his tractor. The kids took their places on the moving mountain, each armed with an assortment of water throwing devices from water balloons to hypo squirts, to baggies filled with water. A couple of the bigger boys were inside the mountain manning the water cannon. They joined the line of parade goers on other floats, army vehicles, the fire truck, a car full of town funcionarios, all led by a brass band. The water fights started from the get go. The kids on the mountain held their own by throwing the water balloons. The boys on the water cannon waited for the right moment of surprise. Shawn milled about in the crowd and watched the float's progress with amusement. Laura was on board dressed as Amelia Earhart complete with leather ace flying helmet, made from scraps. She was supposed to be keeping the kids from getting too wild, but she was really getting into throwing balloons at the crowd. Venting some of her frustrations she threw one at Shawn that glanced off his shoulder. He turned and saw her to be the culprit and was hurt by the anger in her eyes.

The mountain float was a big target for the crowd. The kids on top had the advantage throwing down from above but a limited supply of water. Some of the hijos on the ground mounted an assault and threw lots of water balloons. The boys in the mountain opened fire with the water cannon and it soaked a lot of people, which brought on a bigger assault from the crowd, some of whom charged and climbed the mountain. One of the lads on the float lit firecrackers and went to throw them into the air, but a crowd goer who was climbing up got in the way of the toss, causing the firecrackers to land inside the mountain, which created a surprise that turned to panic when a fire started on the papier mâché float. The warriors of the water war moved to fighting the fire with everything they had. A lot of commands were yelled and no one listened as they all threw water balloons, buckets and used the water cannon until the boys had to abandoned ship. At one point Shawn and Laura were side by side throwing buckets of water from the haphazard brigade, close together yet a great distance between them. The hurt kept them speechless, each enveloped in the escalating madness around them yet so aware of the void between them.

The fire raged on that float and kids in their costumes jumped off the mountain, capes and curly frills flying. It was quite a sight to see. The farmer kept on pulling to get the burning float away from the stores. The crowd followed along, but they gave up fighting the fire and busted out the tequila and laughed heartily. They slapped each other on their backs and shared stories of the battle. The farmer stopped pulling when he got to the soccer field, and the crowd created a circle around the burning mountain and had a grand party as water balloons flew over the fire at the party goers on the other side. Tequila and beer flowed, some guitars and an accordion gathered and played a fast polka beat that blended with the other sounds of laughter, dogs barking, roosters crowing, firecrackers, bottle rockets, full on. Shawn was pulled away from Laura's side by some of the men who had helped to build the float, laughing about what a great tribute this was to their work. Laura, with a heavy heart, went off to check on the children from her class.

Meanwhile Bill finally made his way to the village. He had to hitch hike from the border town because he had been robbed of all his money. He stuck out like a sore thumb in a small Mexican town, a gringo with a suitcase, a busted lip and a black eye. An old man who spoke some English approached Bill in the street and asked him what he was doing in town. Bill told the man he was looking for Laura, an American woman teaching in their school. Of course the man knew of her. He hollered at one of the kids, who ran towards the fiesta to find Laura and bring her back to his tienda. The man took Bill to his little store where his wife attended to his busted lip. Laura was told by the lad that a gringo man was in town looking for her and she needed to go now for this man did not look too good. When she walked into Pedro's store she was very surprised to see Bill, not only because of his present beat-up state, but because she was glad to see him. She gave him a big hug and held his eyes with affection while he told her his story, minus his encounter with Clara. With all the heart felt turmoil Laura had been through in the last weeks, she lost herself in the past with Bill and kissed him tenderly on his busted lip.

Shawn walked in at that moment, and it hit him like a sledge hammer seeing this woman whom he loved kissing another man. In situations such as these, a man either fights or goes into flight. Shawn did both. He blackened Bill's other eye, told Laura to fuck off and walked out of Pedro's. Then he packed his belongings, got into his truck and drove out of town. He ran, he ran just like when he was eight. Ran to that place in his soul of survival, safe and very alone, rebuilding that wall around his heart. He drove down dirt roads in the Mexican night, rerunning the vision of that kiss, the way her hand held his face, letting his heart bleed for the hurt man he was now but also for the boy of eight, devastated by the loss of his mother. Then and now, all coming together and crashing down.

Shawn had been driving for hours, well into the night and off the main road. Not a good thing to do considering where he was in Mexico. But he was not concerned with his personal safety at that moment in his life. He was just thinking back on how callous he was towards his brother Jake after he walked in on his girlfriend with his good friend.

"What an asshole," he hollered at himself. What he would give to be with Jake right then and now. He suddenly came upon a fire in the middle of the road and had to come to an abrupt stop. On each side of his truck a man approached and each had a shot gun pointed at his head.

"Buenos noches, Amigo, we want no harm to you. Just some of your things. Vamos, get out!"

For a brief moment Shawn's first impulse was to go for the gun of the man on his side. But some reason settled in before he followed that course of action. Instead he got out and stood in front of two armed men, looking at their drunken yet lively eyes.

"What things of mine did you have in mind?" Shawn asked with surprisingly impartial concern.

"The truck," said the man wearing a well-worn cowboy hat and faded jeans.

"Oh! Is that all?" Shawn said, which got a laugh from the banditos.

This exchange of humor brought out a gracious side of the two men, who brought out a bottle of tequila and shared it with Shawn. They made sure he had a couple of good pulls on it before the talker took it back, waved it in the air and gave a toast.

"Here is to a good day for us and not so good for you, Amigo," he pulled hard on that bottle. They laughed more when Shawn started talking in broken Spanish. In the middle of some laughter one of the men pointed at Shawn's boots and wanted him to take them off.

"Oh man, come on! Not my boots!"

"Amigo, you look to be a fast runner. We would hate for you to pursue us," the bandito came back with laughter in his voice.

"You boys are all heart," Shawn mumbled as he sat against his truck to take them off. Once he did that, the quiet one pointed the gun at his crotch and said the pants too.

"Fucking hell," Shawn hollered into the night, which brought on more laughter.

The two drunker and richer banditos hugged Shawn and drove off, one in his beloved Ford side step and the other in a beat up Chevy. They left him barefoot and penniless, in just his underwear, warming up by a dying fire in the middle of a dirt road. It did shift his mood away from the drama of the kiss. It may sound strange, but a strong feeling of freedom took over and he felt lighter than he had ever felt before. Ever since crossing the border he had spent a lot of his energy on keeping his truck from being stolen. Now that it had happened he was free of that burden. He started to think of Tilly, the time she robbed Jake of his first kiss by licking Sally. He laughed from the bottom of his stomach as he walked down the road into the Mexican night.

Robert and Manuel Chavez were driving home late that night having sold cattle at the market and spent some time drinking in town. Robert was driving the old Chevy truck and Manuel was asleep under his straw cowboy hat, making their happy way back to the family ranch.

When he down shifted to second, his brother woke up and asked from under his hat, "Que paso?"

"Gringo con no ropa en la calle."

"Si!?"

"Si, loco gringo."

Manuel slowly pulled his hat back so he could see. Still reclined in the seat, he rolled down the window just as they came upon Shawn.

"Buenos noches, Amigo"

Shawn returned their greeting like nothing was out of the ordinary.

"Problemas en la casa, Amigo?"

"Si," he kept on walking.

Robert stopped the truck and talked past his brother, "Banditos, no?"

"That as well," Shawn said, making eye contact with the two brothers.

"What did they look like?" Robert asked in clear English.

When Shawn described each man in detail, both brothers laughed and Robert said, "They have no bullets for those guns, Amigo. In these parts there are more guns than bullets. It was foolish of you to give your truck and other possessions to such men."

"How should I know they don't have bullets in their guns?"

"Just ask, they would be surprised by the question," Robert delivered with a smile.

The brothers took Shawn back to the family ranch and gave him a bed for the night. In the morning they found some clothes that would fit and he spent the day fixing fences with the brothers. They had plenty to talk about and learned of Shawn's farm experience and carpentry skills. The next morning while they sat at breakfast with the whole family, Robert asked Shawn to stay on and work for them. It was an easy yes for him.

He lived in the bunk house that was part of the family compound where four generations of Chavez family lived. Each family member had their own home that faced out onto the open court yard. In the middle was a big rock that was pitted on the top for the women to hand grind the corn into tortillas. Shawn became a part of the family fold, playing with the kids in the evenings and listening to the elders in the early mornings, healing his wounded soul and getting some perspective on his feelings for Laura.

- CHAPTER 18 -

Maine:

"When will you be moving back home?" Marcy asked Jake when she was fit enough to leave the hospital. In that question many were resolved. She was no longer a squatter but the eldest of a family of four. The farm was her home and because of her presence in it, Jake moved back. With each shutter that was removed from the farm house life and light took hold. Brother and sister, learning about each other's lives and who they were. Each day was filled with the hard work of getting the farm back to life, and the nights were spent talking and laughing. They left the murals up that Marcy and Sky had painted of the boys' childhood. Jake told the parts that Moxie did not write about, some of which brought on great fits of laughter. They started to make a plan to get the farm back on its feet as a viable working business. Marcy was an artist but a very organized one. She was a detail girl and had a business mind where Jake did not. They decided to slowly build a herd of milking cows but have fewer cows and add more value with the milk, like making a high quality cheese. Sky wanted lots of chickens and Marcy wanted goats, which made Jake wince when she first suggested it. Trouble and mischief is what he told her when it comes to goats. She just fired back that Sky deserved to have that mischief in her life just the way he did as a boy. What could he say?

One morning Marcy was looking out the window and saw Sky standing in the back field. She was very still and staring into the woods. What struck Marcy was how Sky looked so much older. She called for Jake to come and have a look. He caught the significance of it and commented that Sky was an old soul.

"But what is she staring at? Let's go have a look."

Out on the back porch they saw Tilly standing at the edge of the woods staring back at Sky. The blue, blue eyes of a little girl and dark black eyes of a moose projected love. Sky did not run up to Tilly, for she understood in her old soul the boundary between domestic and wild. She stood and stared, taking strength from the eyes of a moose.

Sky looked over at her mother and Jake and shouted, "Tilly is back."

With that said Jake walked out into the field and gave his war cry. Tilly responded with a full on charge, and Jake had to dive out of the way at the last moment. He rolled and laughed on the ground and felt the lightness he felt as a boy. Tilly stood on the edge of field and woods, took in the sight of the farm and Moxie's offspring coming back to life, and ran off.

It was not all happy times. After the realization of the loss of time set in, Marcy felt cheated not having her brothers while growing up and angry over the lie of who her father was and vented her anger over small things.

One night after dinner Marcy hollered at Jake, "Stop looking at me like that!"

"I can't help it you have his eyes and nose."

"Hey! You just listen here Buddy Boy! I have to accept that the man I thought was my father was not and that your father was. You have to get over the fact, you have a SISTER!"

Marcy stormed out of the room and Jake turned to Sky with a hopeless expression and his hands out at his sides.

"What did I do?"

"Oh, she gets like that."

Jake just stood with his mouth hanging open looking at Sky and thinking "What three-year-old talks like that?"

For Jake it was a great elation to have Marcy and Sky come into his life. It was like Moxie's spirit in living form before him. He had no anger, happy to have a sister in a family that was void of women. Marcy felt anger at times followed by guilt for her actions. She wanted it to work for them to live together as a family and knew her outbursts did not help in that effort.

Alaska:

Brian and Judy were sitting at the kitchen table looking at some drawings they had both done. A rare moment for them to be alone in that busy house. They sat close with both legs touching feeling the heat of desire that had been building for months. It was time for that long awaited kiss. They locked eyes with slow glances to lips. Ring! Ring! The bloody phone took the mood right out of the moment. Out of habit Judy got up and answered the phone.

"Hello, this is Jake, Brian's brother. Is he there by any chance?" he sounded elated.

"Yes, he is right here hold on."

"Hello," Brian said with concern in his voice.

"Hey little brother you are not going to believe this one."

"What now?"

"We have a sister and a niece."

"Don't be foolish!"

"No listen to me! Do you remember that woman who Dad was always writing those letters to?"

"Yah."

"Well, he got her pregnant just before he met Mom."

"Come on! I can't see Moxie keeping a secret like that."

"He didn't know. She kept it a secret from everyone, even her own daughter. She wrote Dad a letter just before she died and that news is what probably kicked off his heart attack."

"Holy shit! How did you find this all out?"

"His daughter Marcy came looking for him at the farm to honor a promise she made to her dying mother and ended up squatting at the farm and found the letter."

"Suffering Christ!"

"Yeah and some. Listen there is a lot more to the story. But right now we are all living at the farm."

"What do you mean all?"

"Marcy, her three-year-old daughter Sky and me. We are going to get the farm back up and running," he said with an enthusiasm that Brian had not heard in his brother in years.

"Does Shawn know?"

"I can't get ahold of him. The village school says he left town."

"Holy shit."

"You got to come home Brian and help me find him. We all need to be together on this one."

"OK, OK I will check on flights. Suffering Christ, Jake," and he hung up shivering with the reality of a new truth in his life.

Maine:

Those first couple of weeks were not just spent with the three of them alone. Many of the town's folk found all kinds of reasons for a visit. All curious to see a child of Moxie's.

"Oh no! Here they come." declared Jake one morning when they were all out weatherizing the farmhouse for winter. Three cars came up the drive with purpose.

"Here comes what?" Marcy asked.

"The gossip hens coming to check out Moxie's secret past."

Jake had warned Marcy about all the talk that was going around town about her and Sky. "Folks will come snooping for a visual to feed the gossip," Jake delivered with extended accent.

"Well Jake, I have learned in life that people will talk about you no matter what so you might as well give them something to really talk about," and she gave him a wicked grin.

That being said, Marcy went right out there and charged up and greeted the parade of ladies. She introduced herself as Moxie's daughter, giving herself the offensive position needed to keep the hens on their heels. They came prepared with baskets of food enough for an army. Well after all they needed to give Marcy and Sky a proper welcome into their town. They kept saying how cunning Sky looked and so much like Moxie. It bothered Sky to no end.

"How come you have two chins?" Sky asked Penny Parker, which brought giggles from the rest of the lot.

Most of the ladies had known Moxie all his life. Many stories were told that helped Marcy to better understand who her father was. Ruth Baxter, who reminded Marcy of Pinch Face Parker from her old neighborhood, took on an air of disapproval and butted in the conversations with cutting remarks. Moxie had written about Mrs. Baxter in one of his letters, a story that involved her and Tilly. One Halloween Ruth Baxter's carefully carved pumpkins that were on her porch steps disappeared in the darkness of night. She blamed it on two of the neighborhood kids. They did have a history of that kind of behavior and more, but not this one. It was all Tilly. She made quite a stink about wanting the boys to be punished and pay her for her pumpkins. The kids were adamant in their innocence, the parents were caught in the middle and Baxter got the town on her side. The two boys ended it by buying her pumpkins and raking her leaves. With total confidence it would not happen again, Ruth Baxter carved the new pumpkins and put them on her steps. That very night Tilly was busted red handed by some neighbors who came home late from a party. The truth then did get around town that Tilly was the culprit not the boys. Ruth took a low profile in town for a month after that one. The town of course took great humor in it. Moxie went over and made it right with the boys, made them see the humor in it and slipped them some bills.

Jake had no need for the hens' conversation. On one of his return trips to the kitchen, Ruth stated that she had never thought of Moxie as a man to hold secrets. The room went quiet for a long moment heads turned towards Marcy.

Henny Carter spoke up and said, "Why Ruth, he didn't know until he got that letter."

"Oh stop it! Of course he knew," Ruth blew back with a self-righteous tone.

Marcy just as cool as a cucumber said, "Why Ruth don't go making assumptions again, after all it was Tilly who took your pumpkins."

All the hens' jaws dropped and Ruth Baxter got red in the face. Jake stood in the doorway and glowed with pride at his sister.

The next day Tug Boat, Clipper and the Chief showed up with a backhoe to replace the bad septic field. Jake never asked, they just showed up and started working.

"What the fuck you boys doing?"

"What do you think? Jake, it`s got to be done so here we are," the chief blasted back, which ended the conversation so they got to it.

All through the day Jake felt a new gratitude towards his life-long friends. It was more than them coming and building a new septic, it was the mountain of guilt over losing the cows. Jake had been running from that guilt, but with his best friends by his side he could face it head on. In the act of tearing out the old septic and building it new he found some footing to forgive himself.

Marcy, Jake and Sky went to the airport in Bangor to pick up Brian. When he walked into the terminal Sky shouted "Uncle Brian!" and ran to him at a full on clip. Any awkward thoughts he had going into it vanished when he saw that smile and those blue eyes. He picked her up and swung her around like a sack of potatoes. Marcy was soon to follow, and she waited for Brian to put Sky down then went to his open arms. Hugging then pulling apart, looking into blue eyes seeing brother and sister. Hugging and both crying for all the words they could not find for all that lost time. Sky hugged around both their legs turning the sobs into giggles. Jake with nothing but smile wrapped his long arms around the three of them.

How is it that a three-year-old can slip right into the comfort of family knowing and expecting love and support when the adults are so awkward in finding their way? Sky broke the awkward silence on the ride home by telling Brian about Tilly, leaning against him with her tiny hand on his leg.

"I spent the night with Tilly when Mama fell down the well."

"Ah is that right?" looking up front at Marcy and Jake for some truth.

"Yes Brian it really happened," Jake responded.

"But we don't have a dug well," Brian stated.

"Remember under the rhododendron bush?"

"Boy! But that was well hidden."

"I fell through the rotten hatch when chasing a cat," Marcy weighed in on the truth.

"Holy shit, how are you still alive?"

"Part of the well cover fetched on the way down and stopped her from going to the bottom," Jake said while turning and looking at Brian to give it some reality.

"Man, oh man."

"Mama slept there all night while Tilly slept with me," Sky took back the conversation.

"Tilly is now coming and going in the farmhouse?" Brian tried to make light.

"No silly. She came to me in the field when I was looking for Mama."

"Well I'll be. What did she do then?"

"Took me close to the barn. The grass is soft there."

"And you stayed there with Tilly all night?"

"Uh huh" Sky looked into Brian's eyes and delivered the wisdom learned that night.

"Wow! And here I thought I was having a wild time in Alaska."

When they got home they finally got Sky to bed after many horsey rides on her Uncle Brian's back. Jake found an old bottle of whiskey and put three glasses on the kitchen table. They sat around that table drinking and talking all night long.

The next morning Linda Crawford showed up to help Marcy bring some women's touches into that long-standing bachelor abode. She walked in after knocking and hearing no reply and found the brothers and sister asleep on chairs and couch. Linda wandered past the lot of them and into the kitchen, saw the empty bottle and three glasses and smiled, and thought "Good to see they done some catching up." She made coffee and did some cleaning then walked on out into the living room and woke them all up. They moved into any kind of conversation, which did not slow Linda down on the talking. She had been looking at the murals that were on the walls in the living room and it had triggered some of her own memories of watching the boys grow up. She laughed, "You boys sure were hell on wheels. Oh heavens to see it all laid out in front of yah like this, really something. What an artist you are Marcy. Oh my look at you all trying to come into it, like I should just throw a bucket of cold water in on the lot of you. Now Marcy I was thinking we could start on the kitchen scrub it top to bottom!"

Marcy was sipping on her coffee lost in thought, so Jake jumped right in and declared top priority of the day was planning on how to find Shawn, "Cleaning will have to wait," he said looking directly at Linda.

"What do you mean find Shawn?" Linda stated with a what now tone.

"He walked out on his girlfriend and is somewhere at large in Mexico."

"At large?"

"Yes, like we don't know exactly where he is and out of communication."

"Sounds like he needs some space."

"Or is he in trouble? Even still we got to find him to let him in on him having a sister. I want to deliver that news in person."

They did some planning alright. Marcy was able to track down Laura from the school where they knew she was working. It took several attempts, but she was able to talk with Linda through the school phone. Laura tried to explain the misunderstanding that caused Shawn to walk out. Then it hit her.

"Wait. Did you say you are his sister?"

"That's right," Marcy found great pleasure in declaring that.

"He never mentioned any sister to me, only brothers, what is all this about?"

It took some convincing, but Jake got on the phone to confirm. Laura struggled to wrap her brain around it all. If it was the truth, then it deepened her love and concern for Shawn. She said he was cooling his heels somewhere and would come to his senses and return to her. Jake really wanted to know where he might go to cool his heels. She suggested the border town they met in and the beach where they first slept together. After some long pauses, each lost in their own concerns, Jake said he would call another time when they knew of their plans.

They made a plan for Jake and Brian to go to the border town first and discretely ask around about a tall gringo redhead with blue eyes. If they found no leads there, they would head on down to that coastal town Laura mentioned. Sky wanted to go in the worst way. Jake told her she needed to keep her mama and Tilly company at the farm. He had a way with her and she did settle down after some small whimpering. Linda of course did chime in that she would be staying some of the nights. Marcy seemed relieved to hear this and put up no objections, so off went the two brothers to Mexico in search of Shawn.

- CHAPTER 19 -

Scotland:

Marcy found, in the attic of the farmhouse, an old trunk which held some diaries and a large folded paper with the family tree. She was up there snooping, searching for some connection to her lineage, something that could tell her more of who her real father was. The McCormack tree held the bold names of Effie Wallace and Boyd McCormack of Bull Island Scotland 1726. "My God, my ancestors. They came over here by ship, from an island in Scotland."

She opened one of the diaries, smelled the aged paper and started to read. Thirsty to learn and discover who her ancestors were so she could begin to fill the hole that was in her. Reading and absorbing, sometimes crying, other times laughing. Such good writing, open and honest. She would steal time in the day and at night, sometimes falling asleep while reading, to awaken just before the light of day, coming out of a dream state and looking up at the rafters to bring it into focus. The comfort she felt realizing where she was. That old attic with the smell of time and soft pine.

The story of Marcy's ancestors was a romance. When Boyd first laid eyes on Effie she was working with her back to him in her father's store. Her head tilted slightly to the side, exposing her neck and the sweet tenderness she held in her soul. Long shiny brown hair flowed down her back. He felt like he could watch her like that for a long time. When she finally turned around and looked into his blue eyes she was pleasantly startled, and Boyd was rewarded with a special and enchanting look from her green hazel eyes. A look like she had a great secret that she had been holding inside for a long time and he was that special person she would share it with.

It was his first time in the store on account of Effie's family being Protestants. He went in to prove his courage on a dare but came out like a lost puppy. After that he found excuses to go back, until the day he made physical contact and all was lost after that. As she was writing down his order she kept asking his name like she did not understand, moving her head close and closer until it was just barely touching, then touching. God it felt great, breathing in her lovely tenderness, she kept so guarded from others.

The Wallace store was outside the village on the island of Bull, run out of an addition on the croft. They had cows, goats and sheep for the wool to make warm clothes to protect against the harsh environment. Effie being an only child had a hard life of doing chores, working at the store and studies. She discovered art after one of the traveling merchants at her father's store slipped her some paints. He was wise on people and recognized something in her that needed a creative outlet. Knowing it had to be their secret, he put it at the bottom of a box he knew only Effie would look into. The merchant was such a breath of life for Effie, who was under the constant thumb of her father. Her mother had died from cholera when she was eight years old, and she had been a warm and loving woman. In the eight years she had with her daughter she left a lasting mark. Effie had so many of her mother's loving traits contrasted with her father who was stern and totally consumed with working the croft and the store. That moment when she found the brush and paints with the paper lining the bottom of the box was forever framed in her soul. It was an instant connection to those tools of art. She knew just what to do. It was in her.

Late at night she would slip into the attic above the store. There, amongst the boxes, with a candle burning she would express what was buried inside herself. She painted the magic of the sea as she saw it with all its spiritual power. The sea had always been her place of solace. She had a secret spot on the shore that was hidden by the high rocks of a jagged spit into the sea. Effie stole her moments there when coming and going to school. She loved how the light played on the water, the moods of the seasons expressed so openly with its dance on the sea. She worked and played with the paints. She had to get the colors she wanted and was persistent in her desire to express what she saw and felt in nature. She hid the paintings deep in the boxes in the attic when they were finished.

Later the merchant gave her a sharp piece of charcoal to draw fine lines with. She drew what she saw in others. Faces, showing their hard character from a life on the island, up to the whims of nature and clan rivals, fishing and subsistence farming on a stingy landscape that was being pushed by a growing population.

She painted the sweet face of her mother, then the hard and stern jaw of her father, the sly wisdom of the merchant, the faces of families cutting peat out in the bogs.

Boyd lived in the family croft on the north side of the island. He too was mostly raised by his father for his mother was very sickly and bed ridden for most of his youth. As soon as they could walk and carry a bucket, they had to take care of the animals, watering them feeding them and cleaning the stalls. Every day regardless of the weather, they trudged out to the well before the light of day to fetch water first for the kitchen, then for the animals. They worked hard but he and his brother Ross would always find a way to steal some time for fun. Of course when tossing flakes of hay down from the loft trouble would start between the brothers. The hay loft had low hanging collar ties that quickly became a jungle gym for the boys, and they swung down and wrapped their legs around each other to get a good wrestle going. They were strong and played rough, bruises and bloody noses a common event. They threw rocks at each other when they were out herding sheep, and while they tried to keep their shots low, some would drift up and occasionally nick some facial flesh. Once Boyd hit Ross square on the forehead bringing a huge bump with a purple spot right in the middle that made it look like a third eye. Even after a bit, their father thought it funny but did make them promise to stop the horse play with rocks.

Boyd was smart and content with his life and studies. He went along with the regimen of a hard life on the island following what was told to him about God and the church and never questioning, until Effie. He went to the store after they had touched heads, when Effie was alone. When he walked in she said, "You finally got it right."

"Got what right?"

"Coming to see me when father is away."

Boyd turned bright red and sputtered out, "I have come to shop."

"Come on you buy the most useless stuff. You come here to see me not shop. It's OK, no shame in wanting to be with me."

"But it is forbidden. You are Protestant."

"Huh so I am a devil to you?"

"No, you don't look like any devil to me."

"Then what?"

"It is just that I will get into trouble for being social with you."

"Then why do you come just to make eyes and never talk?"

"I don't know."

"Well Boyd, I do know. I am attracted to you. I want to spend time with you. I don't give a shit about controlling laws of church."

"That is blasphemy!"

"No it is what I feel in my heart. I trust that more than the church."

"Mother of Mary do you have to be so radical?"

"I have to be me, and some part of you is drawn to me, that is so apparent in your eyes."

"What is so apparent?"

"That you want to touch more than just my head."

"I..." he stammered in such a helpless tone.

"No shame in that Catholic boy. It is a natural thing. We are surrounded by it, the sheep at it all the time."

"But we are not animals."

"No, then why are all being herded so easily by the church?"

"It is belief in God and we are following his will."

"His will is telling you not to be with me, Boyd! What is your heart telling you?"

"Aye, OK, yes I want to be with you."

"Then meet me at the high bluff after the last of the candles go out." With that said Effie gave Boyd a determined and challenging look and went back to supplying shelves. He had never seen anything more beautiful.

It took longer than most nights for his father to blow out the last candle. He slipped out the window past his sleeping brother and into the brisk night. He ran most of the way. The big bluff was a piece of high ground of solid rock that projected way out over the water looking out to the moonlit sea. When Boyd finally got there he stood at the bluff's edge alone and wondered if he was too late. A pit was starting to develop in his stomach when a warm hand grabbed his.

"Looks like there is hope for you yet altar boy." They walked hand in hand along the edge and listened to the crashing surf below them, feeling the magic of place and the special moment of being together. Effie was so much lighter in mood out there.

"I just love it here. So alive yet peaceful. This is my church Boyd. This place gives me my spiritual inspiration. Not that cold damp building they herd us into."

"Have you always been this outspoken?"

"What speaking my mind is outspoken? Come on admit it you feel so much better here than sitting in church."

"Oye what is it with you? Yes I do but maybe it is you."

"Boyd! You surprise me," and she squeezed his hand.

Boyd was in way over his head. He had never held hands with a girl before and here was Effie making it feel like it was no big deal. It felt really good to feel the warmth of her hand and the side of her body that kept touching his. He was heady and light and did not want this night and their time together to end. The desire to kiss her started to overtake him, but he had no idea how to go about such a thing. It started to occupy so much of his mind that he could not think of anything but that. Effie was talking but he could barely listen his desire was so strong. After a bit she asked him what he was thinking about.

"What? Nothing."

"Nothing? You seem very distracted."

"Huh, just, I, you, what?"

"Boyd! Relax. I am a girl, you are a boy. We like each other. Let's talk and be ourselves and just let things happen."

"Oye, I am not used to liking girls, they are silly. You are not like any girl I have ever met."

"I know I am not like the other girls, but you are not like the other boys."

"What?" with a tone of hurtful pride.

"When I first looked into your eyes I saw something in you, a deep compassion. I don't see that in the other boys."

"What boys?"

"What do you think you are the only one coming in and buying useless things? Silly Boy!"

"How many boys?"

"Certainly more fingers than I have."

Boyd stopped walking, looked at Effie and dropped his jaw. It was just too much for Effie to keep a straight face, she started to laugh. Boyd had never heard anything more beautiful and without even thinking leaned in and kissed her square on the lips. She was startled by his boldness but his lips felt so good that Effie recovered quickly and kissed him back. It was a long lingering kiss that left them both breathless. They held each other for a long time afterwards. Effie could feel his hardness through her skirt.

Then whispered into his ear, "Boyd you certainly are not like the other boys."

Now with a tone of jealousy, "Do you do this with other boys."

"No Boyd, you are the first."

"But they do come often, even the married ones. With nothing but intentions of getting under my skirt."

"Mother of Mary Effie, do you have to be so blunt?"

"Direct is more like it. I am sick and tired of social pretense. The hypocrites who sit in church and pretend to be so pious then go out rutting with other women when their wives are home putting their children to bed."

"What are you talking about?"

"I have a special place I go to down by the rocks. It is well hidden. Some nights when the moon is right I sneak out and sit and watch the moonlight dance with the sea. When the tide is low there is a spit of sand that I can see. I have watched several different married men humping women other than their wives on that spit."

"You watch?"

"Not like I am spying, Boyd. I was there before they got there and believe me they don't stay long. The men open their kilts bend the woman over and lift their skirts and do them from behind just like the animals. They don't last long, that is for sure. It all seems just for the man's enjoyment. A few grunts from him and a frustrated sigh from the women and off they go."

"We were kissing, now all this talk of married men. Let's get back to what we were doing."

She took Boyd`s face in both her hands and kissed him tenderly on the lips. She whispered in his ear, "I want it to be special with us," then giggled and ran off into the night.

Boyd went to the store the following week on a day when Effie's father would not be present. There was a man and two girls there. Effie gave him some eye shine, then went back and helped the man. The two girls looked like sisters and were wandering around the aisles with wicked grins on freckled faces. They looked back and forth at each other and made faces and silently giggled and ducked down. They were wearing high boots and man's britches, dark hair pulled back with a scarf, one red the other green. The one with the red scarf caught his eye and raised an eye brow then darted her eyes toward the man, and the one with a green scarf gave him a conspiratorial wink. Clearly, they were making fun of the man. He would say something and the one in red would mimic him and the one in green did some gestures with one of her hands down by her crotch. They both giggled out loud and Effie cracked a smile. She was in on it, too. Boyd was drawn to the sisters' eyes and facial expressions.

Each had lively dark brown eyes that were full of mischief. Their freckled faces expressed their humor so well. He got caught up in it and laughed, until Effie gave him a stern but playful glance which got the girls laughing and Boyd even more. It became so infectious he walked out of the store and down the road cracking up. Not soon after the girls came out giggling up a storm and caught up with Boyd to share in the humor.

"What a arsworm," both girls said in unison.

"What were you two going on about?"

"Mr. MacSwean in there trying to flirt with Effie, talking about things he knows nothing about," the one in red moved her hands and arms in mocking gestures of high social stature. Boyd felt like he was with some of the boys, not two girls and could not help but laugh even more about the situation. When the giggles finally died down the girls introduced themselves. Shauna and Gillia MacClay, sisters and twins. They were well known on the island but he had never met them.

The door of the store slammed shut and Mr. MacCswean came out and huffed up the road, clearly agitated. Boyd and the twins ran back in the store eager to hear why he left so abruptly.

"What did you do to MacCswean my dearest?" Gillia asked with anticipation.

"I just looked down at the condition of his crotch and asked him how his wife was doing."

"Did you really Effie? Oh what I would give to have seen that look. A missus and three wee ones at home, then in here giving you sweet talk while cracking wood," Gillia went on.

"Oh Effie I hope you sent him off for good. Going on with his pious self in town then you saying how he was out in the rocks with some other," Shawna added to the pile of shit on him.

"Well enough of it. Boyd! These two pirates are my best friends Gillia and Shauna."

"Aye we met out on the road," Boyd said with a grin.

"Well Boyd you neglected to tell us you were the kiss," Gillia teased him.

Boyd gave Effie a betrayed look.

"Boyd I had to tell somebody it was burning me up," she gave Gillia a cutting glance.

"I thought that was just for us."

"It was, Boyd. I am a girl. I needed to talk about this grand moment with my best friends. They won't tell a soul. Will yah, now girls?"

"Our lips are sealed," said the twins.

"Shauna! We have been gone too long, we better get on."

With that the twins were out of the store in a flash but not before each one gave Boyd a playful shot in the arm. He could not help but smile at that playful look in their eyes.

When they left, Effie came over and kissed Boyd softly on the lips.

"I have been thinking of you a lot, since last seeing you."

"Me too."

Boyd kissed her with a burning desire and reached down and took a hold of her bottom and gave a wanting squeeze. Effie pushed Boyd away.

"Hey now frisky boy! You been thinking about me or what comes with it?"

"Come on. Tell me you have not been thinking about it."

"Yes of course about the kiss, but also about how good it felt to be held in your arms."

"I did not want the night to end."

He had been doing some thinking on it and realized he had to stop being so foolish on this matter of sex. Show a little more leadership.

"Effie meet me tonight at the bluff."

She made him wait in silence, held his eyes and looked deep inside.

"Ok, now go before my father returns."

This time Boyd was there first and surprised Effie by grabbing her from behind and kissing her neck. She slammed her rear into his crotch and ran off. Boyd recovered and followed in quick pursuit, tackling Effie around the waist and bringing them both to the ground. They rolled in laughter then she surprised him by gaining position on top and pinning both arms to the ground above his head. She was strong and held him for a bit and showed him his equal. Then Boyd bucked her off with his hips and took the top, leaned down and kissed Effie on her eager lips. It was a long and hot kiss filled with the passion of their youth and a building connection between two souls. Boyd started to grind into her and grab with inexperienced hands, but Effie pulled back from the kiss.

"Boyd! It is me you are grabbing not some mutton, squeezing my bum like a merchant at the market," she held his face with both hands. "You need to be gentle with me. I want to feel you touch me with the same tenderness with which you look at me."

They held each other in sweet silence after those words were said, molded to each other's bodies in a natural state, and felt a strong and quiet rhythm resonating in their souls.

A couple of months later Effie and Boyd were in the attic above the store looking at her drawings and paintings. Boyd was the first person to see any of her art. Not even the twins had seen it. It had been her thing. Something that was just about her, no outside judgments. When Boyd came into her life, she wanted to share this part of herself. Keeping it a secret from all was starting to weigh on her. She first showed him the paintings of the sea. Her love of the sea was so apparent. He was touched by the way she brought out each painting and showed it too him like it was one of her babies. Of course they were her babies, she gave birth to them when she created her image of the sea on paper, but also it was the birth of her creative self. They were good, really good. Then she busted out one of her drawings. It was of the twins and Boyd was struck by it. He let out a "Wow" and was quickly hushed by Effie who told him beforehand there could be no talking while in the attic. They could not take the risk of her father finding them up there. All her secrets would then be out. But it was amazing how Effie had caught the twins as tomboys while in the eyes and around the mouth they were all woman. Then she brought out the one of her mother. It was an emotional moment. She was a beautiful woman and Effie had made her eyes radiate out so much love. Boyd felt that loss for Effie, a wave of sadness and overwhelming compassion overtook him. He took her in his arms and held her tight and cried, something he had not done in a very long time.

When they were outside walking well away from the croft, they could finally talk. "Boyd! What is going on with you?"

"I am so sorry your mom died, Effie."

"Darling, it's alright she died a long time ago."

"But to see your drawing of her. It made her so real to me. She looked to be so good. Why did the lord take her?"

"The lord cannot stop cholera. It's a disease, and it plays no favors to God."

"It just not fair."

"Fair! I am well past thinking life to be fair. You have to make the best of what life gives you, Boyd, and right now you are coming into my life and I am going to make the best of it." She gave Boyd a tender kiss.

Marcy was startled by the open descriptions of sex in both diaries. Thinking of the framed photos of her ancestors with stiff smiles and buttons going all the way up with not barely a peek to be had, sex is the last thing you think about. But after all, Effie thought, they are your ancestors and you did not come into this world with them just holding hands.

The time had come to consummate their love. Over on the north side of the island was an old schooner that had washed up on the rocks, its aft cabin still intact. Boyd made a nest for the two of them there. He met Effie in the darkness of the night on horseback. They rode tandem to the north side, mostly in silence. They took in the comfort of a soft summer night. The half moon played its light on the sea as they neared the schooner nestled hard in the rocks. He lit some candles that brought a romantic warmth to the cabin. Excited and scared, the smell of wood and that of the salt from the sea calmed their anxiety. They stood apart and held each other, eyes filled with love and want.

They kissed, explored with wet tongues, fell into the nest and laid on top of one another and rolled their hips. She took his hand and ran it slowly over her face and down over her covered breasts, over her stomach and just over her thighs then back again. She let go of his hand and let him explore, his eyes just visible in the moon light filled with wonder, searching hers. He moved his hand under her long dress and felt first her bare knee, then inner thigh, softer than anything he had felt before. He watched the fire build in Effie's eyes and touched again and again, slow and deliberate, the way she showed him. It was too much, and she took his hand and brought it to her breasts, opening the top of her dress and bringing his hand inside to feel her naked breasts. Both overcome with the building heat, they kissed and explored, and moved their hips as one. All too quickly Boyd spilled his desire into his kilt and lost the will to meet Effie's fire. She no longer felt the burn in his lips and his hardness was gone against her. She knew what happened. He could feel the disappointment in her body, which wounded his pride, but Effie took the sting out of it.

"Boyd I liked the way you touched me just then. Very much so."

She laid partly on top of him and searched his face and slowly kissed. While she teased him, he could feel how hot her hand was through his kilt. Effie smiled with her eyes, touched and squeezed with her hands and built back the heat. She reached into his kilt and felt his raw thirst for her. She took it out in the open and stroked him and looked into his face to learn what excited him most. She let her instincts guide her, slow then fast. Her hot hand drove him to the edge, then she stopped before he fell off of it. Effie controlled his fire so it would last for the both of them.

She got pleasure from giving him joy and played with all that was him. They kissed with a deepening passion while she rolled her hips against his thigh and stroked him. Boyd trusted her to control the pace and rhythm. She straddled him, held his eyes with trust and took off her blouse, exposing her naked breasts in the soft candle light. Such a sight the way her hair played with her wide shoulders, the swell of her bare breasts, the different shades of color around her nipples. Effie's mouth curved in a sensual smile, her green eyes shone with need. He got up and undressed and showed himself to her, then he slowly took off her skirt and fine under layers and took in the wonder of her pink lips that peaked through silky auburn hair. Boyd looked into her eyes and laid on top of Effie as she guided him into her.

They laid there completely stunned by that experience. Just beyond anything they could have imagined. They breathed hard, with blissful sighs, while they listened to the crashing surf.

- CHAPTER 20 -

Mexico:

They just got started riding down the road to town. The two brothers and Shawn up front. Manuel stopped the truck, "Damn Man! You and your fucking garlic."

"Is that what that smell is. I thought it was bad salami," the other brother stated.

"Eats it raw Roberto, he told me to keep from getting the shits."

"Fucking hell, amigo you got to ride in the back!"

"What, it can't be that bad?"

"I am on the edge of puking man, in the back!"

Shawn climbed in the back of the truck. He loved riding back there and making him ride in the back made him feel a part of the family. As they headed up the mountain, the road changed back and forth from tar to dirt. The curves got steeper, and the view opened up to the valley below. The smell of sage and pinyon filled the air. Shawn laid with his back against the cab and took it all in. Roberto passed a beer back to him as they climbed higher up the mountain and passed villages with small homes made of adobe and thatched roofs. The churches were made of wood and painted in bright colors. Small tiendas sold the basics.

You could buy a coke, but not always cold. On the outskirts of the villages people rode along on bicycles and horseback.

They were headed down the other side of the mountain when they came upon a bus lying on its side, some of it hanging over the edge. People stood up on the bus and helped passengers climb out the windows, others just stood for weight on the road side of the bus to keep her from going over. They stopped and got out to help. Shawn climbed up on the bus and the brothers crawled inside to look for the injured. Amazingly there were no serious injuries, mostly scrapes and bruises, so the brothers helped and pushed people out the windows. There was a high degree of tension from fear of the bus falling off the mountain. There was one mama who was big, particularly in her bottom, so the boys with the help of another man had to push her fat bottom in so she could go out. She found it all quite funny and howled in laughter, which eased the tension. Shawn and another man each tugged on an arm and laughed with her. A big collective relief when everyone was out and off the bus.

A big lorry was used to pull the bus back on the road. Getting it back up right was a problem with limited room on the steep mountainside for vehicles to pull her up. There was lots of talk, with lots of hand gestures, some kids from the local village showed up on horseback. Two boys and two girls around twelve to fourteen years of age rode tandem with the girls riding behind, each holding a large basket filled with hot empanadas and Coca-Cola, which were tied in small plastic bags with straws, to sell to the large windfall of customers. Mexico the land of entrepreneurs. One of the lads on horseback sized up the scene and suggested they use his horses to right the bus. He spoke with so much confidence for such a youngster, the brothers bought into the plan and hollered commands to the crowd, which led to an explosion of activity. Ropes of all kinds were found in vehicles and then tied to the bumpers through broken windows all meticulously woven together to makeshift yokes that were put around the horses. Holes were dug into the dirt road at the base of the tires to give the bus a pivot point. The boy hollered at his horses to pull hard towards the mountain. The old Blue Bird, with all that open raw metal, creaked hard and loud protesting against the strain of the ropes. The crowd that was gathered screamed with fury for the horses' victory. When the horses were hard against the mountain and it sounded like the ropes would snap, she righted with a great commotion. The luggage that was still tied to the roof, covered by a big tarp, shot up and over the side of the roof like a big Santa Claus bag, whooomp! It was a wonderful victory that galvanized the crowd. Some bottles of tequila had spilled from one of the roof top bags and were passed around with joyous laughter. They used one of the horses and some rope to pull the fenders away from the tires. The bus driver, with all eyes upon him stepped in and ceremoniously sat down and turned the key. She started with a great plume of black exhaust, and the crowd went wild. The passengers got back on the bus that was covered in dust and broken glass. They had started as strangers and turned family in the course of hours. Off they went down the mountain in a plume of black smoke with no windows and fenders ajar. Shawn and the brothers watched the bus along as they ate empanadas and finished a bottle of tequila.

Jake and Brian made it to the border town a bit after dark. They walked the streets and tried to get a feel for what was going on around them. Mucho gente, a lot of people, and so much action, vendors with push carts who sold hot and spicy food. Bars with working girls who sat provocatively on bar stools, outside men tried to lure in customers by offering deals on shots and beers. The smell of grilled food and leaded gasoline, the sound of hawkers and salsa music, and color, so many bright colors, all so new to the boys from Maine.

"We ain't in Maine anymore, Toto," Brian half whispered.

"No shit! Where do we start?" answered Jake in bewilderment.

"The smell of all this food is getting me hungry. What do you say we find us a place to eat?"

"Si senor," Jake said, while he walked up to one of the hawkers.

The deal they were offered to get them inside sounded too good to be true. They may have been hicks from the sticks, but they knew when things smelled dicey. They walked on and took a look at the girls inside before they moved on down the street. A girl of about twelve approached and spoke in broken English, offering to take them to her family restaurant. They could not resist her smile so they followed her several blocks away to a small cozy place with bright colors on the doors and trim. They were greeted with warm smiles, buenos noches stated in unison from the restaurant. The girl, Maria, seated them at a table and walked into the kitchen declaring she had brought in some gringos.

A boy of about seven walked out of the kitchen with a small tray with homemade tortilla chips and hot salsa. He looked a lot like his sister but showed a bit more mischief in his eyes as he took in the brothers slowly before he put the goods down on the table. Maria came out with an apron and took their orders. The menu was in Spanish and they did not have a clue what to order so they just randomly pointed to things on the menu. Maria gave them a smile beyond her years and walked back to the kitchen. Jake and Brian made faces of anguish from the heat in the salsa. A woman with a wonderful round face brought out their food. She was struck by Jake's t-shirt and her face changed to one with questions.

"Helen B, you Helen B?" She asked while looking right into Brian's blue green eyes with her dark, dark brown ones. His shirt had the proud outlines of a fishing boat with the name Helen B with her name printed proudly below.

"Si, si," was all he could blurt out after he got lost in her eyes. She exhausted her English and asked more questions in rapid Spanish. Brian replied in English as she threw her arms up and ran into the kitchen. They could hear some commands in Spanish, then the boy who delivered the chips busted through the double doors on a small bike, gave 'er one spin around the tables and flew out the door and down the street. She looked at Brian with those dark eyes from the open doors all the way in the kitchen. Brain looked back with his mouth ajar like a trout out of water.

"Hey lover boy, I thought you were smitten with a woman in Alaska?" Jake gave his brother some ribbing.

"What are you going on about?"

"The eye shine you gave that young Mexican woman is not out of cultural curiosity."

"Boy! Those dark, dark ancient eyes, she looked right into my soul and you go and bring up Judy."

"What? After all you went on about her on that plane ride. Don't be foolish."

"Shit Jake! Finally, for the first time in months I am not thinking about her and you got and pop me back to her."

"Ok, ok. Flirt away there, Moon Beam, I am forever your wing man."

Whatever it was they ordered, it was great. Their chatter stopped and they just made noises while they ate away. When they just finished a striking woman came in herded by the little brother on the bike. She sized them up as she walked over to their table.

"You are the brother to Shawn, no?" the woman asked Brian while she looked at his shirt and then into his eyes.

"Woow now, just how do you know that?" Brian asked with an awestruck tone.

"You look like him. Same eyes and eyebrows," she said with a smile.

"My brother Shawn was here in this restaurant?" Brian said in disbelief, still trying to comprehend their luck.

Jake pulled out the photo of Shawn and showed it to Clara. She nodded her head.

"Yes of course, that is him. No not here, I met him in the street," she delivered with a secret in her eyes.

"Like, he asked you directions kind of met in the streets?" Jake played naïve.

"No, I approached him for sex, but he declined. I liked him

for that. I am Clara," she warmly shook their hands. She talked with ease and confidence and told them the whole story. About her uncle, who is the cook and the father of the young woman with the dark eyes who had worked on the Helen B.

"Well of course, I remember him well," Brian said then shared some stories about him on the boat. They could not believe their luck on meeting his family here.

Clara responded to their bewilderment and stated, "Amigos you are in Mexico, things like this happen, especially when you wear a revealing T-shirt. Ahora, your brother`s truck is here in town, parked just a few streets from here. Painted some bright orange color, not beautiful. The story I heard was that the men who stole Shawn's truck lost it later that night in a poker game. The man who won it is very good with motors. He fixed the motor and painted it. Pero, your brother is well, he is staying at the Cruz ranch in Solito."

"How do you know all this?" Brian asked, still amazed.

Clara just looked at him and smiled and said, "Mexico can be too small country at times"

Most of the family was out of the kitchen and sat around and listened and watched for body language, sometimes demanding translations from Clara. They wanted to know more about their uncle, the great fisherman.

While Brian talked Jake sat in the corner scheming. Clara watched him get up and go to the restroom while she gave translations. It was a lively bathroom, handmade tile with bright colors, a urinal and stall with a toilet. Jake was using the urinal with his back to the door when he heard it open followed by a female voice.

"Dega me, talk to me!" said Clara while she openly looked.

"Ahhh, do you mind giving me some privacy!" Jake said while he quickly put it back in his pants.

"Oh don't be shy, nothing I have not seen before. I came in here for the privacy so we can talk. You are up to something. I think you want to steal your brother's truck, no?"

"Ok, guilty," Jake raised his hands.

"Es muy peligroso! Very dangerous, Jake," Clara loudly whispered with concern. She held his eyes for a long moment and said, "I will help you."

Clara went out and waved Brian to come into the men's room, which raised the eyebrows of la familia.

"Shawn has a key well hidden in the back bumper. It must still be there," Jake stated as the three of them put together a plan in the baño.

- CHAPTER 21 -

Maine:

For Sky it was a great change to go from living amongst the shadows in the farm house to one of light. With the shutters off and windows open she felt free, with a need for adventure. She started to explore when Marcy thought she was napping and would slip down the stairs and out like a little mouse into the great woods beyond the barn. Sky would see Tilly out in those woods, where they shared some eye contact, then did their own thing close by. Tilly found things to nibble on and Sky things to observe, turning over rocks and looking for hidden life. The strong scent of moose mixed in with that of pine, spruce and oak trees, whose leaves were in that stage between orange and red, and the distant taste of salt was in the air. Differing shades of green in the pine needles and all the colors of fall's glory. She laid in the deep emerald green of the moss and pretended she was floating on clouds in a blue, blue sky.

When Sky snuck back into the farmhouse, Tilly headed over to Gibson's General Store to eaves drop on the porch goers. Gibson's had a big covered porch out front with benches and rockers. In early mornings it was full of men talking it over before work, then the women and kids came later in the day. Tilly would hang out in the woods nearby and spy on the porch goers. This particular day the winds had kicked up and the fishermen came in from the sea early; some found reason to go to the store for supplies so they could gab.

Duff MacClay, captain of Lucky Boy, sat on a rocker and pontificated to the boys, "See, the biggest wrong assumption people make is that if they tell their story the people are going to get it right. But! The people never get it right. They don't get it right because they are filtering your story through their fucked up story."

"Stop being foolish," Derek Dunkin howled from the bench.

"I am just saying. Think about it as though it is true."

"Jesus Christ, you got so much time on your hands you can be sitting around thinking up this shit," Angus Gillian, carpenter builder, chided him.

Boyd MacCay, another lobsterman, short and solid to the ground, started in on his big problem of the day, "My dog Maggie is giving me the silent treatment today. I left her at home yesterday when I went fishing. Won't even look at me today. Sits way at the far end of the truck. Had to come here and buy biscuits to bribe her with, just to get her look me in the eyes."

"Suffering Christ, MacCay, you spoil that bitch too much. That is why you get the attitude," Duff got back into it.

"Got the same problem with my wife," came from Angus.

"Now, why would anyone want to get married!" Dan Stirling, very much married, stated with conviction but convinced no one.

"You in trouble again Stirling?" from Kyle Campbell stretched out on the steps with his red fishing boots sticking out.

"I am always in trouble. Can't do nothing without her having a say in it."

"Ain't no different than the rest of us, boy," delivered in a high pitched tone from Ian Graham who leaned against the rail wearing his work overalls from the garage.

Duff Aiken, sporting his green suspenders and Bean boots from over in the corner called out, like in victory, "Hey speak for yourselves, I ain't got a missus."

Ross Buchanan, who sat on the best rocker on the porch stated with a tone of authority, "Ayah them scratch tickets you buy every day you're married to them."

"Yah, but they cost less than a wife," followed by laughter.

"What is the tide doing?" Boyd changed the direction of things.

"She is a going," Kirk Wallace spat out with a mouth full of egg salad.

"Christ with this full moon and these wicked tides I better get moving! Them hen clams are far out and there is plenty of honey pots to worry about."

Malcolm Wallace, who sat on the liars bench wearing black rubber boots up to his knees, came out with, "I was out just where that stream cuts in on the flats and fell into one up to my waist, tide coming hard at me. Christ, how I got out I don't have a clue, just a fit of flurry I was."

It went silent as all eyes went to a woman who came out of a Volvo with Connecticut plates and was very much put together. Striking beauty she was, a couple of the boys looked like trout out of water with their mouths hanging open. She walked into the store and did her best to ignore the obvious staring going on.

Old man Walt who had been quiet for some time harped out with all the clarity of the nights watch, "Costs money!"

Just then Effie Gibson walked up and gave all the boys on the porch her assessing eye, then wailed out in a strong and grounded voice, "What a pack of dogs out here. Come on! Step aside there Ian and Boyd and let a lady through. Christ ain't you boys got nothing better to do then sit around talking foolishness?"

Dan blasted back in reply for all the boys, "Why Effie darling we are taking the pulse of the town before getting back to it."

"Dan Stirling if you are so concerned about the pulse of the town I suggest you go home and check your wife's."

"Oh come on Effie I already know its racing."

"Then go home and calm her."

"Yah I tried calming her for the last twelve years. Ain't happening."

"Hmmm I would say in that time you have done plenty to agitate to her with all your running around."

That brought on some laughter from the boys and shut Dan up.

Tilly wandered off and into the woods and followed an old game trail down to the shore. The fog was slowly being chased by the wind, and the murky green water of the sea was restless and choppy with white caps. Hog Island looked harassed out there in the salty mist. Along the shore soft white rocks rode above a black ledge receding to the sea. The sweet high-pitched melody of a warbler, the sharp and regal profile of a pair of loons paddled by. The old wharf reached across the rocks and into the bay, her pilings sculptured by time and sea. The bright colors of the lobster pots piled high on the docks. The assuring sound of distant surf crashed on hidden ledges. The screech of a gull, the soft smell of salt. Tilly went there to sniff that salt air and to go for a swim.

Even though Marcy had been out of the hospital for a while, she was still recovering from her concussion. Confusion and anxiety, and dreams, crazy dreams. She was consumed at times with being lost in the past with the diaries, Effie and Boyd's lives, then being present with the anger she had at her mother. Because of her mother's pride, Marcy had lost the opportunity to know her real father. Being surrounded with Moxie's things, his life, made her ache for his physical presence. With her brothers gone she felt alone and scared.

Mexico:

Shawn and the brothers got to town in good spirits, helping with the bus and the fact that no one was killed put them in a good place. They walked past the market up a cobble stone road that was lined with churches, stores and homes, all tucked in close to one another. One of the churches had a blue steeple and felt more approachable and human to Shawn. He was behind a mother with her two daughters. They all held hands with a little one of two years in the middle; she swung from those loving arms and occasionally touched the ground with those tiny feet. Ponytails on both sides, she looked back and flirted with Shawn and giggled while she turned away. The street came to a huge open market with fresh vegetables and meat from small village farms. It was market day and the town was filled with people from surrounding villages. Each village represented by different hand woven patterns on the women's blouses and the pants of the men, with bright colors of birds from the jungle. A big market with everything from vegetables and fruits, to hardware, tools, furniture, and clothes. Piled in high stacks were mountains of bread, hammers, shoes and fried grasshoppers, a local favorite. Lively action and excitement of street commerce, one woman who sold herbs and potions called to Shawn and told him she had a potion that would help him find love. Roberto joked in Spanish and told her Shawn was running from love. She said her potion would get him to stop running. Shawn ran, which brought on some good laughs from her and others. The brothers bought their wives hand woven scarves, and after that they were guilt free to hang in the bar.

Before the bar, they needed to get the lumber for a project on the bunk house. On the way to the sawmill, Roberto slipped into a tienda and bought some small cakes he held in a wax bag, leverage, he said in clear English while he waved the bag at them.

"What?" Shawn said with a confused look.

"Amigo, this guy Hugo who runs the mill tries to give the customer cuts on the wood that work in his favor. We want a full six-inch board, this guy pushes his cutters to cut in favor of the board. If he only has ten-inch and fifteen-inch boards to cut from, he wants them to cut the ten-inch and leave us walking out with only a five-inch board. So, we always slip the cutters some cakes and they give us just want we want."

"That is funny! Back in Maine we go to the yard pick out stuff already milled to the right size and give the yard man a good

194

joke. Not here, cupcakes. Mexico, what a trip!" Shawn said while he slapped Roberto on the back.

They walked through a hole in a high wooden fence and into a narrow passage through stacks of boards piled very high and came out into the mill yard. Roberto put the bag behind his back so Hugo, who was up in the office overlooking operations from a big plate glass window, could not see the offering for leverage. Manuel walked up the stairs to the office while Roberto raised his eyes brows to the millers, who looked to be about fifteen, and slipped the bag behind one of the wood piles. The boys smiled. Hugo was a large man who spoke fast Spanish, loudly. Manuel started to tell the boys what sizes he wanted when Hugo slid open the window and hollered down for them to wait until they had settled on a price. Manuel smiled and winked at them all.

Hugo came down with the order slip pointed to the pile of wood he wanted them to cut from, then went back upstairs. Roberto took out a small tape he had in his pocket and measured the wood from that pile. After the cutting it would have been three quarters less than what they wanted. Manuel took out a small flask filled with tequila and waved it to the boys with a devious smile and went upstairs to divert Hugo while the cutters took from the pile Roberto wanted. The saw was a huge circular blade with no safety guards and had no way to move it up and down. When they cut the blade was a foot and a half above the boards surface. Shawn knew how dangerous that was and he could not look, so he went upstairs and introduced himself to Hugo and joined in on the drinking while Roberto with his tape made sure all those cuts were to a solid six inches. They neatly stacked the one by sixes and came back later with the truck when the streets were clear after the market.

The bar the brothers took Shawn to was not a male dominated smoky scene he had envisioned. It was an open courtyard with tables and raised flower beds and small trees, with a round bar in the middle. A mixed crowd of families, single women and men, and of course dogs running with the kids. They joined a big table with some locals the brothers knew. The Spanish was fast but Shawn picked out the gist of the conversations. Manuel told the table the story of how it came that Shawn was in their lives. He heard "no ropa" and they all looked at him and laughed. He knew what that was all about and had to laugh, too, it was funny. The pitchers of beer flowed as did other funny stories involving no ropa. A gringa with a Mexican fellow walked in from the back with her auburn hair in a pony tail. She reminded Shawn of Laura. He had been doing really well and kept her out of his mind, involving himself in the farm. At that moment with a good buzz going that pony tail triggered all the feelings he had about her to the pit of his stomach. Manuel could see the change in Shawn and came over and sat next to him. He talked in English so no one other than Roberto could understand their conversation.

"You look like you saw a ghost" Manuel said with concern.

"That gringa reminds me of Laura."

"Ah yes of course, you love her."

"But I feel so betrayed."

"Hey, you really don't know that amigo. You saw a kiss. There are many kinds of kisses. I think you need to reevaluate your feelings on what happened that night and go talk with this woman Laura."

"Fuck that, I know what I saw."

"Shawn just try to be open to something else is all I am saying," with that said Manuel got up and asked one of the women to dance to the salsa song that was being played, that he loved so much.

- CHAPTER 22 -

Scotland:

"I am going to give you a great life," Boyd said while he held Effie after another intoxicating round of love making. Since the schooner they had always been creative in finding other secret hideouts.

"Really now, such bold talk of the future with the both of us still living at home."

"I told you we can go to the mainland and get work."

"Mother of Mary, Boyd! Half the country is starving out there. What work could we possibly find?"

"We have to at least try. We can't keep going on like this sneaking around. I want to be able to walk down the road with you holding my arm it the light of day."

"Well ain't you just a high falutin dreamer. Walking down the road are we now, like high society gentleman and lady? You with a walking stick and me a parasol I suppose? We are crofters, Boyd! We have no time to be walking down the road in the middle of the day when we have to work all the time just to survive."

"I rather like the dream, seems better than the Croft."

"So are you really tired of sneaking around with me Boyd?" Effie kissed him and slowly ran her hand over his naked chest.

"Not this part of the sneaking. No never."

After they made love again in the hay loft, Boyd asked questions about the twins, "I never see them as ladylike. It always feels like being with the boys with them. But your drawing shows the lady in them."

"They really are beautiful. They were born after three sisters, and their father wanted them desperately to be boys. When their births revealed them to be girls he just carried on raising them as boys and never gave it a second thought. The twins have always been doing the work of men. The hard work is bad enough, but having to be around men all day long, the language ya know, going on about women in sexual ways. They have had no chance to explore the women in themselves."

"They don't seem to mind."

"Boyd! What do you know about being a girl? Of course they mind. They are bleeding every moon cycle and tits as well. Gillia especially she has got really big ones."

"How do you know? She seems to hide them."

"She showed them to me. Got naked as a bird out behind the grain barrels. Wanted to know if it was normal for them grow so big."

"What did you tell her?" he asked with some excitement in his voice.

"I said it was more than normal and they were some prize possessions that any man would kill to get his hands on."

"What she say?" he was laughing now.

"Any man lays his hands on these and he won't have to worry about killing because he will be dead," she laughed too.

"How big Effie?" Boyd said with a little too much excitement.

"Just you never mind Boyd McCormack about other girl's tits and take care of the ones before yah," with that said she got on top and fed him hers and looked into his eyes and said, "I think they both have a crush on you. They are always asking this and that about you. Now Shauna wants to know details of what we do when we're naked."

"Effie you don't."

"I do as well."

"Stop your going on, girl. What do you really tell her?"

"That it is wonderful and how lucky for me it is with you."

"Stop shining me up. What now did yah say?"

"Just that. After how hurt you were when finding I told them about our first kiss, I promised myself not to tell so much."

"Oye I was not hurt that much. But you must have told them something. Shauna is always taking curious glances at my crotch?"

"Oh, I may have let slip something."

"See, just can't keep it to yourself."

"Well, with the twins, yah know, they bring it out in me."

"Nooo, they get that talk from you Effie. So forthright and all about men and their affairs in town."

"What yah mean! I get it from them. Hanging around the men since they could walk. Hearing all the naughty talk. Some of the things they go on about. My! Don't we have some laughs."

"Talk about me now, what about you? Telling all to your brother no doubt before sleep," Effie brought the talk around.

"I tell him little. He caught me slipping out the window one of those nights. I had to tell him something. He knows it is a girl but not you. He would kill me if he knew it was you, being a Protestant and all."

"Then we will run away. Far away. To the New World."

"Oye! you the dreamer now."

"No, I am full on. The merchant told me ships are sailing from Scotland often to the New World. It is starting to feel like that is the only place where we can be together."

"That would really be starting over. Leaving family and friends. Could you leave the twins?"

"They would be the hardest."

"This is all I have known, the island, Mum and Pa, Ross, all my cousins in the clan. To go to the mainland is one thing, but to leave Scotland, how could I?"

"Boyd we have to think about it. That we have to do."

"What about paying? What does a passage cost to the New World? Effie what money do we have between us?"

"I don't know Boyd. I will ask the merchant about passage. For money, I have some ideas."

"What ideas? Not taking from the till!"

"Oye Boyd! Come off of it now, you know me better."

"I don't know Effie. When you get your head behind something no telling what you'll do."

"No telling what I will do?" she got right up and put her clothes on. "No telling! Right then. Maybe I go to Oban and start giving wanks to the boys for passage money. No telling? Well, I will tell you! Boyd McCormack you have no idea who I am and got no business laying with me."

With that said off she went into the night. Boyd laid there in the loft wondering what just happened.

That fight was written about in the both diaries. It was the first and it sat heavy on both of them. Boyd thought he had lost her. He was devastated for days and walked around in a blue fog. Effie was mad and did not want to see his face.

He went to the store to talk to Effie but she was out back and her father was there, so he left with a heavy heart. Then he went back on the day her father was gone and the twins were there minding the store with Effie having gone off with her dad for the day.

"Boyd she don't want to see yah, stop wasting your time in coming for her," Shauna told him straight.

"I just want to talk to her and set it right."

"Too late for that. You already set it by calling her a thief."

"Mother of Mary I did not call her a thief."

"She claims yah did."

"I said there was no telling what she'd do. Come on Shauna you know what I mean. She is so strong headed."

"Being strong headed got nothing to do with stealing. You crossed her integrity. Give her time to cool down."

"Cool down?! She ain't right in being angry with me Shauna. It was not what I meant to do."

"You daff headed mule! It don't matter what you meant. It's how she feels from what you said is all that matters, Boyd. You hurt her with your heartless words and now she is angry. I suggest you think to be more careful with your words. Let her go on being angry for a bit then come back with some mighty pretty ones for her."

"I don't need no pretty words. I done nothing wrong."

With that said Boyd struck out of the store.

He did stay away because now he was hurt, he was suffering. He tried to keep a good face around family, lost, aching deep inside. He felt the pain of cutting off his arm would be better to take. Always thought of Effie, so many things would make him think of her, the smell of the sea, the sound of crashing surf, the wind blowing soft in the dune grass. He was in the agony of being in love and was in uncharted waters. After the first weeks of pain he became numb and just headed on a daily course like a helmsman weathering a bad storm.

His thinking changed. For the first time in his life he started to see from the outside looking in. He went to church and listened to the dogma and saw the same rituals without room for personal thought. What Effie had been going on about started to move into his center and he really started to see it. The hypocrisy, the blind faith, the power of the clergy, the use of guilt to control. He started to argue with his brother about it. For the first time in their lives they were not on the same page. The verbal arguments moved onto physical. Fist fights, going at it like mad men. Trying to beat their perspectives into each other. His brother being the oldest felt his little brother should be following his thoughts. To be hearing all this talk of blasphemy, he just could not tolerate it. Just way too disrespectful. He needed his brother to follow his lead, and by God he would beat it into him. Boyd fought back with everything he had. He felt his world was being controlled by the long shadow of tradition from the clan. Just no room for his true self to grow with the narrow walls of religion and clan tradition, his father and now his brother. He fought the hardest for his frustration by being misunderstood and dumped by Effie. To Ross's surprise, he got beat.

From reading Effie's diary, which started when she was little, Marcy learned of the hurt and frustration caused by her first injustice. Her father accused her of stealing money from the till. It was not long after her mom had died and she was really struggling without that constant love. He would not listen to her pleas of innocence. What would she do with the money anyway? He heard none of what she said and took her out to the shed and exposed her backside, which was a great humiliation to her, and whipped her naked bottom. It was like he was taking out his anger on losing his wife on his daughter. She could not sit for a week and it forever changed the relationship with her father. At that time in her life she desperately needed someone she could trust and depend on. He destroyed that with an unjust act of anger. She became an island to herself, keeping a candle burning in her soul from her mother's love. She was forward and to the point in her dealings with her father, but inside she was a wounded bird that through many years of solaced time by the sea and painting had nurtured her soul to being healthy. The twins were such inspiration to her healing, they helped her to laugh at herself. She loved their insights about the rawness and shortcomings of men. But most of all they really loved her.

She did not trust men until that day she turned around and saw Boyd's eyes looking at her with such compassion. She blossomed after that and loved with all her heart, until that night in the hay loft when it all came crumbling down with Boyd's accusation, then up went the barricade. During that time Effie was done with him and for that matter the whole lot of 'em. Tensions were building again between the clans with such bravado talk in the store and village of fighting. She hated violence and could not understand why they all could not work it out in council. She did not have the strength of heart to see the fallout of another battle producing dead and wounded men, mourning women and children. Effie started to plan to go to the New World on her own. After she showed the merchant some of her paintings she decided to take up his offer to sell them to some of his rich customers on the mainland. Hopefully they would sell and she could have enough for passage across the sea.

- CHAPTER 23 -

When Marcy got to the part about the big fight she saw how Effie's accusations were more about the incident with her father. Boyd had just pushed that old button. She wished she could go back in time and set things right. Tell Boyd why she was so upset, that it had more to do with Effie's past, but she could not. Marcy went back and forth between diaries and got completely absorbed. She noticed Boyd's diary was written later, like he was looking back and writing about his life trying to find some solace.

After a month of having not spoken to Effie, Boyd walked down the road away from town and the family croft after another fight with his brother. He wanted to be on his own, away from the building tension between himself and his brother and the clans. He felt it building in the air; violence wound soon erupt. It seemed his whole life was being torn upside down. He loved the island, the clan, the church. But now he did not know, he was losing faith in the clan. In his heart he knew that he and Effie were not done. He just could not imagine either one with their lives apart. It was just plain as day that as long as he was a Catholic and she a Protestant, they could not be together on the island, which meant leaving, possibly all the way to the new world. He was distraught and angry enough that he was starting to see it. It was early summer and the air was rich with the smells of wild flowers and salt air. He had an urge to go for a swim in one of the island ponds that was close. Boyd headed down a trail to the pond, when he walked right into Shauna, who was coming up. Her hair was wet and loose about her shoulders and she wore a simple shirt and skirt, but she looked more womanly than he had ever seen her. She was startled yet happy to see him. He had a cut over his left eye that had a lot of dried up blood around it, making it look worse than it really was.

"Boyd what have you done to yourself?" Shauna said with tender concern in her voice.

"What?"

"What? Mother of Mary! You are all bloody above your eye."

"Just a scratch, Shauna."

"A scratch don't bleed like that! Let me mend you some, now Boyd."

"I'm fine, just going for a swim."

"No let me," with that said Shauna took some of her loose shirt sleeve and made it moist with her spit and started to clean off the blood. She stood close touching Boyd with her chest. Normally she had them wrapped, but now after a swim it was just a thin summer shirt and her naked breasts. They were big, firm and soft and they were warm and getting warmer as they pressed into him. Her face was close to his and he saw the beauty that Effie had captured in her drawing. She smelled of the pond she had just came out of and the croft was in her clothes, but her breath smelled sweet like something he wanted to taste.

"The clans been battling already?" Shauna chided him.

"Might as well be the clans. My brother Ross."

"He look worse or better than this?"

"I think I broke his nose."

"Ahh going to a take a while for him to live that one down."

"I don't care anymore Shauna."

"Don't care? Boyd he is your brother."

"Yes my brother not the lord above, always trying to control me. Done with his ways."

"Ahh, yah just still hurting over Effie. Sore at the world."

"Yah sore alright" and shook his hands, which got Shauna to look down and see his open knuckles. She went down on her knees and started to dab the wounds with her sleeve. Her shirt was loose and open at the top and when Boyd looked down he was given the full view of what she had shown Effie in the stock-room. They were wonderful and very desirable. Heart break or not he was only a young man, he got rock hard. It became very apparent to Shauna the condition Boyd was in, his kilt was askew and open a bit from the fight with his brother. Shawna had a good view of his nob and very much liked what she saw.

"God Effie was right," they both said to themselves.

Shauna's nipples got real firm as she stood up and stuck them back into Boyd`s chest.

"I did not know you liked me in that way Boyd."

"I did not know until this moment. You are very much a woman."

So there they stared into each other's eyes and felt the growing desire.

"Shauna and Boyd what are you doing?!" It was Gillia coming down the path for a swim.

They moved away from each other, both clearly in a state of arousal, with his kilt sticking out and her hard nipples poking through the thin shirt.

"I was just cleaning the blood off of Boyd."

"Looks to be more than that," Gillia stated while blatantly looking at the protrusions.

"Nothing happened here Gillia," Boyd defended the both of them.

"Looks to be that things are happening."

"It just happened but nothing happened."

"Hmmm really now?" with that said she just locked her eyes on Boyd's crotch as did Shauna.

It was all too awkward and embarrassing for Boyd, and he gave his farewell and ran off down the trail.

"Mother of Mary! Shauna, you gone mad. Effie is our best friend."

"For Christ sake Gillia nothing happened."

"Right look at the state you are in. All flushed with hard nipples."

"You would have been the same if you saw what I saw."

"Which was what?" now clearly curious.

"I was on my knees cleaning the wounds on his hands when it come jutting out for a good view. God Gillia! I got to see the lot of it."

"Really! And?"

"Effie is right he has a magnificent prick."

"Really and yah got a good look at?"

"Yes and very close. I wanted to kiss it."

"Yuk Shauna what's got into yah?"

"I never even thought of it, but once I laid eyes on it I felt a strong desire to give it a kiss."

"So you stood up and kissed his lips instead?" Gillia scolded again.

"No, but we were about to. I felt it for sure until you came and ruined my chances at my first kiss."

"Shauna he is for Effie!"

"Oye I love Effie too, but if she is going to toss him I want first dibs. He is a good one compared to the rest. He sure has desire for me."

"Listen to yah, all greedy with your lust, now out with your nipples so all the world can see. Effie and Boyd belong to each other, plain as the peat in the bog."

"Yah you are right. But still, I want that kiss before she comes around to him."

"Shauna!"

"What?" Shauna said then laughed and Gillia could not help but join in.

When Boyd got home there were horses tied in front of the croft, which meant visitors from away, not a good sign. When he went inside it was men he recognized from the MaCsween Clan. His father gave him a strong look and motioned for him to sit and join them.

"We have no choice now. We have to get them when they first come ashore," MaCsween stated with conviction.

"Why not attack the ship when she comes through the narrows? Take her by hooks from the shore?" Boyd`s father asked.

"No, they have a lot of cannons on board. We would lose too many men gathering to go over the sides. The best way, Cam, is to get them when they are bringing their men to shore in small craft away from those bloody cannons."

"Alright then and you are sure it's just two days away?"

"With the wind the way it is, yes. We will have to gather a good half day before they arrive and have all our men hidden in the bogs."

"We will be there with all of our clan. Until then God speed."

They all left Boyd alone with his dad and brother. His father took a good hard look at the both of them.

"Oye, at it again the two of you. Bad enough we have to fight the monarch. You boys need to resolve your differences quick like. In two days time you will be against the English, side by side, and you will really need each other then."

"Father are we uniting with the MaCsween Clan?" Boyd changed the subject.

"For now, yes. The English monarch is trying to divide us by offering deals of land and power to other clans if they fight for them. They are shipping in men to tip the odds. We need to stop them before they unite with the betraying clans."

"But father, why does the monarch want to divide the clans?"

"Divide and conquer, son. They want to be done with our ways, for us to stop speaking Gaelic and speak English so they can completely control us for their own economic gain."

"Well we can't be having that. Let's go fight the bastards!" Ross showed his bravado.

The sea smoke hung low around the bogs, which made for good hiding and a great element of surprise. The English soldiers were heavily armored and moved awkwardly over the sides of the landing skiffs. It was an easy victory for the clans. During the battle while Boyd fought side by side with his brother and father he was so focused on staying alive he thought of nothing else but fighting and killing his opponent. It was the first time in over a month that he did not think of Effie. During and after the battle Boyd felt a part of something bigger than himself. All the questions he had about the clan were lost.

The twins were all astir over the battle, worried over losing Boyd, each for their own reasons. Effie was worried as well. She was angry at Boyd but wanted no harm his way, and the thought of him hurt or killed sent a chill through her heart. Word had traveled that the men were coming back and the road they were on would bring them close to the store. The twins could not stand to just sit and wait, so they got Effie to walk with them up the road to try and get a glimpse of Boyd and see if he was alright. They were just bustling over the crest of a hill when they saw the clan coming towards them. When Effie caught sight of Boyd all the emotions that she had blocked, with her anger, came pouring out and were revealed in her face. She gave Boyd a look, and that look, that lasted in the briefest of moments changed the lives of many people. To Boyd, he saw the love she had for him and knew they were destined to spend their lives together. His father saw that his son was in love with a girl who was a from society's secular view, a Protestant, but for him a connection to a forgotten past. For there to be love between them, it would have been going on a long time behind his back. He was furious. Boyd`s brother saw the love and felt betrayed by his brother for not being included. He then saw the anger in his father's eyes and had a deep premonition that things would never be the same in his family after that moment in time.

That night a storm lashed out in the Wallace croft. Boyd`s father lost control and struck his son across the face with an open hand. The emotional pain of that slap scored deep into his soul, the look in his father's eyes of raging anger felt like hatred. A cord was broken between father and son, and when he retreated to the solace of his bed his brother plagued him with guilt. All that feeling of belonging he experienced in the days prior had been tossed aside. After the storm subsided and all in the house were asleep, Boyd slipped out with a few of his belongings and headed for Effie.

He found her going through her art work above the store. Effie was waiting for him. She had lit a candle that could only be seen from a certain spot outside. She recognized the sound of him coming, and when he came into view with his ruck sack over his shoulder, his face said it all. Effie got up and held him close and tight. They both wept for a long time.

Nothing had to be debated now. They knew what they had to do: go where there was a different way of living. Effie was prepared for this moment. She had sold her paintings to the merchant who had a rich English client that paid dearly for her art. With his connections he'd secured passage on a schooner sailing to the New World. She had originally asked for only one ticket, but the merchant convinced her to secure two in case she had a change of heart. She could easily sell the passage if she ended up traveling alone. It was through a shipping company out of Glasgow, and they had ships sailing across the Atlantic several times in a month. She only had to say when and he would get her a spot on the next outgoing ship. They had to get from the island over open water to Oban then make their way to Glasgow, which would take weeks on foot, less if they could find horses. The twins had access to a fishing dory and they would need their help in sailing it to the mainland. Effie had to quickly choose from all her possessions the most essential items to cross the Atlantic and start a new life. She grabbed her journal first, then a good pair of boots, some paint brushes, paint and paper. She packed warm practical clothes and left the fancy dresses behind, not that she had many of those. She moved fast. No doubt Boyd`s father would come looking at day break.

When she was packed up and writing a parting letter to her father. the light of day was coming on the horizon. They had just gotten outside when Effie's father came out of the croft. Both Boyd and Effie had expressions for expecting a row.

He held his hand up and said, "I have not come out to stop you. I want to give you this book that was your mothers favorite and hope its contents will help you in times of need."

He went over to Effie and held her with a tenderness she had never felt from her father. He kissed her forehead and looked into her eyes and said, "It was a dream of your mother's to go to the New World. She wanted to be on land by the sea that had never been plowed and listen to the crashing surf and birds from a virgin meadow."

"How do you know where we are going Father?"

"I have known this day was coming since you first started seeing Boyd."

"But we were so careful."

"A father knows what is going on in his own home."

After Effie kissed him goodbye, he walked over to Boyd, held both his shoulders and looked into his eyes, "I know you will take good care of her, better than I. God be with you both. Now you must be off quick. Your father will be looking for you soon." He led them a ways down the road, then gave one last look in their eyes and ran back to the croft. Not long after he was back McCormack came knocking.

"Right then Wallace, where are you hiding them?" Neil McCormack bellowed as he came through the door after Wallace opened it.

"They left. Heading lord knows where."

"You damn fool Wallace! You let them leave?"

"Neil! There is no stopping them. They can't live here where religion divides them against the people they love. What does love know of religious boundaries?"

"Damn you and your daughter. My son belongs here," Neil came after Wallace and grabbed him by the throat with seething anger in his eyes.

"Go on do me the favor. My soul died when my wife went years ago," Wallace choked out. The lack of fight and those words cut through Neil's anger and reached his heart. He had known Wallace`s wife. She had been in his church when he was a boy, before she converted over to the Protestants. She was beautiful and always defiant, beating up boys in the church yard and challenging the law of the nuns. He was in awe of her and later in love, crest fallen when she left his church and married Wallace. When he saw her around the village it always warmed his heart to see her move about, those familiar mannerisms ground into him from childhood. When she suddenly died his heart ached and suffered from the loss. He saw that old pain in Wallace`s eyes and the anger left him. For a moment he was without the dominant perspective of father, clan leader and devout Catholic, but a man with buried wounds in his heart that needed to be expressed.

Wallace saw the anger leave Neil`s eyes, then the hands left his throat. Neil fell back and sat down on the floor with his mouth hanging open then started to talk.

"Shit man! She was the last person in this village who should have been taken. What a loss, I was angry with god for taking her. She was not afraid, filled with free will and human spirit. What a gift to have such a soul in my childhood. I miss her too, Wallace. When I saw Effie coming over the rise of the road yesterday she looked so much like her. It knocked the scab off that old wound. It was like feeling the loss all over again. Christ, I got angry and took it all out on my son. Wallace! I hit him right across his face. Man, the look in his eyes. I lost him right then and there."

Niel sat there and looked into Wallace`s eyes and saw an old childhood friend. They used to explore the wonders of the moors and talk forever about having adventures at sea. That friendship torn apart by their rigid religions. The pain from all that was lost in the tear filled eyes of both men.

Effie and Boyd could not leave knowing what might happen to Wallace if Neil McCormack`s anger got the best of him. They snuck back to the croft and hid in the barn and planned the best way to cope with the situation. Boyd crawled in the high grass then leaned low below the window. He could hear the two men inside talking, and he could not believe what he was hearing. They were going on about Captain Jack and the mystery of his missing chest of gold and silver. He took a quick look in and both men were sitting on the floor passing a jug back and forth looking like school boys.

When he got back to the barn, Effie looked at him with anxious eyes.

"Don`t tell me they are both dead on the floor."

"Well they are on the floor but both quite alive. They were drinking and talking like boys about buried treasure."

"What? How could this be?"

"Maybe they are glad to be rid of us."

Effie smacked him on the arm. "Well, whatever is going on between those two it ain't bloodshed so let us be gone."

They slipped through the wooded glades and made their way to the twins, who were in a field herding sheep. When the twins saw them with packs and satchels they knew what was up and it hit heavy in their hearts.

"Oi, it is nice to see the two of yah together but not the packs. Ah Effie! You warned us of this day but we did not want to believe it. Now here it is," Gillia declared.

"I can't believe it. It will be so strange without you guys," Shauna said with a lost look on her face.

"Girls! We can't have sad goodbyes right now, we need your help to sail the fishing scow to Oban," Effie stated with conviction.

"Sail to Oban, now that is a proper adventure!" Gillia yelled.

Effie and Boyd hid in the woods while the twins snuck around the rest of the day and gathered supplies. As sad as it was to be losing their dear friends, they really enjoyed being involved in their escape from the island. It was well after dark when they all got aboard the scow and drifted out of the cove with the tide. They raised the sails in the dark of the night and caught a good gust of wind off the point of the island. It was exciting to be out there exposed to the wonder and power of the sea under and a star filled sky. Effie and Boyd stood at the stern and looked back at Bull Island for the last time.

They did not linger long in their mood, for the wind and sea picked up quickly and the twins needed help reefing the mainsail. It was like trying to hold a bucking calf, the way the power of the wind heaved the sail and boom about. Gillia was at the helm while Boyd and Shauna worked the reef and Effie tended the jib lines. Shauna was behind Boyd and worked very close, at times grazing her chest across his back. He looked back to see if it was intentional and was greeted with naughty eyes. If that was not enough trouble a, rogue wave came over the bow of the scow and soaked them, almost knocking Shauna overboard. A raw cold wind bit through them. They would not last long in wet clothes. Gillia and Effie yelled at them to go below to change into dry clothes. The scow had a small cuddy cabin that they squeezed into. They fumbled with cold wet fingers with way too many buttons to be undone. Shauna shivered badly and could not work the buttons.

"Boyd I can't do it you will have to," she said in a panicked voice.

Boyd gave her a look, realized she really needed help and fumbled with her clothes to get them off. He found a sail bag that he used to dry her off. He tried not to mind her raw beauty but could not help but take it in. After all it would probably be the only naked woman he would see other than Effie. He wrapped her in a blanket and took off his clothes with cold fumbling hands. He rubbed himself dry and started looking for dry clothes for them but realized Shauna needed help. Her lips were blue and she was shivering beyond control. Boyd very concerned and wrapped only in the sail bag stuck his head out of the hatch.

"Effie I need your help down here with Shauna, she is shivering badly."

"I can't come below, Gillia needs my help up here. You have to tend to her," Effie looked at him with deadpan eyes while she held the jib sheet, ready to ease it fast when the next gust hit them. It was getting gnarly out there.

"But she is naked!"

"Boyd! This is no time for modesty. Keep yourself wrapped in that sail bag and get under the blanket with her and warm her with your body. It is the only way to save her out here in the cold!"

He gave her a look of a sheepish boy that brought laughter from both girls, and went below.

He did what he was told and got under the blanket. He wrapped his body around Shauna and rubbed his hands up and down her back trying to get some circulation going, taking in with his eyes the beauty and curve of her back, her naked bottom that was different from Effie's. Her breasts were cold but the nipples hard and they pierced into his chest. Oh man! What a predicament to be in.

Up on deck Gillia and Effie were busy tacking through a narrow passage between two islands. The wind sheer that came off the islands was strong and demanded attention on tending the jib and main lines to ease sheet. It was a fishing scow not an ocean going sloop, so they had to be mindful of healing over too much and taking in water that could swamp the wide and open cockpit of the scow. Hands at the ready, they looked and listened for breaking surf on unexposed ledge.

"Aren't you jealous?" Gillia asked.

"What? With Boyd down there naked with Shauna, no. She will shiver to her death otherwise. I could not live with that happening. Besides it will give them both something to remember," she said with a giggle.

"I will never hear the end of this from Shauna. Laying naked with a man and Boyd at that."

"Well she has had a crush on him."

"Effie, you knew?"

"Of course. It was so obvious."

"Why did you not call her on it?"

"Why? How can I blame her? I have a crush on him."

Gillia looked at her with awe and said, "You really are something Effie Wallace and I will dearly miss you."

Shauna finally stopped shivering and fell asleep in Boyd's arms completely exhausted. With her guard down, the tenderness that was in her was exposed, hidden by a tom boy persona crafted by her father who raised her as a lad. With the mystery of her nakedness revealed, his energy moved away from the wanting in his groin to that of the heart. He realized he loved her, not out of lust but for her as a person with her playful and raw honesty. After this day he would never see her again and he felt sad. His hardness that was against her thigh with only the thin cloth between them went soft.

"Hey what happened?" Shauna whispered in a sleepy pouty tone.

"I thought you were asleep?"

"I was. Feeling safe with your wanting me, now the want has gone soft."

"Mother of Mary, Shauna. It can't be that way between us."

"Boyd! You wanted me plenty that afternoon out by the pond. If Gillia had not come along it would have been between us, a kiss for sure."

"We have to forget that afternoon, Shauna."

"Forget! Boyd I will never forget that day nor this right now, laying naked with you and wanting that kiss that was coming to me."

"Shauna! I am for Effie."

"You will be with her the rest of your life. You are leaving mine and this is my last chance to get my first kiss and I want it to be with you," she held his eyes with conviction and desire.

Just then a strong gust tipped the scow over hard on its side, knocking the two out of the small bunk onto the floor boards. Shauna landed on top of Boyd with her legs open and around him. With the cloth between them lost in the fall her soft and wet lips touched his penis. Her want for him was too great and she placed her hungry lips against his and found his tongue with hers. Just then the hatch opened and Effie stuck her head in.

"Well! That is one way to get warm."

"That gust knocked us out of the bunk," Boyd said in surprised defense.

"Right and the gust knocked your lips together."

"Effie! That was my doing. I could not help myself, laying naked together and all."

"Shauna he was trying to save your life by keeping you warm with his body not for this."

"Oh God Effie it was just one kiss and my first at that. You are both leaving my life and never coming back. What more can possibly happen?"

Effie looked at them both. Boyd looked like a guilty school boy and Shauna pleaded with her eyes for forgiveness, a pathetic yet endearing sight. How could she be mad at them, she loved them both.

"Oh Shauna, I have to forgive you, we'll see it as a going away gift. Now Boyd pull yourself together, get dressed and come and help me on deck."

The wind was building and the they were being overpowered by too much sail. Effie and Boyd had to take the jib down. They worked together to gather the sail that was wildly flapping from the wind and kept it out of the sea and unhooked it from the fore stay.

"Effie I did not want that kiss. She came on me so fast."

"Boyd, I have known of her desire for you for a while now."

"So you are not cross with me?"

"No, nor with Shauna. She is right this is the last of us being together. Now She won't have to lay awake at night wondering. She can lay awake knowing."

"So, was she a good kiss?" Effie looked at him with a playful challenge in her eyes.

"It happened too fast."

"Well then, maybe you should go back down and go for another to find out."

"No Effie, I would much rather kiss you," with that Boyd wrapped his arms around her and went for a kiss.

She pushed him away and very sternly said, "Boyd McCormack don't be letting all this go to your head. Just because I am forgiving you for kissing another woman and crossing the ocean with yah does not mean I will jump right back into bed with yah. You are going to have to work for it all over again and even harder than the first."

He looked at her with a crooked smile that showed awe, confusion and love. Thinking a guy can't win today.

The fight came out of the wind at daylight, just as they came into the Oban harbor. The local fishermen were on their way out for the day. It was not normal to see a boat come in at this time of day, too many unseen dangers out there in the dark. They drew plenty of attention, what with three women and a man tending a fishing scow. They came into the town wharf with the main sail topped up and spilled the wind. Gillia nailed the landing with grace, which impressed the men on the dock. The twins took off to follow a lead on buying horses from a family member who fled the island life and was making a go at farming on the mainland. Boyd and Effie went off to buy more provisions for the long trip to Glasgow.

The twins scored two horses at a good price and helped to pack the saddle bags. The trick was to keep the loads balanced. They all found more things to do to avoid the unwanted good bye. It was the hardest thing, saying goodbye to the twins. Effie cried the most, and the twins quickly wiped away tears. Boyd tried to hold it together as he took in their image to last a lifetime.

They rode in silence for a long time after that, the reality of leaving their family and friends sunk in and the lonesomeness of it held their mood blue. As they moved further away from the familiar smell of the salt from the sea to the visual beauty of the highlands, their somberness softened.

In the days that followed they eased into a routine of riding side by side. They talked with ease about whatever came to mind without any pressures of time. Just before twilight they found a safe place to sleep for the night, set up camp and built a fire and cooked under a dark sky filled with stars. Slept in each other arms all night long without fear of getting caught. Effie did honor her word. She held out on making love with Boyd for many nights. To hold her close and feel the heat of her body only to be shut down left Boyd with a deep ache in his balls.

They met other travelers on the road and heard their stories, which was a great delight to the both of them. One night a boy of twelve showed up at their fire riding a pony. He was out looking for lost sheep and spotted their fire. A talker for sure, spent too much time alone out tending the sheep. With his mother dead and his father drunk every night, he found solace out in nature. He had a strong accent that was different from what they knew on the island. Some of his words they could not even understand. He had lots of sheep stories, felt they got a bum rap on being labeled as stupid. That's because most folks don't get the quality time with 'em that he did. Under his daily observations he found them to be quite bright. Boyd and Effie just let him go on and found silent humor in his theories on sheep.

The next day was one of those eerie mornings in Scotland. The fog seeped its way from the bogs out onto the road and hung low to the ground. They came through a bit of woods and the trees were tight to the road. Effie and Boyd felt it first in the pits of their stomachs, a tension in the air. They gave each other a knowing look and went into high alert and used all their senses for signs of trouble. They had one sword between them and Boyd reached back from under the saddle bags and got it to the ready. It was so hard to see out into the woods with the heavy fog, and loaded down with supplies they felt like fat prey. The horses, used for working the fields, were big and strong, but they felt the stress from their riders and changed the pace from a slumbering walk to a trot. Just the sound of their big hooves hitting the road echoed out into the murky woods.

Effie felt the need for a weapon and took out the rope they used to tether the horses and tied a monkey fist to one of the ends. The silence was broken by the crashing from the woods as two men came out on horseback and onto the road and rode fast at them with swords held high. Thinking fast Effie gave Boyd one end of the rope and told him to tie it to his pummel and gallop towards the charging men. The two bandits had faster yet smaller horses, so they were much higher off the ground on their strong steeds. Just before they crashed into the men with horses and swords, they split apart and the rope between them caught the men chest high and knocked them to the ground. Their horses charged off down the road and Effie and Boyd chased not far behind.

When Effie and Boyd got a safe distance away they stopped their horses. The adrenalin raged in their veins and the relief of escaping death enveloped them and they fell apart in giddy laughter.

Later that night when they were naked under their Scottish wool blankets, Boyd laid on top of Effie and looked at her with shiny eyes filled with love and admiration and asked, "What made you think of that rope trick so fast my love?"

"It was the twins."

"What?"

"Well, when you were out with the clan battling they were scheming on how they would come and save you. That was the plan they came up with, except the men would be on foot and the rope was to take 'em at their necks."

"Mother of Mary, the twins! I miss them already."

"Aye, me as well but I felt 'em with me right when those men came out of the woods. They would have loved that little adventure."

- CHAPTER 24 -

Mexico:

Jake and Brian looked at Shawn's truck from where they stood eating snow cones from a street vender.

"Man that is one ugly color," Brian said while he bit into his cherry flavored ice.

"I kind of like it. Blends in down here," Jake countered while he looked at it with an appraising eye.

"Blends in? Jesus boy it is so ugly you can't miss it."

Jake casually walked across the street and leaned against the old side step, crunching on his blueberry flavored ice like he did not have a care in the world. Brian stood in front of him to block the view of the street goers while Jake sat down on the side step. Right under the wheel well just after the step Shawn had placed a key with tape and a thin layer of Bondo over it. All Jake needed to do was to puncture that layer with his knife then pull back the tape for the key. He smiled when he had the key in his hand. Brian sauntered over to the passenger door and was surprised to find it unlocked. He slid in while Jake opened the driver's door and slipped and started the old girl up. He did not waste any time and put it into gear and gun it down the road. They heard the distant sound of Spanish hollered in the streets and saw men in the mirror running for their vehicles to give chase.

"Holy shit! That guy knows motors. Feels like she's got more power!" Jake hollered while he pushed the pedal to the metal.

"What? You telling me Shawn let you drive his little darling?"

"Hell no, I used to take it for spins when he was off in Moxie's truck."

"Shit you got balls. He would've killed you if he found out."

"I think he was suspicious but what could he prove? The odometer had been disconnected for years."

They made their way through the city streets and headed out of town. The plan, under Claire's initiative, was for the street venders to block the cars that would follow in pursuit. There were men loyal to Carlos and others who thought he was an ass-hole. The snow cone man was of the latter, so he took his sweet time getting his cart out of the way. Word had gotten quickly to Carlos, who was in a back bar nearby playing poker. Nothing pisses a guy off more than having the truck he won in a poker game from men who stole it, stolen from him. He hollered a bit then found a fast car to use. It was quite the posse of cars that ran down those streets and chased a few blocks behind the Ford. Once the brothers were on the highway heading south they gained more ground on that open road. Jake turned off the head lights and focused on getting his night vision.

"What do you think will happen if they catch us?" Brian asked while he looked out the back window.

"Boy! Don't even go there. Failure ain't an option on this one," Jake stated with conviction.

"Yah, well if you don't want to fail you better come up with a better plan than thinking you can out run the headlights gaining ground on us now."

"What?"

"I can see their head lights passing all the other ones. Oh man they are fast."

"We have got to get off this road!"

"Yah, well there ain't any other roads for a long ways."

"Fuck the roads, go four wheeling."

"Shit looks like a lot of sand out there."

"We got to risk it Jake. Go between the cactus it will be firm ground there."

"Alright then, let me know when I good spot comes along."

"Right up ahead between those two big cactus."

Jake flew off the road onto a hard pan of sand and dirt, never once touching the brakes.

"For Christ sake you trying to kill us?" Brian hollered while he pushed on the roof with both hands to keep from hitting his head.

"I don't want them to see my tail lights, just hang on."

"How is it you got to drive anyways?"

"I had the plan to get the key. The man with the plan drives," Jake delivered with a smile while he looked over at Brian.

"Yah well it feels to me more planning was needed. Won't be long before they figure we left the road. We got to find a place to hide."

"Boy! Where are we going to hide out here in the desert?"

"Ravine, we need to find a ravine. Turn a little to the right. Looks to be some bigger shadows over there."

Brian had good instincts, because those shadows were a clump of small trees and cactus along a dried up river bed. Water only ran in that bed during the rainy season. Jake drove right down onto it and parked close to a high bank that had a small overhang. They found some big tumbleweeds that had been collected by the wind against the dry river bank. They were both pleased by how well they hid the truck.

"Let's hide on the other side so if they do find the truck we have a chance to make a run for it," Jake stated as the next plan of action.

"You think we need to worry about snakes out here?"

"Shit, Brian. We got enough to worry about without you trying to bring in more shit."

"Hey I am just trying to be proactive. Keep your eyes on the ground."

"Ground? Man! Eyes on the road. Look they are already doubling back."

"Shit they are on to us."

Good thing it had been so dry that hard pan sand made it hard to read tire tracks. Carlos and crew were city boys, not trackers, so they knew they had left the road just not exactly where.

Back at the brother's farm:
"You are afraid" came an old female voice from the shadows of the courtyard. It was the abuela, grandmother, of the family. Shawn was surprised by the words themselves and that they were in English. He had only spoken Spanish with her.

"What?"

"You are running from love because of fear. I see you still as a boy, holding onto a way of being that no longer works. The walls you have built to keep your heart safe are taking away your joy, mi amor. You are no longer that boy, let go of your fear."

With that said she walked up and touched his arm with a warm small hand and walked off to get some sleep. Shawn stood for hours after that and leaned against a porch post, took in the sky and moved his thoughts through a new window.

When he finally went to sleep he dreamed of Moxie and his mother back at the farm in Maine. There they were so real in his mind's eye, surrounding him with so much love. Then his mother vanished and he felt that loss he had as a little boy. He awoke and felt that pain through his whole body. He took it all in until he was no longer afraid of it, then he let it go. That night his subconscious started the slow process of tearing down those walls that surrounded his heart.

Maine:

Still dark and feeling the morning cold, Marcy set the fire and took the simple joy of watching it build, which eased the loneliness out of the house. She was learning the different sounds of the fire in the old cook stove. Full of life with the constant chatter of crackling and popping. A big gust of wind blew hard off the sea and rattled the sash windows. The wind brought in the storm. She could hear the rush of the rain against the glass then the beating rhythm on the roof. The flames leapt steadily against the logs and built to a soft roar. The metal of the stove creaked from the expanding heat, and the kettle whistled with the howl of the wind in the trees and the whine of it across the open chimney. The flames of the fire held comfort as the storm started to rage outside.

Marcy struggled with so many emotions. The euphoria of surviving her fall and finding out she had brothers had worn off. That morning the pain over the truth of her real father hit her hard. The sadness of knowing she would never hear the comfort of his voice or feel the love of his touch. Anger towards her mother built in her like the storm outside. The lies, the lies, re-running them over and over as she and Sky hid from the storm inside close to the stove doing crafts. Sky felt her mother's anger and shut her out, both silent through that dark day. They had an early supper of soup and a story on the couch, and Sky went to bed early with no complaints.

Sky laid in bed and listened to the night. The storm had finally ended, still except for the sound of the distant surf crashing on the ledges and the call of the coyotes. It sounded like a chorus, then one would break out in a higher yelping pitch. It made her think of Tilly, she wondered where she would be just then. Probably listening to the calls as well right out there in the woods. There in the comfort of her warm bed she looked out the window into the darkness. She whispered into the night and sent her angels out to look after Tilly and to look after her uncles in Mexico.

Marcy sat by the wood stove and struggled with her emotions while she listened to the coyotes. That yelping expressed so well her pain and anger. She was exhausted from the anguish of those emotions. She started to read Effie's diary and was taken away to the world of her ancestors.

- CHAPTER 25 -

Scotland:

Boyd and Effie came into Glasgow, sold their horses and proceeded to look for the offices of the merchant. After Effie had looked at the letter from the merchant, she laughed.

Boyd wanted to know what was so funny.

"All my life we have called him the merchant never thinking to ask his full name, but here it is, Logan Mac a Chlieirich, now that is Glasgow royalty. All these years I figured him for a well-connected merchant of the road. Well, should be easy to find this place then."

His office was modest in size but lavish in wood working and well-crafted furniture that held stories from his travels. He greeted them warmly and was not surprised to see Boyd there with Effie. He explained to Effie that while she paid for passage she still had to work as a stewardess to the captain's wife, who was pregnant.

"There are so few crew members on this schooner that all hands must work. Boyd will be expected on night watch. I trust you know something of holding a helm, and if not you will learn quickly," Logan stated while he held Boyd's eye, then continued,

"Sailing this schooner across the Atlantic will give you a far better chance of survival. So many die on those blasted square riggers where they pack hundreds in steerage like cargo. You will have your own cabin, which is a true blessing believe you me," Logan placated the questions he saw in their eyes.

When Captain Allan Flannagain and his wife Belieg walked in the merchant's office it was like meeting old friends. There was a connection between them. They were kindred souls for having left their places of birth, but also they were couples in love. As the ladies talked of symptoms of pregnancy, Allan told Boyd the story of the schooner. Anaitis, for the Persian goddess of water and nature, was a two-masted schooner with a 124-foot hull, an eighty-foot bow sprit, and a beam of 23` 6``. Her draft was 13` 9``, foremast 77`, and mainmast 85` with the top mast making it 110`. She had seven sails and 7,500 square feet of sail area.

"You and Effie will make it a crew of seven, not including my wife."

Anaitis came with a colorful history. When she slipped off the ways in England she was named Elizabeth, built by the royal navy to see what kind of a fighting ships the fast sailing schooners could be. It was overtaken early in its learning curve by pirates well better experienced in naval warfare with a schooner than the cocky English captain. She did not fare as well as Elizabeth. The pirates took off the forty-foot bow sprit and added the eighty-footer. To do this they had to change the bow and stern to hold that extra weight and sail strain. But it gave the schooner additional sail, and they souped up Elizabeth to be a very fast schooner with commanding lines and renamed her Black Mermaid. She pillaged vast amounts of merchant and royal navy vessels, until she was stolen by Scottish buccaneers in the Bahamas. They had created a grand diversion for the crew of the Black Mermaid, who were all in port with the ship with a lawless party that started in the streets and turned into a parade that went to a beach on the other side of the island. The booze flowed freely with music and the illusion of willing women. The meager crews watch on board the Black Mermaid was easily overtaken by the experienced Scottish buccaneers. With the help of some locals, who did not like the captain of the pirate ship (he had scorned a local woman for a rich merchant's wife), rowed the schooner out to sea under tow with a fleet of dories. She was renamed Anaitis and carried high priced cargo for those willing to pay. On this particular trip it was one Scottish engineer, Fife MacGregor whose mission was to design and build sawmills on some rivers in Maine with all the sterling silver on board to back him.

They met him at dinner later that night in a small pub, called Graham's. Fife was in his sixties and had a humble demeanor for a man so accomplished. He gave the impression of being a listener, since he talked very little of himself. He came from good Scottish blood with a full head of dark hair and hazel eyes that spoke more than his words.

It was a wonderful meal of tender cooked fowl and seafood. The owner, George Graham, came out and shared some island rum and then left them so Allen could inform them of what was to come. The arrival of Boyd and Effie meant the crew was complete, so the schooner would sail in a week's time, which gave the crew time to get their lives on land in order before they headed for sea. The other five crew members who were not present were all well experienced mariners from different countries around the world, from the Bahamas, Tito, to the highlands of Scotland, Jamie Gail, to Andre the Frenchman and the German boatswain, Luke, who would help Fife build sawmills. The first mate was Ross Morgan from Glasgow, who had sailed with Allen for many years as fellow mates then became his first mate on the Anaitis.

Allen was anxious to cross the Atlantic so their baby would be born in Maine. Allen felt confident with the speed of the Anaitis he could cross in sixteen days given the prevailing southwest winds. He made it clear that while September was a month for gales on the northern passage, it would be clear of icebergs and hurricanes.

"We will be sailing through some gales. It will be a rough ride for a few days, so get your heads wrapped around the fact that will be happening soon," Allen stated with the clarity of a captain delivered with wide eyed contact.

During the week in port, Boyd and Effie lived on Anaitis and got the feel for life on board and learned all the names and functions for the lines for the seven sails. Ross taught them the lines and how to fire each cannon on board. There were fourteen in total, but all were well positioned by the pirate retrofit. It was a fast moving fighting machine, which they would use only for defense of the vessel and crew. The Atlantic coast of North America was swarming with pirates who were taking advantage of the increase in merchant vessels they could pillage. What they could not outrun they would have to fight, and Ross assured Boyd all crew members were not just top notch mariners but fighters as well.

"Being a clansman I would assume you know how to fight," Allen said while he gave Boyd a knowing look.

Boyd returned that look with a confident smirk, which was all Allen needed to see.

Then in response to the look of concern on Effie's face he said, "Anaitis is very fast. We should be able to avoid the fight."

It was a cold, sunny early November day when they headed out with the morning tide on the River Clyde. The two couples left Scotland for good but the first mate and crew would take over and operate the schooner and its profitable business after Maine. They would always return to Scotland. When they got out into the Firth of Clyde and raised all the sails, a somber mood overtook the four lovers leaving their country of birth. The crew were anxious for the wide open sea to fill their lungs and free their hearts with the salt of the deep sea. They busied themselves with putting up more sail so they could to make an impressive time out of the bay. They hollered across the open deck about what they had been up to while on land. To hear it all broke Effie out of her somber mood. She found it funny, the men had obviously had known each other for a long time, the way they held nothing back.

Andre gave Jamie Gail a really hard time about his woman situation and pushed Jamie to respond, "With the way you run your mouth, how in God's name are you still alive?"

"I deliver with charm, mate, and I know how to swing a cutlass," Andre said with a strong French accent and devious smile.

Boyd suffered the worst for leaving. As angry as he was with his father, he loved him, his brother as well, the whole clan. The reality of leaving hit him hard as he saw the land that was all he had known become less and less and the open and unknown sea became vast and unknown before him. He grasped hard for a foothold. Effie had her sad heart felt goodbye with the twins, she had suffered her hearts sorrow when her mother had died and for years had wanted to leave Scotland. She was on the mend and was looking forward to a new start. Boyd was looking back. Those two opposing energies did not mesh. They had a silent battle of the wills, each stubborn and holding to their needs and independent ways. Boyd needed Effie's support but refused to ask. She was not going to coddle him because she felt it was his own struggle to get through.

Boyd's help was needed in raising the top sails, and Allen called Effie over to take the helm. She was surprised Allen trusted her on the helm, but Allen explained that all crew on the schooner needed to take the helm and learn her well. Every crew member had to go on watch as helmsman and lookout, two above deck at all times. It was not a fishing scow, but more elegant and swift, she cut into the swells of the sea with a galloping grace. Effie played with the helm, headed away then back into the wind, Anaitis was very responsive. She was thrown across the helm on some of the gusts, but Effie was strong and caught on quickly to the feel of helm and sea. She really loved it and could not keep a huge smile from her lips. Allen's eyes lit up watching her first time connecting to wind and sea. It laid a seed for their friendship that would be long lasting.

They laid there with the silence heavy between them and listened to the constant rhythm of the water against the hull, the creaking of the rigging and the sound of the wind whistling through it. The eeing and awing of the hammocks down in the crew's passage. They were side by side in a bunk, but there was a gulf between them.

Effie broke the chilling silence, "Boyd don't be cross with me."

"Mother of Mary Effie if ever there was a time in my life I needed support it was today, and you just ignored me and found humor in the crew's folly."

"Boyd you listen to me, I will not play nurse maid to your emotions, that is your job. Now, I know it is hard leaving everything behind, all the love and support, but that is all behind us now. Looking back with longing is not going to get us across this ocean. I need you to be strong, to be my partner and for lord knows what is ahead. You need to be real clear on why you left and find peace with that decision and be willing to live with it for the rest of your life, because I do not want you to one day wake up hating me for feeling like it was for me you left."

Boyd was silent for a long time, "You're right. It's my job to make peace with leaving, mine alone."

With that said he kissed Effie on her forehead and rolled over, his back and the warmth of his bare ass touching Effie's. Having said her piece eased the tension and Effie fell asleep and left Boyd to his own struggles. Just below the surface of her conscience she dreamed of her mother. She felt her presence, her special way of being that was so filled with a giving love. The dream world of her subconscious showed her how she was becoming more like her father, stingy with her heart. Effie awoke with remorse for the way she had dealt with Boyd. She rolled over and wrapped her arms around him and sang an old island ballad, which brought tears to both of them. They were good after that.

Marcy was up in the attic in the Maine farmhouse going back and forth from Effie`s to Boyd`s diaries. Effie wrote every day with the date right there at the top, while Boyd wrote in spurts, usually when he was confused about something or very excited about life at that particular time. Plain as day when they crossed the Atlantic in 1727, Effie was more together than Boyd. They were young, sixteen and seventeen. The male brain is not fully developed at that age. He was very self-centered at that time, for most of his life he had followed his father and brother's example without question, so the life of rebellion was new to him. It took some ego to do that, but it blinded him to the bigger picture of all that was around him. He did write about that day and the days that followed. Clearly he was lost during that time. He had only known life on an island with long established culture and customs, which he left behind.

Boyd was in love and way in over his head with a very smart and independent woman, starting a new life from scratch. He had yet to find that solid rock within himself. Homesteading, finding land, clearing the land and building home and barn, growing food. Could he do it? He was scared and Effie challenged him to stand up to his fears. He just did not know how. Lucky for him they were not on a square rigger packed in like sardines with a hundred and fifty other passengers, desperate for a new start in life willing to risk the high odds of mortality. He was on a sound vessel with a sane captain and an old crew with good character. Those old sailors recognized Boyd's plight and took the time to school him on sailing and life. They were well beyond the drive of ego to prove themselves and make their mark. They had lived full, adventurous lives and knew who they were and what they had done, no need to prove anything. But to help out a kid who was just starting out and maybe make up for some of the stupid mistakes from their fucked up pasts, they were all in on sharing some hard learned lessons.

Effie on the other hand had long ago discovered the harbor of her inner self when her mother died and received that beating from her father. She was alone at sea after that, emotionally on her own. She held onto the presence and love she had received from her mother and brought that into her inner core. This was her dream to sail to America. It was her mother's dream as well, which empowered her even more to make it happen. Effie was being present and leaning forward. She really loved being on the schooner and around such salty characters who were free of so-cial and religious norms. There is no room for any pretense at sea. She had craved the open raw honesty she received from the crew after so many years of playing a role to survive in a rigid house and island village culture. It was like she was just starting to really breathe and feel her potential for what she could do in life.

They awoke to the sound of waves crashing against the hull of the schooner, which was heeled over hard. Above deck they were greeted with menacing gray skies. The crew had taken down the top sails and the two cutter jibs and replaced those with one smaller storm jib. When they had come out of the bay at twilight the previous day and into the North Channel, they had ridden the current on a broad reach with a good, stiff southwest wind. That morning the wind blew northeast and hit them right on the nose. The current in the North Channel moved southerly and the wind went the opposite direction, and the opposing forces created a short choppy wave that made it hard for Anaitis to get a rhythm and cut through the sea. Allen and Ross both kept the helm steady as they tacked on a close hull. The ship felt small against the open sky and sea that was before them, and the reality of being out in the Atlantic hit Boyd and Effie very hard. Allen recognized those looks and knew they needed to be active and get away from the fear that was taking over their heads.

"Boyd come spell me on the helm. Effie help me up on the bow with that storm jib."

When they got to the bow, Allen explained to Effie that she needed to walk halfway out the bow sprit and adjust the storm jib so they could heave-to. He kept her from falling into the sea by wrapping the other jib halyard around her waist and keeping tension on the other end, which came from a pulley atop of the mast.

"Quick and confident steps, the spar is no place for hesitation!"

She had good balance from walking atop the narrow walls around the island. But to be out over the water on a bow sprit that swung up and down at least twenty feet, now that was a ride. The feel and tension of the rope gave her some comfort and sense of security. It was an adventure for sure, suspended out there, blown in the wind and being pitched by the anxious sea. She unwrapped the cleat and eased the down haul until Allen hollered at her to stop and cleat it off.

"Good job out there, Effie," Allen cheerfully told her when she got back on the deck.

It helped to move about, but the sea rolled all around them with increasingly bigger waves, and the gray sky turned to a dark bulging blue. Effie went below to fetch storm gear for both herself and Boyd, and while she pitched down below she started to feel seasickness come on incredibly fast. When she got back above deck her color said it all.

Tito was close by, "Miss, better to stay top side, keep your eye on the horizon, don't get lost in the gray of the murky waves," which he delivered with a sincere smile that resonated compassion.

Such a simple gesture, that smile, but it helped Effie immensely at what was a very vulnerable moment. She had never been sea sick before and for a brief period there she wanted to die.

The rain lashed out at them, big cold drops that stung the exposed skin. The wind picked up and hit them hard and cold out of the northeast. They sailed with just the storm jib and a reefed main staysail. Waves occasionally broke on the deck of the schooner, which to Boyd and Effie felt increasingly smaller. All crew were on deck except Luke, who was in the galley cooking. Carpenter, cook and ship's doctor, he never went to medical school, but as a boy he worked closely with a ship's doctor who did go to medical school and had learned the art of patching men up quite well. It was in him because it was such a part of his daily life in his youth. He ran away from his father, who was a tyrant beating him at most day's end, so the sea meant freedom from all of that.

The crew ate their meals in the wheel house, right behind the main mast and before the helm, which went partly below deck and was quite big for a wheel house. The pirates had retrofitted it to be a mess hall and battle point. It was fortified for naval warfare with double oak side wall planking with iron plates and had mounts for swivel cannons that could be put in place in times of battle. It also had a small wood stove that was kept company by a pot of soup or beans. Allen ordered all crew except two on the helm to go into the wheel house or down below. The frequency of the waves that washed over the deck had increased, and keeping his crew safe and alive was Allen`s top priority.

Effie went below and checked on Belieg, who was throwing up in the chamber pot when she came into the cabin. She held her hair back and kept her from being thrown out of the tossing bunk while she leaned her face into the pot. Boyd stayed on the helm for another hour, then spent time by the wood stove and dried off talking to Ross, Fife and Allen. Andre and Tito were on the helm. Jamie talked to Luke in the galley and ate. He could eat in any storm, that boy of the highlands.

"Boyd! You look to be blue the in eyes out there. Not good, mate, we need you present on that helm. All lives on board are depending on yah. Now, I know you have left your clan and feel like you betrayed them, but let me tell yah straight the sea don't give a shit about what clan or religion you are from. It will gladly take your soul no matter, add it right to the batch. We are all out here alone but for our wits and strength of character, so get your head out of your ass and get front and center," Ross laid it out as the first mate should, the ship was no place for a moper.

Boyd took it well. It just added to what Effie brought on the night before, and it was easier to take it from Ross, who got a bowl of soup and handed it to Boyd, then sat right next to him and said no more. Allen and Fife talked about the weather and wondered aloud how long the wind would keep blowing from the northeast. The sea, the wind and the rain lashed at Anaitis, and it made very little headway, heaved-to just on the margin of control. Allen did not like it. It felt like it would turn into a full blown nor'easter, which meant gale force winds and rain. For days they would get beat backwards, losing time, and that he did not have much of with a baby coming.

"Do you think it will ever end? How could there possibly be anything left to come out?" Belieg whimpered while curled up around Effie, who was sitting on the edge of the bed.

"It has to end. Oh, you poor dear, I bet you want to die right now, but please don't," Effie blurted out, which brought a child-like giggle from Belieg.

"It is true this is the worst feeling. If it weren't for this baby. Oh God! What am I saying? But thank you for being here, Effie, it does help. Not easy duty for sure," she said in a sickly, sleepy voice before she fell asleep from exhaustion.

Allen came into the cabin and relieved Effie so she could lay down and sleep, which she was able to do despite all the heaving.

Boyd and Fife sat close to the stove deep in conversation.

Ross had gone below to catch some sleep before the long night that laid ahead.

"I felt so sure of my decision when I left the island. I felt rejected by my father so I was right in leaving, and he was wrong in striking me. But now I don't know. I feel like I am betraying my family and clan," Boyd confined in Fife.

"Lad, you made a decision based on some heightened circumstances. You can't be looking back now. You have to live with the choices you made and make the best of what is before yah, and right now that is crossing the Atlantic. That needs to be your biggest focus. Guilt will not give you the will to survive this journey. As all sailors learn, fuck guilt," Fife stated with conviction.

"But sir I thought you were a business man, not a sailor? You are the reason the Anaitis sails for Maine."

Fife laughed a light chuckle, "Yes I am that, but before I was what I am now I sailed for years, shipping the lumber my family milled all over the world. My family encouraged me to spend my rambunctious years as a youngster on a square rigger and see a bit of the world, feel some its harsh ways, but they had no idea how I would take to it. I loved it. You see I had a choice to be out there, which makes a world of difference. I started as lowly crew but was under the caring eye of the captain who was a good family friend. I had it easy compared to most, but I loved the challenge of it, the navigating, the planning, trying to figure the weather. Love took me away from the sea, then the sea drew me back and took away the love."

"What do you mean took away the love?" Boyd needed clarity.

"Clara was her name, and she was a beautiful and a strong

woman just like your Effie. I married her and got into the mill-
ing, then built mills for the family. We were happy for a bit, then
I started sailing again to get to places to build new mills, sailing got back into my blood, then, I needed more of it. She was
hurt by my absence and in the end left me for a merchant, and a
personal friend at that. I was angry for a long time. Now I don't
blame her for leaving. When I married her I told her she had
more of me than the sea and I would be there for her, but the sea
had more of me then she. Do you understand now lad?"

"Yes, I am really sorry, sir," when Fife heard the sincerity in
Boyd's voice he realized what a caring soul he was.

"Well past the hurt and sorrow of it, lad. Now, let's give those
boys a rest on the helm."

When they came out of the door of the wheel house, a huge
rogue wave came over the starboard side and landed in the middle of the schooner. It knocked all four men down and tossed
them along the deck like landed fish. The volume of water was
so great when it hit the main staysail, it broke the yoke that connected the boom to the mast. Free of the mast the boom lurched
about above the deck like a wild serpent. The sail parted ways
from the mast, setting the gaff free to swing wildly in the wind
and damaged the upper mast and rigging. When Andre got on
his feet he was struck back down by the swinging boom, which
broke three of his ribs and tore open a big gash in his right forearm that was a real bleeder. Jamie helped Andre and was hit by
the boom on the side of his head, which knocked him out cold
to flop around on the deck. Boyd and Fife were washed down
the deck on the port side, protected from the flying boom by

the wheel house. They came to their feet and took control of the helm when all the other crew appeared, brought topside by the impact of the rogue wave on the hull. Allen yelled orders competing with the loud cracking sound of the sail luffing in the howling wind. The rain turned to hail when Tito and Ross took a long rope and, one man each holding an end, ran down the port and starboard sides ducking and dodging that bloody wild boom. They got that rope just above the boom and into the clue of the sail and with tension on the rope, gathered the luffing sail and tied it down to the boom. Luke helped gather and furl the sail, and all three men were bucked about by the wild boom.

After the boom was secured they brought the gaff down and were treated to another wild bronco ride when they tied it down. It beat them up some more, but then they could safely attend to Andre and Jamie. The blood needed to be stopped from flowing out of Andre's arm. Luke had thrown out his shoulder when he tried to hold down the boom, and without the use of his hands he had to instruct Effie on what to do. They had no clean bandages on hand, so Effie took the knife out Andre's sheath and reached under her rain gear to cut off a peace of her dry shirt to stop the bleeding. Andre, who was partly in shock but still conscience, got a look at Effie's bare midriff and beautiful belly button and felt like he had found some salvation on that schooner in a brewing nor'easter.

The captain was tending to Jamie who was conscious and bleeding from a deep gash on the side of his head. Allen cut a peace off of Jamie's shirt and stopped the bleeding. The crew got Andre and Tito into the wheel house and set up a field hospital by turning the tables into operating tables close to the heat of the stove.

"You will have to stitch up his arm, but you must clean that wound first," Luke gave orders to Effie while he held his arm, clearly in a lot of pain.

"I have stitched men before, women's duty on an island of the highlands. Do you have alcohol to clean this wound?" Effie asked in a tone that implied she was ready for the task.

"Plenty of that around, for cleaning that wound use the moonshine from the colonies and save the island rum for Andre and me to drink for the pain," Luke said while he pulled one bottle at time out of the food locker with his good hand.

Effie took the cork off the jug of rum and supported Andres back so he could take a healthy slug to help cut off the impending pain of needle and thread. After he had several good slugs she handed the open jug to Luke and unwrapped and exposed the wound on Andre's arm. She then took the bottle of moonshine, pulled the cork free with her teeth and told the Frenchman to hold tight before she poured clear one hundred percent alcohol over that big open gash.

"Oye you bitch of the sea!" Andre yelled at Effie.

"Bitch aye, well take some more then," Effie yelled back while she poured another batch over the wound.

"Oye! No more, madame please, you are wasting good alcohol."

"How good?" She took a big pull off of the bottle and drank it down without struggle. "Oui! that will give me the grit to stitch you up."

"Oye, madame that was impressive," Andre said while he

reached out with his good hand for the bottle and took a moderate pull. "Ahhhh that is smooth stuff! Those boys in the colonies know their moonshine. Here's to the colonies," with that he took a big swig and coughed.

With only the storm jib up Anaitis floundered hard in the pounding North Atlantic Sea. Captain Allen ordered the helms men to put the stern to the wind and head northeast. With this new course they rode the waves and cut across at an angle to keep from breaching.

Fife told Boyd to not fight the helm so much, "Work with the sea. Follow each wave and keep with its momentum."

The two men learned to work together on the helm. It was a silent language of feeling each other's strength and understanding how each reacted to the sea. They learned a lot about each other in a short period of time. Boyd was surprised at how strong Fife was for his age and how intuitive he was in reading the sea. He worked with it instead of fighting it, and more importantly he felt his calm confidence. It was dicey with no sails to power the ship on waves that were big enough to capsize her. The two men at the helm, entrusted with all lives on board, had a clarity of purpose that was beyond fear, reading the sea and feeling the hulls respond to the waves. Nothing else mattered at that moment but staying focused and working with nature. It was a powerful moment for Boyd in which he let go of his guilt for leaving and his fear of what was ahead. He knew he was on the right course in life, for at that moment he fought a storm that was eager to take their lives but he felt more alive than any other time in his life.

The course change took the strain out of the ship and crew, but they went in the opposite direction of their intended course.

The captain and Ross went forward and held dearly to the cap rail for the deck was a sheet of ice. They pulled a sea anchor out of the ship's locker that was just aft of the bow on the port side. The anchor was a large hoop woven with round rope that had canvas attached to it. It was like a big bag that held water to slow the ship from the will of the sea. They tied that to the end of the anchor line and threw it overboard, making sure the line stayed slack for several hundred feet before they tied her fast. Allen gave the order to swing the helm all the way to starboard. Anaitis was on a crest of a wave when the anchor took hold of the sea and jerked the ship into the wind. It slowed them from moving too quickly off course and kept the bow into the waves. It was a last resort, all they could do at that point.

Allen ordered Fife to lash the helm and all crew into the wheel house. Effie put the final stitches into Andre and Luke watched while he sipped on the rum.

"Work of art her stitching skills. You boys care for some of this island rum?" Luke greeted them while he waved the bottle out into the air.

"Brothers of the sea, may I suggest the moonshine here, more taking to the present climate. Ifffff youss know what I mean!" Andre stated with drunken gusto, feeling no pain.

"Be still Andre, I ain't done yet!" Effie scolded him.

"Oui madame, what the bossy boots you are."

"Right I am," she leaned into his ear and said loud and clear, "and don't you forget it!" Effie then grabbed the moonshine and took a good pull.

"Done with the stitching. Not a pleasant chore that one," Effie stated while she washed her hands in a warm basin of water and then went over and stood close to Boyd and gave him a warm tired smile. He put an arm around her waist and looked into her eyes. She saw the change in him.

Tito took care of Jamie through all the commotion. He had taken a cloth from the cupboard and dosed it with the clear alcohol and padded the bleeding wound on his head. Jamie was coming out of it and wanted a pull on the jug, but Tito would not allow it.

"No man! Not good now for you. Your head must heal," Tito was insistent.

"Tito, he is from the from the highlands, there is no hurting his head," Luke interjected.

"Look who is talking nothing, more hard headed than a German."

"Ja but we put it towards being efficient not stuck in old traditions always fighting with our neighbors."

"Aye, but at least we are loyal and back our word."

"Ja all for the glory of clan. What about the rest of the world?"

"Alright enough! Listening to the two of you is caving my head in," Ross demanded while he stood with his back to the stove with a coat of thin ice over his rain gear.

The Anaitis floundered for the next twenty-four hours in forty foot seas, bobbing up and down with every wave. It was hard to sleep with the noise of the storm pounding that schooner, the slamming of the hull against the massive waves, the screech of the wind against the rigging and cabin tops. The only ones not sick were Luke and Jamie who hung tight in the galley. Despite all the heaving Luke was able to keep a pot of soup going on the stove. Effie spent some time with them until even she could not take the banter between the two and found Andre and changed the bandage on his arm.

"How long have you been a mariner, Andre?" Effie asked while she wrapped the wound on his forearm in the first aid cabin slash storage room.

"Since twelve, madame. Not my choice believe me. I was fishing with my grandfather off the coast of France when a pirate ship over took our small fishing boat. They wanted food and water. My grandfather was killed defending all that was his, and I was pressed into service on a pirate ship."

"At the age of twelve?" Effie's voice raised in indignation.

"Oh yes, madame, very common practice to take boys to sea."

"But what did they have you do?"

"I was very small, so when we were broadside and the grappling hooks were held firm on a ship we were fighting I would crawl through the cannon holes and steal gunpowder. Other times on the captains words I would light a long fuse in one of the barrels of powder and get out quick as we disembarked from the pilfered vessel. The cannons were still hot from just having fired so I would wear thick wool, a hot maneuver if you know what I mean, madame," with that he gave Effie a flirting smile with a shimmer in his eyes.

Effie ignored his flirts and asked further questions, "But why destroy a good ship? Why not take command of her?"

"Oye! The madame speaks like a pirate. It is never that simple, sometimes we attack the last ship in a convoy and it has to be a quick pilfering, for they send the cutters after us. The ship must go down to leave our mark, something to sit in the back of their brains that are filled with their queen's desire. We would get them, one at a time."

"But Andre are you still a pirate?" Effie said in a tone that left Andre wondering if she was now playing him.

"That too was taken from me. The British Royal Navy captured my ship and captain. I was then pressed into the Royal Navy and learned to sail and swing a sword, madame."

"My word what an extraordinary life Andre, and you still serve the sea after all that?"

"Madame, you have a way of arranging words. I thought for so many years I was serving a captain, but I have come to believe how you just said it, we are all serving the sea. It is all I know, it is so much a part of me now. I can't live on the land with any peace in my soul. Working on the Anaitis is a blessing for an old sailor, very little climbing and the food, ahh madame, the best on any ship."

"I can't imagine all the climbing there must be done on a square rigger, with all those sails."

"Oui, and each sail has several lines and each with their own name. Fuck, madame, so many names and you had to know them all."

"Do you still remember?"

"I try to forget, believe me, but it is in me, been some years now since my time on the riggers. I like sailing the schooner, slick buggers on the sea they are."

Effie finished up with Andre and went to check on Belieg, who was tended to by Allen and was not hungry. She did not want to be back in her cabin so she went aft and found an open hammock in the crew's cabin and fell asleep with the storms rage on the schooner, the screeching wind, the pounding waves. She focused on the sounds that were closer and not as loud, the language of the swaying hammocks, their lines on the hauls beams. Effie fell asleep and listened to the eeing and awing of the gossiping hammocks.

When Boyd shook her awake, the ship was not slamming into the sea and the wind was no longer howling.

"Effie! I've been worried sick about you. What brings you to be sleeping here?"

It took her a moment to gain her bearings. She looked at Boyd`s worried face and it took her a bit to get it. Then she said in a sleepy groggy voice, "Boyd, sorry to cause you worry but I could not sleep in our berth. Always feels like I will be pitched."

Her tender vulnerability changed his worry to desire and he kissed her with hunger. She responded with a suppressed need and the kiss led to some well needed love making to heal the divide that was between them. They swung and swayed, eeing and awing to the rhythm of the sea.

Later when they came out on deck they were met with a grand mystical sight. The schooner's rigging was all covered in ice, and the early morning light shone through a break in the clouds and reflected through the ice crystals which created little panoramas of rainbows. The sky was rich in color from the storm's clutter of remaining clouds and the sun was hungry to gain control of the day. The sea had a good swell, but the waves were no longer breaking. Effie and Boyd stood on the bow and held one another in awe of the beauty before them and felt grateful for having survived a nor'easter at sea.

The wind changed to southeast and Anaitis got back on course with the wind behind them on a broad reach. Luke had repaired the goose neck and Tito and Jamie spent some time up the mast and fixing the rigging. She was at full sail, but they had lost a day doing the repairs. The captain was worried about reaching their destination in time for the birth of his child. His fear and stress moved from the top down and infested the schooner's crew. They pushed Anaitis hard and took advantage of the favorable winds and put up all sails. They found the Gulf Stream, that strong current ran south westerly and they made good time.

Effie was summoned to the captain's cabin and handed the ship's medical book and told to study the chapter on child birth. She might be needed to deliver the baby. Luke was sidelined with his arm in a sling and could give only oral advice, but they needed Effie's hands to have some knowledge behind them so she studied that book by candle light in the rolling cabin far into the night.

- CHAPTER 26 -

Mexico:

Carlos drove a street car, no way was he going four wheeling with that. Between all the vehicles in the posse only one of them was a truck. Two of the guys stayed back to safeguard the cars while the rest piled in the back of that old truck. Carlos drove and bitched about how bad it needed a tune up. One of the hombres in the front spotted for tracks. He would see something and holler to stop and get out with a flashlight to take a good look, and then with great poise he'd point in the direction they should go. This went on many times, and the boys in the back lost their spirit for the chase the further they got away from the road. A bottle of tequila was passed around to bolster the spirit back.

Jake and Brian laid on that desert sand behind a small cactus and some tumbleweeds and watched the head lights of the truck. One minute they were coming at them, then they would stop and change directions.

"Looks kind of foolish don't it?"

"Real foolish. Jesus Christ, we could've out run that operation. Looks like they only got one truck."

"Lucky for us we got city boys chasing us in the desert."

"Ain't no lucky yet, boy, we are laying in the sand like sitting ducks."

"OK, let's change the plan and get back in the truck and out run those fools."

"Now you are talking, vamos mi hermono!"

"Ah si, si," the both of them laughed as they ran for the truck.

They were pulling away the tumble weeds from the old Ford when the cactus on the river bank above them lit up from head lights.

"Shit they're coming right for us. Now or never Buddy Boy!"

"Hold on Jake, they may not be certain yet. Still just looking, let's wait it out in the truck."

"Fuck! Awful too close for comfort."

Brian jumped in the driver's seat and was surprised when he got no protest from Jake. They could see the approaching truck by the head lights getting brighter on the far bank of the ravine. The truck stopped on the overhang the boys were under. They heard the men climb out and talk in Spanish. Jake made a face at Brian to make a run for it. Brian shook his head no. When they heard and saw the sand and gravel rushing down, they knew the men would find them. Brain fired up Shawn's truck, slammed her into gear and stepped on the gas. He knocked over two very surprised men with the bold Ford bumper. Slightly bruised and a bit dazed, the men got up and opened fire. They hit the back of the tailgate several times but somehow missed the back window. The hombres on the overhang had guns but none had bullets in them, and they could only watch in frustration as the truck they were trying to catch drove away.

"Does that answer your question on what they might do with if they caught us?" Jake hollered from under the dashboard.

"Yah I get it loud and clear, asshole!"

"Hey, just be glad they are bad shots."

"Or drunk."

"Yup we got a drunk posse chasing us," Jake clarified when he came out from under the dashboard and looked back at all the stumbling going on.

Carlos was in the truck and hollered for the guys to climb in. Those hombres were very excited and drunk when they jumped back into that truck. Brian and Jake had a good head start and a faster truck. They out ran the posse that was in the one truck and kept on going even after they saw them head back to the road. An hour later they stopped the truck in a small ravine and found some tumble weeds to hide the truck. While they felt safe they fell asleep.

When Laura got past the initial shock of Shawn leaving, she was relieved. It had been really hard those last weeks between them. She had been so afraid of him leaving that once it happened and it was a reality, Laura could cope with it. Bill was so pathetic with his Romeo act, complaining about his bruises and the attackers. She eventually gave him some money so he could go home and get out. She was disgusted with men and put her focus on work and the people before her.

After a couple of weeks, thoughts of Shawn worked their way back into her mind. She started thinking of all the things they had done together, realizing how much she loved him. Questions of concern, where was he now? Still in the country or out? She missed him and after talking with Marcy her feelings got even more intense. The fact that Shawn was out there not knowing he had a sister really made her yearn to find him. She asked a few men in town that were connected about any sightings of a gringo driving a green Ford pickup with Maine plates. Some days later she got word back about a Ford truck that had been won in a poker game, painted brown and had been seen up at the border. Laura, being who she was, borrowed a truck from a friend and drove to the border town to look for answers.

Laura did not know that the brothers had stolen back Shawn's truck. Jake told her that they would come see her after looking around the border town. She did not think they would find out much without knowing the language but said nothing figuring it couldn't hurt. They needed to jump in on the learning curve on the ways of the local culture anyways, and she needed to be there and look for herself. If it was his truck, then it was stolen. Was Shawn hurt or killed when that went down? Was he left in the desert? So many questions. Laura knew where to start looking. Shawn had said the decoy girl's name was Clara and she knew what she looked like. She might have heard something about Shawn, so Laura went back to the bar where she had first laid eyes on him. She waited a while, but sure enough Clara did come in and Laura went right up to her and asked to speak with her.

"Señora if you have come to ask about what your boyfriend or husband has done, I cannot help you. So many gringo men come. They get what they are looking for, buenos noches," Clara delivered with confidence and went to walk away. Laura held her arm and said she was looking for Shawn, the tall redhead from

Maine. Clara stopped and looked right into her eyes and asked what led her to believe she knew anything about this man.

"He told me you helped him that day in this bar when the fire happened. I am his girlfriend and very worried about him. Please! Do you know anything?"

Clara sized her up one more time and told Laura to meet her in one hour two blocks over at a small cafe and whispered the name as she walked off.

Jake heard the sound of giggling. He was in that state between dream and reality. In the dream the laughter came from Brian as a boy, all of them out in the old barn playing hide and seek. He was giggling when he found Jake in the grain bin. Jake opened his eyes, his face puttied to the window, and looked into the dark brown eyes of a Mexican boy. The boy was on small horse, leaning down and looking into Jake's open eyes.

"Amigo, is your truck so ugly you have to hide it with tumbleweeds?" the boy said with laughter still in his voice.

"You got that right and a good morning to yah there young fellow," Jake said while he stepped out of the truck. "You the greeter of the desert?"

"Si amigo, I am Roberto and this is Sadie," he waved down to the horse, "on my way to my tio`s ranch." Delivered with much confidence from such a boy.

"I am Jake. They got you herding cows?" he asked with interest.

"No, we are building a new barn."

"So you are a builder as well as greeter."

Roberto liked that comment and smiled with pride. He looked

back into the window of the truck at Brian and then at Jake with a questioning look.

"Don't worry about him, he is a sound sleeper."

"Sound sleeper? That is funny kind of English."

"It's an expression, and yes funny now that you mention it. Where did you learn to speak English?"

"Not far from my home is a bad turn in the road. Trucks often overturn there on stormy nights. The whole family goes out and collects the cargo while the trucker has his wounds healed at my tia`s house, or shares a bottle of tequila with my uncle. I go with my father to the border to sell the goods to the gringos. We have a tape recorder that he lays on the seat between us teaching English. My father, he never got it, but I did. So I make the deals on the prices with the gringos, language is easy for me."

"Less luggage in the attic," Jake delivered.

"What is this English?"

"It means you are young and have less things in your head getting in the way of learning a language."

The boy giggled again, "My dad said the same thing in a different way."

Now it was Jake's turn to laugh.

"Well I would say you have enterprising family, Roberto. I should wake my brother and get back to the road."

"Amigo I would not do this right now. The men who put the bullet holes in your truck are out on the road."

"Ah, smart little bugger. Seen the damage and know our plight."

"They came to our ranch late last night. Said to keep a look out for you."

"Ah, so now you are a spy?"

"No, I really am going to my tio`s ranch. But I knew what I might find when I saw this ugly truck trying to hide in tumble-weeds. Carlos is asshole. I am no spy. You need to do better with hiding this truck and lay low."

Jake studied the boy for a while and looked at the truck covered in tumbleweeds. He then roared in laughter, which brought the boy into it and woke Brian.

"Is there some new development in our predicament that would bring on such laughter?" Brian said with a grouchy voice.

"Not really, just a new perspective from our friend here Roberto. And good morning to you little brother!"

"They will be better shots today, Jake, nothing good about this morning," Brain said with grouch and gloom in his voice.

"But we now have inside info. Ain't that right Roberto?"

"Si, I heard them say they will stick to the road today. Knowing you will eventually need to get back to the road because the can-yons will limit your options. By afternoon most of the men will be bored and want to go home."

"So what are you saying, it will be safe to leave after dark?" Brian asked.

"More or less. I will have to lead you through the canyons to get past where they are waiting for you. They won't be looking there. The ones left will be way too lazy for that."

"I don't think it will be that easy, Roberto," Jake said while he looked out at the desert.

They spent the day lying low. Roberto left and came back with water and food. Somehow he got leave from barn building and helped burn the long desert hours in the day by teaching the boys Spanish. After dark and with good scouting info from Roberto they headed out and went no more than a mile before running out of gas. They did not know that the gauge was off and had to confirm the tank was empty by sticking a stick down and seeing the tip was dry. A classic, out of gas in a desert canyon, standing around a truck that can't move while the stillness and solitude seduced them and the stars lit up the sky and calmed them. The constellations so vivid it brought the words to Jake.

"Man, you can see why the Mayans got into the stars."

"Mayans amigo? I use them every night to guide me," Roberto said while he headed off with empty jugs to siphon gas from one of the cars at the road block, slippery boy that one.

Just before sunrise they followed Roberto through a maze of canyons. They got back to the main road just before sunrise, and when they gave their farewell to Roberto he refused the money that Jake tried to give him and said the adventure was enough payment for him. Then they headed off down the road for Solito to find Shawn.

- CHAPTER 27 -

Atlantic Ocean:

E arly one morning when they had just sailed over what is known as the Scotian Bank, a hundred miles off the coast of Nova Scotia, they spotted sails far off on the horizon. With the smaller mast in front they could tell she was a three-masted schooner. It came about and sailed directly at them like a hawk after prey. Given pirates had preferred the schooner for naval battle and that they were in prime pirate territory, Captain Allen ordered the crew to ready for battle. There was no mistaking the proud lines and long bow sprit of Anaitis. In the pirate world the Black Mermaid was legend and a prime prize to capture and command. Allen knew they would want to minimize the damage in battle and that the pirate ship would first try to overtake them with their speed, then raise the pirate flag showing their intentions and giving captain and crew option to surrender ship before battle. If no surrender flag was flown, they would get in musket range and try to shoot out the helmsman and anyone else on the poop deck. Followed by scatter shot from the ships cannons to rip sails but not take down any masts. Then they would come in with the grapple hooks and many men would come over the side with cutlasses in hand. A three-masted schooner could have over a hundred men on board. There would be no chance for the crew of Anaitis. For sure the three-masted schooner was faster, but Anaitis had the advantage of pointing higher into the wind and could come about faster. Surrender was not an option; they would have to out maneuver the bigger ship with a clever strategy.

In all the commotion on board Effie went instinctively to Belieg. She was surprised to find her so calm.

"Finally something to take my mind away from my suffering body," Belieg said with determined eyes, which gave Effie needed strength.

"I know my husband. He is experienced and very clever. With the help of this crew on board we will prevail through this coming battle," she stated with a confident and caring hand on Effie's arm.

There was a lot of commotion on the cannon deck and in the wheel house. One of the changes that Allen made to Anaitis was to fit it with two long barrel cannons specially made by some of the finest blacksmiths in London. They could shoot farther than most cannons on ships that size, and the best part was no one but the crew knew they existed. Tito, Jamie and Luke were preparing the long barrel cannons on the starboard side. The protocol was to fire one cannon to see the range so the next would better hit the target. In the wheel house Fife, Ross and Andre took windows out and put the long barrel musket guns in their pivot stations.

Allen looked through his spy glass and saw that the oncoming schooner flew the Union Jack and looked like a naval vessel.

It was a sign to him that it was a newly acquired conquest and the pirates had yet to retrofit it for their purpose of taking over ships. The captain and crew had no time to fully know the capabilities of the ship they were sailing, a weakness he would use to his advantage.

He set a course that put them on a long reach and it looked like the Anaitis was on the run. The pirate vessel did likewise and after some time Allen gauged the amount of time they had before the three-masted schooner would overtake them. He was impressed with the speed of that schooner. They had only a couple of hours. His crew got the ship ready for battle, then all they could do was wait and anticipate what was to come.

When Allen went to his cabin to check on his wife he found her and Effie playing string games with their hands and singing the rhymes that went with them. Both were smiling and calm. Not what he expected to find.

"They are fast, Belieg, should be just four bells before we engage. I won't be able to come check after this," Allen delivered with a tone of love and concern.

"Their speed will make them cocky, and their greed for this prize vessel will make them foolish. I know you will use it to our advantage. I believe in you, my love. I can see this through and have our baby, now come and give us a kiss."

Effie was impressed how Belieg anchored her husband. He was more assured when he left the cabin.

As if reading her mind Belieg explained, "It is always before the battle he is afraid, but once it starts he is too engaged in the present to have fear. We will be fine."

Allen could see the officers on the poop deck. They were dressed in British naval uniforms, which forced him to blurt out to the crew, "The cheeky bastards are wearing the Union Jack uniforms like we will fall for their games. Let's blast 'em good with the long guns when they raise the Jolly Roger."

When the three-masted schooner was just out of normal cannon range of Anaitis, they raised the pirate flag and showed their intentions, expecting to see a white flag in return. Allen gave the order to jibe ho and fire at will. Ross had the range figured for the distance of the oncoming ship, and he aimed for the forward and center masts to slow it down and even the odds. The real skill came in timing the swells of the sea with the angle of the cannons. He ordered to fire at will! The first cannon ball was just shy and splashed the hull with water just off the starboard bow. It alerted the pirate captain and crew of the danger they were in. They tried to head up wind when the second cannon blasted from Anaitis hit the top fore staysail, which broke the front mast and brought the gaffsail down with it. Splinters of spars and torn sails crashed down on the crew on deck. The crew of Anaitis cheered, Allen ordered them to fall off on a long reach and they made their getaway. All on deck looked back and watched the pirate ship. There were a lot of men on board and they wasted no time and cleaned up the deck and salvaging what they could to get back more sail.

"Well lads they may not know their ship but they know how to salvage and fast. It won't be long before they are on us again, all cannons ready."

It no longer looked like a proper naval vessel. Makeshift spars stuck off the bow and the sails billowed from them like spinnakers, and it was fast approaching. Allen could see from his spy glass that they had moved and mounted two long range cannons on the port and starboard bow, "Lads, I thought wrong. They are equipped for long range battle. Ready all cannons!"

When the first cannon shots were fired, it triggered the first labor pains for Belieg, sharp and sudden. She screamed out in pain and yelled out, "Mother of Mary Effie, this baby is coming! You best get ready to deliver."

Effie felt a surge of energy and focus, which diverted her fear from the cannon blasts that had shuddered through the ship. She gathered her wits and supplies to bring a newborn into the world in the middle of a naval battle.

Belieg and Effie heard the blast of gun powder then the whistling of the cannon ball just off the stern of Anaitis. The second shot was more terrifying as it whistled louder and closer and shot right through the stern cabin windows. Splinters of wood and glass flew everywhere. A piece of the window frame hit Effie in her forehead and knocked her off her perch at Belieg`s bedside.

Allen's first impulse was to go below and check on his wife, but he knew he had to stay on deck and lead his crew to fight back with all they had or else become the pirates' whim. Boyd, who was on the cannon deck, headed for Effie when Ross grabbed him and with a stern voice said, "We need to save this ship Boyd, let's have faith they are alive. We need you here to win this battle."

Allen ordered to jibe ho and Andre swung her hard and away from the wind. It was a gutsy move given the high winds but it paid off. The pirates did not expect that. Anaitis was on a port

tack and headed towards the pirate ship. The pirates were prepared for a starboard side attack and their make shift sails off
the bow were a problem. They got weather helm from the bloat-
ed weight of the sails off the bow, and they could not get into
position fast enough to attack. Allen gave the order to fire and
all seven cannons on the port side blasted in succession. Four
missed but three hit the ship, taking out the center mast and
blasting into the wheel house. The pirates scrambled like ants
all over the deck of their ship and removed the bow sails and
regained control of their ship. All too quickly they were in position to fire the twelve cannons on their port side. Allen ordered
to come about when the cannon blasts were heard and all on
deck of Anaitis braced for incoming cannon balls. Two struck
the fortified wheel house but the other cannon balls whistled by
overhead. A rogue wave that was not in the normal sequence of
the waves threw the cannons off their target. It was a very lucky
break. In position for attack, Anaitis fired cannons on the starboard side, which took down the forward mast and the upper aft
mast and left the three-masted schooner with just its main stay
sail flapping in the wind. The pirate ship soon fell behind barely
afloat in the devastation.

Allen ordered Andre to fall off on a long reach and hollered
through the deck hatch for Ross to come topside and take command. He ran below to see if his wife was alive. Allen and Boyd
arrived at the broken cabin door at the same time and stood in
silent shock at what they saw. The cabin was littered with broken
glass and splintered wood. The only place that was not was the
white bed sheet where Belieg laid with her knees up, naked from

the waist down. Effie was between her legs with the blood covered remains of her blouse barely covering her breasts and the missing bottom half wrapped around her head.

"Don't just stand there with your mouth`s hanging! Get in here and hold her hands," Effie hollered at the two men.

Belieg pushed and hollered, the crown of the baby's head started to show. Both men were impressed with how hard she squeezed their hands.

"Come on darlin' almost here, give me another hard push with all you got," Effie coached her.

Belieg pushed and screamed into the bowels of that ship, and just as the baby's head came out the severe pain caused her to lean over and bite into her husband's shoulder. It was a solid and deep bite. Allen screamed along with his wife as their baby girl was born into the waiting hands of Effie. She clipped and tied the cord and held that precious baby, struck hard with the miracle of life, and slowly and with tender love handed her to her mother. Boyd saw a bolt of maternal love overtake Effie and knew they would have children soon.

They sailed into a harbor that was under British rule and Allen found a doctor to check on the health of his baby and wife. It felt strange for Effie and Boyd to stand on dry land. The rhythm of the sea was set in their bodies and to not be moving in that same beat was a major adjustment. The rest of the crew got a kick out of their reactions. Andre and Tito were on watch on board with muskets ready. The port was a bit unruly with merchant ships from all over the world mixed in with buccaneers and pirates trying to blend in and look like merchants. 1727 is marked in history as the end of the golden era of pirates. The rise in the number of buccaneers turned pirate had gotten so out of control, instigated by countries who encouraged the pillaging of merchant ships from the countries they were at war with and shared in the pillage with the buccaneers. It became so lucrative that many skilled mariners left the low pay of the navy and merchant vessels and took to the pirate life, pilfering vessels of any country and keeping all the bounty to themselves. The British, French and Spanish had naval convoys out on the seas and took back control of major trade routes. When captured, quick tribunals were set up and many mariners were convicted and hanged, some of which were mere victims of the rogue culture of man and sea.

Nova Scotia in 1727 had an interesting mix of ethnic cultures. The French at Port Royal in 1607 started the Arcadian culture, which mixed in with the Wabanaki. The Scottish Colony in 1621 only lasted a couple of years but later brought scores of Scots to the Maritimes. The British did not establish a colony until 1746. After Queen Ann's war in 1710, some treaties were signed and gave control of Cape Breton and Port Royal to the French. So at that time it was the law of the biggest guns in the rest of the Maritimes, with many battles for control. Amongst all of it a vibrant trade came across the Atlantic from Europe and spilled down into the colonies. Not to mention the ethnic blend of seasoned characters from all over the world enriched by their adventures at sea. It was very exciting for Effie and Boyd to walk around the port village absorbing a new land and the cultures that struggled with it.

"Can you believe it Boyd? We are finally here in the new world! Maine is not far from here. Soon we will be there and find land to settle. Such a journey to cross the sea!"

"Aye Effie! It feels so new and nobody here knows our business," they both laughed and ran through the narrow port streets holding hands.

A British naval officer with six men in tow bearing muskets announced himself at midships of Anaitis and hollered for an audience from the wobbly dock. Andre sashayed himself slowly up to starboard gunnel and peered questioningly over and called out with a tone of bullshit authority, "Captain is away yah have to come back later!"

"May I have a word with you then, sailor? It appears you have taken cannon fire. May it have come from a three-masted schooner masquerading as a British naval ship?"

"Well there, a British officer with a crystal ball. How could you have known?" Andre stated in mock sincerity.

"That ship was stolen from this port by a former British naval officer by the name of Fenton who went rogue years ago. He created a diversion by blowing up our small garrison with all our gun powder in it. While most of the crew were fighting the fire, he easily took control of the ship and sailed out on a night zephyr."

The naval officer was clearly and plainly embarrassed and deeply agitated by confessing this painful truth, which immensely pleased Andre given his history of being pressed by the queen's navy.

"You don't say, Governor, now let me get this straight for the log book, under your watch a fellow officer stole a prize ship of the British Navy and then proceeded to attack our ship, which left us with no choice but to defend our ship and fight back. Your prize ship, which I might say was a beauty until she come under our cannon fire, is floating with just her main staysail and a crew of over a hundred men, which I would say by now are very hungry for a good fight. You could easily overtake them with your two frigates I see here in the harbor and give some of your lobster backs a bit of action," Andre delivered with a broad cunning smile.

The officer got very red in the face and tried to compose himself, "How am I to believe you could escape a battle with a three-masted schooner equipped with twenty-four cannons?"

"Go find out for yourself. Head northwest by west more than half a day's sail and you will find the truth."

To assert himself the officer moved the conversation to the problem of a lack of gunpowder due to the destroyed garrison. All ships in harbor were asked to donate kegs of powder from their ship stores to the Royal Navy.

"Aye we are about run dry of powder from blasting your lovely three-masted schooner, but I will report your request to our captain," Andre then left the rail and went into the wheel house and left the officer and his men standing on that wobbly dock.

It was well into the night when Andre heard a squeaking noise coming from the cannon deck. When he went below to investigate he found a blond headed boy, stuck between a cannon and its opening, squirming like a fish to get out. Still clutched in his hand was a bag of powder.

"Aye! You little rascal! Trying to steal our powder," Andre wrenched the lad from his stuck position and shook him with his strong hands, but when he looked into those young eyes he was struck with the memory of his youth and of being forced into doing this very same act. He stopped shaking the poor lad and asked in an uncharacteristically kind voice if he had been pressed into the Royal Navy.

"They said I was a stowaway and had to pay for my food by working, slopping the officers' tables and stealing powder, sir," the boy delivered with truthful innocence and sorrowful gray eyes.

"Now how is it that you came to be a stowaway on a British naval ship?"

"It was my cousins. They dared me to go on the deck of the ship when it was on the pier in Portland. I had to show them I was not afraid of any Bloody Backs, but when I was on the ship the deck's watch came around and I had to hide in one of the topside lockers. I had to hide so long I fell asleep. When I woke up the ship was at sea. I hid for a week before they found me stealing food from the galley one night. I had to steal, sir, I was starving!"

"Aye lad you done good, cunning rascal you are to have slipped their watch for a whole week. Now how long ago was that you come into this misfortune?"

"Not exactly sure but I would reckon six months."

"Aye, your parents must be sick with worry and grief. Well I will tell you what, lad, your misfortune has changed because this here ship is heading for Maine. I reckon you should stow away here until I straighten things out with the captain."

"But the Bloody Backs will come looking for me," the boy was clearly very afraid.

"Don't you worry about those crackers, lad, Andre here will take care of them," and then winked at the boy. "Now what say your name?"

"Finn, sir, Cabin Boy Finn."

"Ok then, Finn. You find a good place to hide and I will bring you some food," he then reached out and put his strong hand on Finn's shoulder, "Don't worry, I will get you back home. And stop calling me sir. We are all common sailors on this ship."

It was the human contact of a hand's empathetic touch and eyes filled with compassion that convinced Finn to trust this crusty Frenchman of the sea.

When Andre entered the captain's cabin he looked very much out of character, which broke Allen and his wife out of their trance with the baby.

"Sir, may I have a word?" he looked uncomfortably at Belieg.

"Feel free to speak, Andre."

"Well sir, I caught a boy last night trying to steal powder. I know I should've thrown him off, but I could not. I fed him and he is hiding now in the ship's hold. Sir, I want to bring him with us to Maine, bring him back to his parents."

"So I gather the lad was pressed, by whom?"

"The Royal Navy, sir, the bloody officer asks for donations of powder then sends a boy to steal it."

"They will no doubt come looking for him, Andre. You are putting us all a great risk."

"I know, sir, but they would never find him on this ship. The lad is a crafty one, hid for a whole week on their own vessel before they caught him. It ain't right sir. I see myself in his eyes, but he can have a different life than me, one he deserves, to grow slowly from boy to man, not have it thrust on him like a hurricane."

As the captain, Allen had to always think of what was best for the whole of the ship and limit the risks, but before him were the pleading eyes of Andre, who had a chance to somehow redeem some of his lost youth as his wife held their new born girl and her eyes pleaded with a mother's love."

"Ok, Andre, bring the lad here."

When Finn came into the cabin, Allen did not have a chance to address the boy. Belieg with baby in her arms and Effie were all over the poor lad. They hugged him and fussed over his tangled blonde hair, empathized with the look in his eyes that showed a frightened boy fighting to survive in a world of men and sea. The lad had not felt a warm and loving touch since he was last with his mother, and it took him some time to let go of his guard. When all was said and done, Finn was hired on as cabin boy to help Effie and Belieg. He would actually receive a wage.

The lobster backs did come looking but did not push any further when Allen asked if the missing cabin boy had anything to do with the shortage of gun powder. Under normal circumstances the officer would have ignored the comment and gone through the ship, but his ego had been bruised by Fenton and he was a bit insecure at that moment in time. They slipped out of Port Royal after Anaitis was in good repair and headed for their final destination on the coast of Maine. Fair winds for that time of year helped relax the crew on the ship and bring in a culture of family.

Finn and the baby quickly bonded. It was uncanny how the little one stopped crying when in his arms, affirming for Belieg and Effie to witness. Those three bonded in a special way, fulfilled their various needs after some trying times in life. He spent time alone with Andre and learned the language of sailing a schooner and built back trust in men. Fife and Luke spent a lot of time together as well, and the elder shared some of his hard-earned wisdom with the young man.

"You are out of the mold now, Boyd, free to make your own niche, express what is inside you and how you live. There is no place for you now. You will have to make it yourself. Carve out a piece for you and family. Don't get addicted to the sea. I can see you are starting to get seduced by her. Stay honest with the land and it will serve you well, not as fickle as the sea."

Luke`s eyes held the conviction of this hard-earned wisdom and he laid them on Boyd in a way that had an impact. He then went on, "Me I am done with it, going to build mills in Maine and stay put. What a cutlass can do to a man's body, horrible, never got used to it. I am done with patching men back together, done with the violence, the mad greed. I was given a second chance early in my life. A good man showed me forgiveness and taught me all he knew. I have lived a good life even though he could have had me tossed in prison, been a way different life then."

"Prison? What did you do?" Boyd asked in disbelief.

"I come into the city of Amsterdam without pence and hungry as a tom cat. I broke into his kitchen to steal food and he caught me on the way out, grabbed my arm hard the way my dad did, but he saw the desperation in my eyes and he found his heart and gave me a chance. He gave me a room and chores to do, saw I was smart and then started to teach me medicine. That knowledge has given me privilege but with that came the price of enduring other men's suffering. Now I have a chance to build something and be away from all of it."

On the last night of their voyage there was a calm sea off the coast of Maine. On the stern of Anaitis the majestic glow of twilight cast a silhouette of Finn holding the baby girl, and Effie and Belieg, who sat on either side of him. They were connected by their sufferings, needing one another to help heal some deep wounds. Finn needed to feel the complete trust of a child and the loving touch of a woman. The women, who both grew up surrounded with the hardhearted love from men, were blessed with the innocence of a boy who needed their love. A moment set in time by unconditional love.

The next day Anaitis entered a wide mouthed river and drifted with the incoming tide into the land of the New World. A still and clear afternoon with a deep blue sky and a wonderful shimmer of the sun's dance on the sea. That light on the sea felt familiar, so when Boyd and Effie stepped ashore on the land that would be home for so many generations to follow, they felt a strong connection. They staked a piece of land to homestead up on a hill that was cleared by a fire caused by a lightning strike years before, the stumps of the old growth having time to break down to soil. The deer and moose grazed hard on any new growth except for some young pine and birch trees that were left to grow big. It was good fertile land to grow potatoes and vegetables and corn for grain for feeding cows. Together they cleared the land of rock, wrestling them from the earth with strong fingers and holding them dear to chest and heart and stacking them for rock walls around the field. They lined the well with field stone and both labored so hard to dig. Always together and very much in love as they produced three boys and a productive homestead.

Effie wrote about small everyday things, how the boys were growing, some funny stories about them, some not so funny, the weather, the changing seasons. She wrote about a letter she received from Andre telling of the great reunion with Finn and his family. Andre had a flair with the pen and wrote a good story about this emotional event. What was surprising was that the family took to Andre's unvarnished ways and asked him to stay and live with them, and so ended his sea faring days. Then one lazy late fall afternoon she saw, through a shadowed twilight, the beautiful silhouette of Andre and Finn walking up the farm road. They had sailed up in small sloop from Portland taking a bit over half a day. What a wonderful reunion they all had on that day which was followed by many more visits. Finn's cousins coming as well through the years, all getting well with her boys, at bit wild at times she wrote.

Then the pages changed. A dark storm came into Effie's life and her past floated up to the surface. She missed her mother and wondered about her father and his health. She tried to put together some of the broken pieces from her past and fill a hole deep inside of her. Effie also wrote about being angry with Boyd, he had pushed that old button with a gruff off-hand comment at a moment she felt insecure and it made her feel rejected.

Those were the last words from Effie. The entries into her

diary stopped cold, just blank pages to the end of the old tablet. Marcy searched deep into the trunk and looked for another diary and found instead Effie's self-portrait, done with a mirror. It was the eyes and the way she held her chin that struck Marcy so hard. Effie looked very much like her. Eyes that shined out love with crinkled lines around them that showed it to be hard earned. She felt a connection at that moment, the likeness in the portrait and knowing so deeply the story that went with it. With that felt connection came a dreaded premonition, and Marcy headed for the family graveyard to find the truth.

- CHAPTER 28 -

Mexico:

Laura and Clara drove out of town later that night. After meeting and talking at length, the ladies decided to go together to find the brothers. When Clara heard that the boys from Maine were still being pursued she felt partly responsible and wanted to help. She did not think the men would have lasted this long in their hunt. They were both in stitches laughing about the story of Laura setting the trash can on fire so she could meet Shawn and save him from Clara. Laura slowed the truck down when the road came to a sharp curve and the terrain changed into a canyon. Just after the curve was a fire with men standing around it and three cars parked so traffic had to slow down. They heard one of the men say "Chevy con chicas," followed by catcalls as they passed. Clara concealed her identity by wearing a baseball cap and a plain scarf.

"Typico hombres, so aburrido! Borracho as well but that might help if the brothers have to make a run through them. Unless they try to sneak around in these canyons, this road is their only option."

"Maybe we should help them out and teach those men a lesson!" Laura stated while she looked back through the rear window with disdain.

"What do you mean?"

"Let's go back and slit their tires."

"They are not that drunk, Laura."

"I could divert them while you slip in for the slit."

"Divert them how?"

"Stand on the rocks and flash them."

"Oh you are a feisty chica, me gusta, vamonos, let's do it."

They pulled over around the next curve and walked to the back side of a steep knoll. From the crest they could look down on the men. It would be a safe spot for Laura to put on her show. There was no way they could climb up that rock. Clara helped her get ready by fixing her hair to look like a helpless yet sexy gringa and told her to set her bra just under her nipples so they would show through her blouse but not to show the full breast, "Keep the mystery alive." Then she walked down to the side of the road and circled back to where the cars were in the shadows of the night. From there she could see the men and Laura.

"Ayuadame," came the alluring and helpless call from Laura.

"Que paso," in unison from the five men.

"Arriba!" cried one of the men as he stood and pointed to the top of the rock.

"Mama cita, que paso?" asked the same man that was standing.

"I am lost," Laura said with a helpless and naughty tone and threw her arms and shoulders back in despair and showed more cleavage in the process. The men were spell bound by Laura's show. Clara had to admit she did a great job of it and laughed to herself as she slit those tires. After Laura saw Clara slip away from her high view point, she told the men she would walk down and around the rocks to them.

"Increible," exclaimed some of the men as they went back to the fire and drank some more in anticipation of meeting this sexy gringa.

Clara was making her way back to the truck when she was met by one of the men who had wondered off to take a piss. He was none too happy when he saw the knife in Clara's hand and realized what she had been up to. She recognized him from town, but he could not see her face because of the scarf she had wrapped around her mouth and nose. He had a bad reputation, particularly on how he treated women, and she was scared but tried not to show it as she put the knife in front of her and let him know he was in for a fight.

"Ah, so this chica likes blood, huh, we will see whose blood!"

She did not want to speak for fear of him recognizing her voice, so she just waved the knife aggressively in front of her. He had a sick grin on his face as he danced around her, taunting with words of what he would do to her when he took the knife away. Clara was a strong feisty woman of the streets. She was going to fight him with all her grit. She focused on the spot just above his eyes so as not to get lost in his and to show him no fear. She was also worried that when Laura did not appear the men would come looking and then she would have no chance. She had to end his dance of violent sexual expectation and win this fight quickly.

Laura was back at the truck wondering where the heck Clara was. She had seen her leave and should have arrived about the same time at the truck. Something must have gone wrong, and she had to go find out and help Clara. She was careful running from one big outcropping to the next. She got to one cluster with high cactus and peered around a big boulder to see Clara lunge at a large man, with a sick grin, with her knife. He was quick and moved to the side but not before the knife sliced open the shirt on one of his arms. With his other hand he struck Clara across her face with a closed fist, which sent a chilling smacking sound of pain to Laura's ears.

"Ah perra, you will regret this when I am done with you. You ruined my favorite shirt."

Laura ran behind the man and brought her shoulder low behind his knees and tackled him to the ground. Clara could not believe her eyes. She had dropped the knife when he struck her and could not find it in the dark dirt, so she grabbed a big stick instead and ran up and smacked the man on the back of his head before he could get up.

"Come on you crazy woman, let's get out of here quick before the other men come," Clara said as she helped Laura to her feet, and both chicas of the night ran for their lives for the truck.

Right when they got to the Chevy, Laura was startled when a strong hand grabbed her by the arm. One of the men had also gone off to take a leak and had seen the last of the ruckus and ran in pursuit. Her reaction was immediate and without thought she brought her other arm around with a closed fist and smacked him square in the jaw with a round house punch, which dropped the drunken man right to the ground. She got in the truck just as

Clara fired up the motor, put the Chevy into to gear and peeled out of there.

"Holy shit woman where did you learn to throw a punch like that? Here I been thinking gringas were nothing but sour milk and honey," Clara said while she accelerated the truck down the road and looked over at Laura with awe and respect.

"I grew up with older brothers," Laura delivered with a smile of relief.

Maine:

Marcy knew where she had to look. In the back of the small cemetery was a jumble of overgrowth that looked to be hiding something. She went to the barn first for tools, then with a lantern to light the night, big clippers and bow saw she clipped and sawed her way to where she found a head stone that stood a couple of feet above the ground. It was covered in moss and lichen, and when she peeled off some of the moss from the right-hand corner she could see the indentation of a letter. She brought the lantern close and could see the top of what looked to be an E. Her heart sank to the pit of her stomach. Driven for the truth she went back to the barn for a stiff brush, a bucket with some splashes of water mixed in with baking soda and vinegar and another bucket with clear water to rinse. She watched the solution react to all the hardened bacteria and slowly open up its tight fist around the letters. She scrubbed away and revealed the name Effie Wallace McCormack with the dates 1707-1737. It was like a severe blow to her gut. She doubled over and cried, then with tears in her eyes and a heavy heart she pulled away moss, washed and scrubbed the black bacteria from the space that tells cause of death. While she howled in anguish to the heavens above, "Why so young?!"

Marcy scrubbed away with that stiff brush until the devastating words were revealed, "Died from a tragic fall down the well, October 18,1737." Effie fell down the well on October 18, the same day Marcy fell down the well two hundred and forty years later! The enormity of it was too overwhelming. She went into a state of shock, sobbing uncontrollably for a long time until she passed out from emotional exhaustion.

Linda found her by the flickering light of the lantern, curled up in a ball against Effie's gravestone. She knew what was on the stone from past explorations with Moxie after he shared the diaries from the attic chest with her. But the similar dates on the day of falling down the well hit her hard. She sat on the ground and held Marcy like a baby, rocking her in her arms. Marcy was deep in her subconscious, hanging onto the embers of her soul. In her dream state, Moxie appeared, asking her to find forgiveness. When Linda Magee took her in her arms, it was Moxie holding her in her dream, his likeness strong in her mind's eye. She looked up into his blue eyes and felt nothing but love. Then she awoke into the sheltering eyes of Linda. She felt wrung out, emotionally beat but finally at peace. Her storm had moved on.

Later, after a couple of cups of mint tea, Marcy put into words her feelings of loss, "I always felt a deep ache inside of me. As I read her diaries I felt like the ache was being soothed by having those feelings explained and knowing their story, those words from my greatest of grandmothers I feel so connected to. For those words to suddenly stop, oh God!" Marcy stopped talking and tried to control her tears, "She died so young Linda!" She held Linda's eyes for a long moment and then continued, "Now to find out I fell down the same well on the same day two hundred and forty years later. What is that all about?" Marcy paused for a while, then with a troubled and lost look she asked, "Why did I survive?"

"Jake"

"What?"

"The re-bar he pounded into the sides of the well for foot holds stopped you from hitting bottom." Linda explained to Marcy that Jake found and read the diaries in the trunk when he was a curious boy. He too burrowed through the overgrowth and found the dreadful truth on Effie's gravestone. He did not stop there. He wanted to go to the bottom of that well, like he could still save her."

"How do you know this?" Marcy asked with a perplexed look.

"Moxie knew what Jake was up to and told me about it. He left a trail of clues for a loving father to follow. He did not want to intervene. He knew Jake needed to explore and struggle to find the story of his ancestors just as he had. Jake loved Effie and Boyd. Their presence is still so strong here at the farm. His love for Effie saved you. Love that has been stolen by tragedy in your family for generations.

"When Moxie was twelve his mother was killed in a boating accident. He held that pain inside and became stoic so he could help raise his brother and sisters. She was so happy for him when he married and started to have children and then to lose his wife was too much for anyone to bear."

She looked at Marcy to see if she was ready to bear more and continued, "Moxie talked about his research about his ancestors and found the loss of loved ones was all too common. Almost as if Effie's early death cast a die for generations to follow."

As hard as it was to hear this, those words helped Marcy to define some of the pain she carried around and to get some understanding of who her father and her family was so she could begin to fill in the gaps in her life.

Marcy told Linda about her dream with Moxie holding her, "It was like he was right there for real, not a dream."

After she heard those words Linda had a warm inward smile and said, "Marcy, that was Moxie. My father comes to me in my dreams all the time. Death cannot extinguish spiritual fire. He may not be here in the flesh, but by God he is here and with you in spirit and soul. It is not too late. You have a relationship with him now and always will."

Marcy eyes watered over and Linda reach across that kitchen table and held her hand. Then with a lost and troubled look she said, "Was I just a mistake?"

"Oh my no! Marcy, Moxie loved your mother from the bottom of his heart." She got up and took her in her arms and continued, "You are from love darling." Marcy was held dear by Linda for a long time and then looked her in the eyes which said, I will always be there, I will always care.

As Marcy washed dishes after putting Sky to bed, she wondered how her brothers were doing. She thought bad things were happening to them when the phone rang. It was Judy wanting to know what was going on. Brian had only called once since leaving Alaska and said he was going to Mexico to look for his brother. It did not seem to her that he had a real plan. She wanted to know more. Marcy told her what she could and then confessed that she was worried, too. They comforted one another and moved on to their own lives. Once they found out they both were artists, on and on they talked. Judy then felt it safe to ask what it felt like to all of a sudden find out you have brothers.

"I knew of their lives while growing up. I used to pretend they were my brothers. Now it is official," Marcy delivered with a funny laugh.

"How did you know of their lives?"

Marcy told Judy the whole story of Moxie's letters.

"His descriptions of the boys and life on the farm made me feel like I was right there. Now to learn he was my father," she cried some and Linda was there in silent comfort breathing into the phone.

"Sorry, it just comes over me at times. I don't try to stop it anymore. I completely lost it the other night. Moxie came to me in the middle of it all. I know it was a dream but it felt like he was there, so real and alive. It really helped. For just a moment in time I looked into his warm blue eyes and felt his soul."

Now Judy started to cry.

"God listen to the two of us."

"I know, I know we have to talk about something else."

"OK, so are you and my brother an item?" It was a direct question that did change the course of the conversation and was met with a laugh.

"In the short time I did spend with him, your name seemed

to come up a lot. When I asked if you were his girlfriend, he said no. But here you are calling in concern like a girlfriend would."

"Ah, a family trait of directness. To be honest I am asking myself the same thing. I lost someone I loved to the sea. I have been afraid to love again. But Brian has been such a good friend to me. Just before he left there was some sexual tension between us but we have not even kissed. So does that answer your question?"

"Yes, thank you. I am glad I asked. Here I was thinking you had done the deed," they both fell into laughter on that one.

They talked for hours about things they'd only thought about but had never found the right words or the right person to express them to. They were both ready to listen to each other's struggles and open to being changed by what they heard. That long conversation ended with Marcy inviting Judy to come to Maine for Thanksgiving.

The next day Marcy and Sky took a walk along the sea. Late afternoon light broke through the shadows on the water, shimmers of hope reflecting on the surface then onto the banks of the shore, dancing on the greens of the moss and browns of the downed leaves. The clouds in the sky, crimson and dark blue, brought on the twilight. Still warm for that time of year.

Sky had kicked at an old log lying across the trail. It was home to an ant colony and they ran around like mad. Those worker ants always moved towards their goal. They picked up their dead, carried them home and rebuilt what was destroyed without even breaking rhythm.

Marcy stood transfixed watching the ants. It was a powerful revelation that brought on the realization that, I can't change the past, and I need to take all that I have and move forward with that, giving love to myself and all who are before me.

Mexico:

"I did not know your grandmother spoke English," Shawn said to Manuel while they were out mending fences.

"Who do you think taught us English? Don't let mi abuela fool you, she is a very smart and gifted mujer."

"I believe you after the other night."

"Que paso?"

Shawn told him what she said that night. Manuel smiled inwardly with pride and then said she was a reader of souls.

"Some come from the village when they are struggling with themselves. She can see who they really are and what is the root of the problem. Many have been helped by her gift of seeing souls."

"You are right, Manuel, I need to talk to Laura."

"Claro que si amigo."

Bordering the fence line was a dirt road. A bunch of kids made their lazy way down it, taking turns pushing a boy on a wheel chair who was paralyzed from the waist down. When they had seen them in the past, Manuel had told Shawn that the kids of the village go to his home every day and take turns pushing him to school. That boy had just made the kids laugh when a truck pulled up to the group. It was a way's off, but Shawn could see it looked an awful lot like his truck but a shit color and covered in dirt. The kids all pointed up the road at Manuel and Shawn. The truck drove towards them, and the closer it got the more he was convinced it was his. Shawn crawled under the fence and stood in the road. There were two men in his truck. Holy shit it's my brothers, what the fuck? Shawn stood there with his jaw hanging open and looked at his grinning brothers. When they came to a stop Shawn approached the truck from the back and saw the bullet holes in the tail gate. He strode with anger up to the driver's side window.

"What did you bastards do to my truck?"

"Can you believe what he just said?" Jake told Brian as the two got out.

"Great seeing you too big brother," Brian said with a tone of sarcasm while he grabbed Shawn in a bear hug and Jake wrapped his arms around the two of them.

"We stole your precious Ford back and had a little car chase. Lucky for us those bullets are in your truck and not in the back of our heads," Jake delivered with a smile, then he smacked Shawn on his arm.

"How did you even know it was stolen, and why are you two here in Mexico?" Shawn said while he tried to wrap his head around the sudden appearance of his brothers with his truck.

"Your truck ain't even the half of it, brother! Have we got a story for you."

After being introduced to Manuel they all stood around the truck and leaned in with their forearms on the side rails, telling Shawn the bigger story of having a sister and a niece. Shawn's jaw dropped again for the second time that day. He looked from brother to brother, then to Manuel and muttered, "I can't believe it." Then he broke out with, "We have a sister, suffering Christ!"

Manuel took it in stride. In his world this kind of thing was no surprise. He saw it as a blessing and congratulated Shawn with a handshake and slap on the back, then did the same to Jake and Brian.

Along came another truck with two mujers in it. The four men looked with all eyes, then Shawn recognized the two women and yelled out, "No fucking way!"

Laura stepped out of the truck when it reached the men. With eyes only for Shawn she stood and waited for him. Her face had scrapes on it from the tackle and her right hand was bruised from the punch. For the third time that day his jaw hung open and he stood frozen, but those warm brown eyes filled with love drew him in. They embraced for a long time and both felt that familiar comfort. Clara got out with a big bruise on her left cheek and a black eye and kissed Jake and Brian on the cheek.

"Nice to see you two are alive," she said with a big smile while they looked at her black eye with questions in their eyes.

"Just a little skirmish but nothing two chicas could not handle," Clara said with a tone of pride in her voice while she looked at Laura.

While Shawn held Laura, he whispered in her ear, "What the fuck is going on here?"

She whispered back, "It is a long story."

They made their way back to the ranch and had lunch with the Chavez family. Many stories where told from the different perspectives around that big table. The abuela took it all in with the inward knowledge that a big shift was taking place for the McCormack family. She looked at Laura and Shawn with eyes filled with affection and wisdom. The brothers from the two families really enjoyed getting to know one another, and it did not take them long to start ribbing each other.

Clara held her own. She sat with regal poise amongst this old established family of Mexico. It was interesting for Shawn to see the respect the Chavez women showed towards her, given the way she made her living. They were a family of privilege but were no fools to the hardships of life in Mexico. They were aware of the personal sacrifices she had made to keep her family alive.

Jake was very happy to be together with his brothers. Knowing they were going back to Maine and the farm and that everyone was safe. After much discussion Shawn decided to leave his truck hidden at the ranch and go back with his brothers. He would come back another time when things cooled down to get his truck. He asked Laura to come and spend Thanksgiving with his newly expanded family. That was a no brainer.

Later that night when alone with Shawn, Laura asked, "What happened to us?"

"I am trying to figure that out, but what I am realizing is that I got really scared. I felt so vulnerable with you because I love you so much. I got worried that you would be taken from me. I did not know how to cope with the fear. Then when I saw you kissing another man I just totally lost it."

"Shawn that kiss meant nothing. He is not a part of my life. He is my past. Why can't you trust the love I have for you?"

"What I am realizing is that it has to do with losing my mother. It is so hard for me to trust love. Man have I missed you," and he went to kiss her.

Laura let him, relishing his taste then gently pushed him away.

"I am not ready to have sex with you, Shawn. You really hurt me." She went and sat on the bed and looked him in the eye, "God, those last weeks we were together were horrible. Just hold me tonight, I really need to be held."

Maine:

Marcy and Judy each drove a vehicle to the airport to collect the brothers and Laura, who were flying in from Mexico. Sky and Marcy waited at the gate to greet them when they got off. Judy hid behind a coffee kiosk. When the group from Mexico walked down the hanger they pushed Shawn to the front to be the first to be greeted by their sister and niece. When he entered the airport, there were Marcy and Sky holding hands with a lot of expectation in their eyes. It was a powerful sight when he saw those two, such a strong resemblance to Moxie. He opened his big arms and took them both in.

He whispered into Marcy's ear, "Man oh man, life."

Sky hung onto Shawn's leg. He picked her up and looked into her eyes and then held her while Jake and Brian gave Marcy a group hug.

"I was so worried about you guys," she exclaimed.

"We were worried too for a bit there," Jake told her.

When Judy felt the time was right she stepped out from behind the kiosk. Brian could not believe it. She ran into his open arms and with both hands held his face and finally had that long-awaited kiss.

When they all got back to the farm they hung back and let

Shawn go in first. Seeing those murals of his childhood was a revelation after his long journey. As a boy he felt alone and lost without the love of a mother. It became a mantra, a lens that he used to filter his life. Love leads to the loss of love and then pain, so he blocked love out. But now with his experience in Mexico he had a new lens. With that new lens he looked at those murals and saw just how much love there actually was in his childhood. From his father, his brothers, from Tilly and the community. That was all in him and for so long he kept himself from seeing and feeling all that love. But at that moment it tingled in his inner being and it all came out in a grand smile. He was home.

The light of late fall cast its intoxicating spell over the farm. Low angled rays, shining clean and bright on the bark of the trees, alive with the spirit of life. The shadows of the branches brought contrast to the light that held the magic, timeless. They were all drunk on it, giddy with joy, positive conversations with so much laughter. The McCormack family and loved ones were all together. They had just eaten a grand meal and walked through the field and on into the woods. It was a grand moment that marked a great transition for all of them, as individuals and as a family. They were all present with the realization, these are the people, this is the place they wanted to be and no other, no longer afraid to love, ready and willing to love with all their hearts.

Tilly watched them through woods and saw that the family she had known her whole life were full and complete, past the struggles of buried sorrows and onto the higher ground of a loving, truthful, well-functioning family. In certain indigenous cultures, the moose is a symbol for moving to you higher self, for it is in the eyes of the moose that we see and believe in our better selves, that we push from hanging dearly onto a plateau that is incomplete to finding a place where we achieve what we need to get done in this life, to find the natural gifts given us and express them out into the world.

- EPILOGUE -

When Effie went to the well to haul water she was lost in her old feelings of having no love from her father. She felt a strong sense of loss, something she could never get back, and she feared the loss of the love she had in her life now. That pull of fear came from deep in the well. It created a moment of vertigo, and she fell. She did not intend to end her life. She was weaker than the fear at a vulnerable moment. The fall killed her and set a pattern in her family for giving into the fear of the loss of love for generation after generation. After Effie's death, Boyd shut down and could not bear the pain of hearing her name or talking about her. He had lost the opportunity to celebrate her life, sharing her interests and passions for life with her children. They felt the loss so deeply because they were afraid to express their loss of their mother with their father. Everything was buried alive and kept their feelings deep inside and not released. Trauma early in their lives that was then set in their DNA and passed on, thus starting a pattern in the family of the men giving into that fear and the women placating that through early departure.

Moxie made the giant steps towards breaking that destructive pattern by researching the stories of his ancestors beyond what he found in the family chest. He was captured by Effie's story and started to make connections and see the patterns set for generations, which in a way soothed some of his old wounds. He left a trail for Jake to follow, and with the brave adventurous heart of a boy the pattern started to crack when he pounded those pieces of rebar into the sides of the well on his way to the bottom to find truth. That courage from a young boy put a big crack in that wall of family fear, and the pattern changed when Marcy was saved by the pieces of rebar. When Jake got to the bottom of the well he felt Effie's sorrow of not being honored. He cried and wept for a very long time, shed the lost tears for so many generations and properly honored Effie's soul so she could be free of the well and do her angel's work. The pattern that kept away love through fear broke and let the light in.

The End

She sat on that wall feeling the strong spirit of Effie, knowing her stories and passions and desires and mourning the loss of a life ended way too soon. Unfulfilled goals lost and wandering around for generations left an unexplained, empty ache. Marcy had her own desires and passions to fulfill and had been conflicted with that ancestral ache. So while sitting on that wall feeling a deep connection to her great, great grandmother, she could now explain that empty ache and put words to it and let it go for her and all her surviving siblings to be free to live their life's purpose.

ACKNOWLEDGMENTS

The act of writing is a solitary endeavor but to publish a book is bringing together a collective of different people with talents and perspectives that help the book flow to the reader. Three women edited this book that I would like to thank: Elizabeth Peavey who looked at eighty pages of the first draft and gave me a critique on substance of character and plot. Reminding me of the reader and to not get lost in my inside jokes with my father. Kate Kearns who worked on grammar and sentence structure and in going over her edits I learned something of the English language. Gwedolyn Erin Cremers came in for the final touch up on historical dialogue and grammar she helped in the final sanding and varnishing. Consulting readers: Thank you to Roger Hutchins for his help on local dialogue and marine mechanics. Mike and Finn Fleming for helping in character development and interior cabin design. Fay Simpson, my cousin, for her guidance on matters of the heart and body. Lee Huston for his help on Schooner rigging. Special thanks to the Chapin Family for their friendship over the fifteen years that I worked on this book. In ending I want to acknowledge that I am dyslexic. Before I got help at the age of fourteen I was reversing letters that kept me from comprehending what I read and I was failing in school. My Eighth-grade year I went to a tutor everyday he took me back to first grade and explained the alphabet to me and the sounds that vowels make explaining to me all the while how my brain was reversing them. I adapted so I could comprehend and write. It is a slow process from my heart to my head but here it is, and through the struggles I have to say I see dyslexia as my gift.

Thank you to Mike and Sara for over the last fithteen years being my anchor to come home.

special thanks - photo by Nicole Cobbs

David Rankin Johnson lives on the coast of Maine in a home he built powered by harvesting the sun. His low over head allows him to travel in the winter, at times enjoying local music, dance and food with people from all over the world, who laugh with joy and listen with open hearts. At times he has worked as a volunteer teaching carpentry to children in Guatemala, Nicaragua and Bolivia. He works as a carpenter renovating homes some luckily by the sea. But really "Sailing is what feeds my soul and blows away the stress."

CPSIA information can be obtained
at www.ICGtesting.com
Printed in the USA
BVHW031310100619
550608BV00001B/6/P

9 781733 941006